Abi walked toward Keith, stopping a foot from him, and his heart felt like it would explode.

"Keith, you're a great catch for Silver Valley, I'm sure. But we're both professionals, and we both know the intensity this case is going to require. Hanky-panky isn't on the docket."

"Did you just say hanky-panky?"

"I did. And we're adults. Let's get it out in the open so that we can let it go."

"Like hell."

Abi didn't resist as he grasped her upper arms and pulled her body up against his.

"I'm sure all the girls like this Neanderthal move. It's quite slick, actually. Do you practice—"

Keith planted a firm kiss on her lips. No tongue, no seductive caresses. Just pure lip-lock.

Abi shoved against his chest. "Really? Is that all you've got?" As she challenged him she fought the warmth that blazed from her lips to her midsection.

"You've no idea, Abi," he growled.

* * *

We hope you enjoy the Silver Valley P.D. miniseries.

If you're on Twitter, tell us what you think of Harlequin Romantic Suspense!
#harlequinromsuspense

Dear Reader,

Welcome back to Silver Valley, the small town in Central Pennsylvania that has more than its share of danger and bad guys waiting around every turn. Fortunately there's love all around, too.

Secret Agent Under Fire is the fourth Silver Valley P.D. book. We finally get to see the True Believer aka New Thought cult get its due—after it has plagued Silver Valley for the past four books.

It was my honor and privilege to write about Keith Paruso, a firefighter who is fighting to keep his professional reputation intact after being slandered by cult members in *Wedding Takedown*. Abi Redland is a former FBI agent and arson expert hired by the secret government shadow agency the Trail Hikers to help solve a series of arsons in Silver Valley. Abi and Keith immediately butt heads, as they are both fire-science experts and have definite opinions on how to catch their criminal. I loved writing how they fall in love no matter how dangerous the setting. I had a hard time saying goodbye to Abi and Keith at the end of the book. I hope you'll feel the same.

Thank you for your wonderful response to the Silver Valley P.D. series. It's a joy to write, and of course I love to highlight the area I call "home."

I adore connecting with readers! Please sign up for my newsletter at my website, gerikrotow.com, and join me on Facebook, Twitter, Pinterest and Instagram.

Happy reading!

Peace,

Geri

SECRET AGENT UNDER FIRE

Geri Krotow

 HARLEQUIN® ROMANTIC SUSPENSE

Recycling programs
for this product may
not exist in your area.

ISBN-13: 978-0-373-40207-6

Secret Agent Under Fire

Copyright © 2017 by Geri Krotow

Printed in U.S.A.

www.Harlequin.com

Former naval intelligence officer and US Naval Academy graduate **Geri Krotow** draws inspiration from the global situations she's experienced. Geri loves to hear from her readers. You can email her via her website and blog, gerikrotow.com.

Books by Geri Krotow

Harlequin Romantic Suspense

Silver Valley P.D.

Her Christmas Protector
Wedding Takedown
Her Secret Christmas Agent
Secret Agent Under Fire

Harlequin Superromance

What Family Means
Sasha's Dad

Whidbey Island

Navy Rules
Navy Orders
Navy Rescue
Navy Christmas
Navy Justice

Harlequin Anthology

Coming Home for Christmas
Navy Joy

Harlequin Everlasting Love

A Rendezvous to Remember

Visit the Author Profile page at Harlequin.com for more titles.

To my dearest Stephen—looking forward to the next thirty years.

Chapter 1

Abigail Redland had never heard so many different bird-calls in her life. Hunched on the dirt floor of a long-ago abandoned play fort, she hard-swallowed a laugh. Imagine, she was having more fun in the deer-tick-infested woods of central Pennsylvania than she'd ever had in her office at FBI headquarters in Washington, DC. Cramped muscles from the long night of surveillance included. She stretched her legs in front of her, careful to remain silent as her hamstrings protested with sharp spasms.

"You still there, Abi?" Rio Ortego's voice sounded in her earpiece and broke through her mental distraction.

"Here. Nothing."

"Roger." Rio was all business, as usual. Not only was Rio the Silver Valley Police Department detective who ran their current op, he was also a fellow Trail Hiker secret agent. Abi still had to pinch herself that she'd landed her new job with the autonomous government shadow agency so quickly after she'd left the FBI.

Because of its secrecy, she'd never heard of Trail Hikers. The fact that it was headquartered only two hours north of DC and yet a world away in Cumberland County, Pennsylvania, had intrigued her. As had the scope of their missions, international and domestic, outlined to her by the Trail Hiker CEO, Claudia Michele, a retired Marine Corps General. That had been almost three months ago, and Abi would be forever grateful to Claudia for finding her via the FBI's database of departing employees. Abi figured she'd have to take a job that wouldn't use her arson expertise as a cushion between the FBI and whatever came next. Being a Trail Hiker agent was a godsend, even if she still didn't know what was going to come next. All she knew was that she didn't want to be taking down bad guys for the rest of her life.

Abi used her binoculars to go over every visible part of the house across the woods for what had to be the hundredth time in two hours and she all but willed their target to appear. She was at most one hundred yards from the house but the binoculars were invaluable. At least she didn't have to rely on the night-vision goggles any longer—the sun had been up for a good hour.

As if summoned by her thoughts, two ominous *booms* preceded a thin line of smoke wafting on the early morning breeze—her only warning before the sight of graceful flames registered as they licked up the side of the old, abandoned home.

"We've got heat. Flames. Heading in." She dropped her binoculars and began to unfold herself from her hidden position on the ground.

"No, Abi, stay put. We've called the fire department in. Watch for the arsonist."

"We'll never catch him if you keep relying on the SVFD, boss."

Rio didn't respond and Abi didn't expect any different. She didn't have anything against the local fire department—Silver Valley Fire Department wanted the bastard as much as, if not more than, the Trail Hikers and Silver Valley PD combined. They'd all been tracking this loser for the better part of three months. He'd set building after building on fire, each time leaving a fireproof message in his wake, either outside near but far enough from the blaze, or, in many cases, in a fireproof lockbox. Always a warning for Silver Valley to "listen to God" and "revert to the old ways."

The mental image of the printed, computer-generated messages, all part of the evidence file, made her grind her teeth. Chances were that the fire starter was long gone, as most arsonists fled the scene immediately after committing their crime. He may have set the stage for the flames a day ago, to enable a quick entry and exit from the scene. Anger engulfed her as she faced the hard fact that he'd somehow sneaked in and out without her or the police or fire department's notice. Certainly none of the SVFD's walk-throughs had yielded hard evidence, either.

Abi resumed her vigil anyway, which was automatic from years of FBI fieldwork. She forced herself to still and listen intently for any telltale signs of a human being. There had been none when she'd arrived four hours ago, well before sunup. The fire department had searched the house, along with several other empty buildings, last night and, from what Rio had told her, SVFD had found no indication of flammables or explosives in any of the suspected structures.

She stared at the old farmhouse. A farmhouse that probably should have been razed decades ago judging from the weathered clapboards and rusty hinges visible from the outside. She hadn't gone in to inspect it with the firefighters; as a secret Trail Hiker operative she had to remain as invisible as she could. Her cover as a special contractor to the police department worked but there was no need to push it.

Only a handful of Silver Valley PD officers knew about the Trail Hikers, and the secret government shadow agency put a capital *S* in *secret*. It was easy enough to blend into the police department, though, as it regularly had civilians coming and going. It would be much more difficult to do her work in a fire department without loaded questions regarding her identity. Besides, she didn't think any Silver Valley FD firefighters had been read into the Trail Hikers or she'd have met them as part of this case. Trail Hikers was so classified that she wasn't privy to who was a part of the agency and who wasn't. Abi didn't care about that, anyhow—she was damn grateful to have this job. It was the perfect transition to her new life, whatever that would be.

Twigs snapped and a loud thud made the ground quake. Her spine stiffened and she looked through every crack in the fort, taking care to stay as quiet as possible.

"Crap!" The oath was followed by the sound of heavy steps on the forest floor and jeans-clad legs entered her field of vision.

Carefully and intentionally, Abi crawled toward the entrance of the fort, her weapon drawn. When the feet began to sound a pattern moving away from her, she burst out of the shed.

"Police!"

She made out a tall figure, male, in a hooded sweatshirt. He turned in her direction and revealed a face covered with a ski mask. His single, deliberate hand gesture made his intention clear before he turned and ran. He zig-zagged between trees and bushes, eliminating her chance at a clear shot.

Abi began pursuit.

"We've got the building surrounded, Chief."

"Roger," Keith Paruso replied to his team leader over the wireless audio system. The fires were never difficult to put out, as long as they caught them early. In this case they'd narrowed the arsonist's next target down to three abandoned farmhouses and, sure enough, he'd struck the first one on their list. His team had been here in less than three minutes, pre-positioned on the main highway.

It was almost *too* easy.

If it was up to Keith, the son of a bitch wasn't going to get away this time. As he scanned the perimeter of the scene, his spine stiffened when he spotted a hooded fig-ure running along the far edge of the farm clearing. "I've got a suspect and I'm going after him." As he spoke he shucked off his gear and then ran straight for his target, grateful he hadn't donned his firefighting boots. He'd hoped he'd get a shot at capturing the criminal.

Was it his job to catch and apprehend an arsonist? No. That was for SVPD and other law enforcement. Keith's job was to run his fire department and make sure they put the fires out and kept Silver Valley citizens safe.

But this criminal was different; the entire case was different. He was certain, as was his sister's boyfriend, Rio, that this fire starter was connected to the True Be-liever Cult. A cult that had been led by Leonard Wise, who'd convinced vulnerable single mothers that he was their savior. That their daughters would be the mothers of the "new community" he envisioned. The cult had been disbanded by arrests and incarcerations two decades ago, after a twelve-year-old girl reached out for help. That girl had grown into Zora Krasny, a woman relocated and raised in Silver Valley under the witness relocation program. Unfortunately, prison terms ended and the perpetrators had regrouped in Silver Valley over the past eighteen months, hundreds of miles from upstate New York, where they'd caused trouble all those years ago. Now the True Believers, still with Leonard Wise at the helm, were calling themselves the New Thought community. Suspicious activity that turned criminal and life-threatening had occurred in the usually quiet town of twenty thousand. As soon as Rio and SVPD could get the needed evidence, they'd take Leonard Wise and his cult down for good. Trail Hikers was involved because of the potential for disaster; the local law-enforcement agencies, or LEA, could handle only so much.

Keith adjusted his stride to leap over a Civil War–era fence, stomping down on thistles and brambles as he landed. The fence was a keen reminder of the violence central Pennsylvania had endured almost two centuries ago. It was ironic that the peace that emanated from the surrounding Appalachian Mountains was being disturbed again, but this time by a modern-day cult.

The toe of his running shoe caught on a tree root and he pitched forward but regained his balance quickly. When he did, he noticed a second figure on the run; a woman with her weapon drawn and in the fist of her pumping arm as she chased after the suspect. She wore a Kevlar vest. What the hell?

Was it an SVPD officer? He personally knew only one female SVPD cop, Nika Pasczenko. He didn't know the others. Nika was taller, leaner than the definitely feminine figure streaking across the field. This woman was a stranger to him.

He ran across her path toward the suspect, figuring either he'd catch up to her or they'd corner the arsonist.

But the bastard disappeared from the horizon, only to be seen again on a dirt bike that roared as he made his escape, holding on to an accomplice who drove the vehicle.

He kept running, until he was almost even with the woman who stood stock-still, her arms still raised as if she'd get off a shot at the now long-gone bike.

He slowed to a walk and approached her from behind, and was treated to the most colorful string of epithets he'd experienced since becoming a firefighter. She was speaking to someone, probably mic'd for the stakeout he knew Rio had set up.

"Yeah, the SOB's gone. What do you mean there aren't any SVPD units to cut him off? Why the hell did I just spend the last night using my rudimentary camping skills if you didn't have backup?"

His foot snapped a twig and she whirled on him, her pistol in his face.

"Whoa, there. Hey, I'm on your side. I want to catch the bad guy, too." He held up his hands and offered a grin, still marveling at her effusive dirty language. Marvel turned to awe as huge doe eyes rounded and, after looking him over, she spoke into the small mic he saw pinned to her bulletproof vest.

"I've got someone here with me. What is your name?" Eyes on him again.

"Keith Paruso, Silver Valley Fire Department. Chief."

Whoever spoke to her in her ear confirmed his identity because she lowered her weapon and holstered it, keeping her dark gaze steady on him.

"Roger. I'll meet back up with you in a bit." She yanked her earpiece out, her gaze steady and sparking the wrath of the devil as she leveled it on him. "Sorry. I wasn't expecting you, Chief."

He ignored her insincere apology. "May I ask who you are and what the hell you're doing at my fire scene?"

Dang, dang, dang, *dang*.

It wasn't like she didn't have an alibi, a practiced reason for being here. But as a Trail Hiker it would have been better if she hadn't been tagged by the chief of SVFD, for God's sake.

"I'm Abi. Working under contract to SVPD to support the apprehension of this arsonist."

"Uh-huh."

The studly fire chief didn't buy it. She could tell from the way his hands, raised to show her his harmlessness, had lowered and were fisted on his hips. His brows, even and straight across his eyes. Brilliant, cornflower-blue eyes not unlike the sky above them appeared anything but soft and summery. More like a blast of arctic wind over glacial ice.

Sighing, she pulled out her ID. "Here. Check it yourself."

He reached for the card and their fingers touched. The immediate sexual awareness caught her off guard. Sure, Fire Chief Keith Paruso was an attractive male and obviously in outstanding shape, but she worked with fit—even hot—men on a daily basis. Not one had ever made her feel so instantly turned on, been so quick to remind her that she was a woman underneath all the body armor and cargo pants.

"It says you're a free agent, *Abigail*."

"I am. I told you, I'm a contractor. And it's Abi." No one called her Abigail. Except Dad, when she was a kid, and she'd left home almost fifteen years ago. And even he called her Abi these days.

"I didn't realize SVPD employed contractors, especially ones as prepared as you are, *Abigail*."

He was clearly who he said he was and, as she looked past him, she saw the fire trucks, the firefighters hosing down the house.

"I don't know many fire chiefs who'd leave a fire to run after a suspect. Where I'm from, you leave that to law enforcement. Unless you have a problem with SVPD? Don't you trust them?"

His eyes narrowed and she thought he was going to either throw her ID on the ground, spit at her or turn and leave. He looked pretty pissed off.

Instead he laughed. A lot. Not a snort or chuckle, but a warm, rich sound that seemed to roll over and around her, squeezing her tight, cutting off her breath. If he hadn't already turned her on, this would have done it.

"I've got a job to do, Chief Paruso." She held her hand out to retrieve her ID. He ignored it.

"The 'job' you have is a case I've been working intensely on, along with SVPD, for over three months, and it's affected my job for over a year. A case that could have resulted in us catching the bad guy. Since your weapon was drawn and you were at least a quarter of a mile ahead of me, I'm thinking that you had a decent chance to catch the loser. Instead, we're here exchanging pleasantries while the dirt bag's free to light up his next target. So forgive me, Abigail, if I'm not too impressed with how you do your job."

How the hell had SVPD Chief Colt Todd found this one? And why hadn't he been informed that someone else was working this case? Keith made a mental note to see how much Rio knew about Ms. Abigail Redland. Thank God he knew Rio well enough to ask him, since Rio and Keith's sister Kayla were a couple. He was supposed to meet them for dinner tonight. Soon enough.

"I'm not being paid to impress *you*, Chief Paruso." Her eyes glinted with the morning sun and her chest moved with the deep breaths she drew—was she trying to calm down? Was he making her angry, too? Not that he was looking at her chest. Although...

"You have leaves on your, um, Kevlar."

She looked down and brushed off the dried oak leaves that were ground into her vest. Her hands were small but capable, and he imagined they'd be the perfect size to fit around his—*no*. He was not going there, not while this investigation was open, not with some pseudo-law-enforcement agent who probably didn't know the difference between arson and a bonfire.

"Interesting that you have such keen observation skills, Chief Paruso. I'm curious as to why your talents haven't caught this criminal yet."

Anger dowsed the searing line of awareness between them, his focus no longer on his crotch but her snide comment. "How I run my investigation is none of your goddamned business, whether you're working for SVPD or the CIA. In case you missed it, I'm the chief of the fire department. In reality, it's law enforcement's job to get the criminal, as you pointed out." Who the hell did she think she was?

"Trust me, I know what your job is, Chief." She said it as though she really did understand firefighting, and it made him even hotter under the collar. Unless she'd had firefighting training herself, she had no business saying she knew his job. None.

"What's the problem, folks?"

Keith all but jumped at the familiar voice behind him. He'd been so wrapped up in his emotions he hadn't heard the approaching steps.

Way to go, Keith.

"Hey, Colt." He held out his hand to the Superintendent of the Silver Valley Police Department, Chief Colt Todd.

Colt gripped his hand firmly and gave it a quick shake before he grinned and nodded at Abigail. "Glad to see you two have met. Abi's new to SVPD, working with us to fill in the gaps around the arson case."

"So she said." Keith wasn't budging.

"Yes, we've met. Speaking of the case, Chief Todd, I need to get back to headquarters and compare notes with Rio and the team. If you'll excuse me, gentlemen." Abigail walked off as if she owned the entire field they stood in. As if she was in charge of the case.

"Those weren't nice words I heard you two exchanging, Keith."

"Damn it, Colt, we need to be working together on every single aspect of this case or we're never going to get the dirt bag. Not to mention bring down the cult, if they're truly connected. Why didn't you tell me you had a contract employee working this? And how is it that a civilian is carrying a weapon and wearing Kevlar as if she's more than a contractor?"

Colt's eyes narrowed but he maintained a neutral expression. "We have several civilian staff members, Keith. Take Claudia Michele, for example. She runs our social media efforts but she's also been intrinsic to solving a few cases." Colt spoke about the woman Keith suspected was involved with, if not in charge of, the kind of undercover ops he suspected went on in Silver Valley. He knew that Silver Valley's status as a quiet small town was at times lost because of the major highways that ran through the outlying area. A state turnpike and three interstate routes, heavily traveled, made Silver Valley attractive to criminals of all types. Criminals that committed crimes that required LEA ops to counter their stinging effects on the population. Ops he wasn't privy to, not officially, but it was difficult to work as closely as he did with SVPD and not notice that some of his LEA colleagues appeared to be involved with more than local operations. And since his sister had become romantically involved with Rio, he'd had his suspicions validated by Kayla's obvious avoidance of him when Rio was working "on a confidential case."

"So who is Abigail Redland, Colt? Is she FBI? ATF?"

Colt shook his head. "It's not important. And I'm not blowing you off, but just as I can't always discuss all aspects of any one case—it's the same with SVPD employees. I know you understand, Keith."

Keith watched the older man's face closely. Colt ran a tight ship over at Silver Valley PD and never let the backlash of public opinion or fellow law-enforcement officers keep him from doing his job. Clearly he wasn't going to budge on the Abigail Redland issue.

Keith relented and let his shoulders drop.

"Sorry, Colt. It's been a long night, a fruitless morning, and we still don't have the arsonist. I'm not convinced it's just one person any longer, either."

Colt's eyes lit up. "Yeah?"

Keith debated how much to tell Colt. Because he wanted to nail this fire starter himself. He had to. To repair the damage to his professional reputation, which had been crushed under the lies and corruption of Silver Valley's most recent administration, including an outsider mayor who was now behind bars in the state prison at

Camp Hill. Worse for Keith, a couple associated with the cult had falsely accused him and his fire department of negligence at the Silver Valley Community Church fire two Christmases ago. It had cost Keith his job; he'd been placed on administrative leave for several months. Even though the charges had been dropped, thanks to Rio's hard work, Keith felt the cloud of judgment that hung around his neck like a lead weight.

"There have been a few signs that the fires are being set differently. Same propellant, gasoline, but with different starters. This house reeks of chemicals from fireworks, and I heard two large explosions before the flames started. My firefighters staged a mile away heard them, too. Yet we saw nothing on our walk-through inspection last night." He wondered if Abigail had heard those explosions, if that was what had alerted her to the assailant. That must have been what had prompted her to take off after him, at least.

"The first few were definitely started with matches. Maybe one was a butane lighter," Colt mused aloud. "It's not unusual for an arsonist to change starters, is it?"

Keith looked up at the blue sky, watched two red-tailed hawks circling each other. Freedom. That was all he ever wanted. Freedom to do his job in peace, knowing he was serving the citizens of Silver Valley, enabling them to sleep at night, knowing that if the worst happened and a fire broke out in their homes, SVFD would be there and all would be okay.

Home fires and car fires from accidental means were one thing. Pursuing an arsonist was another.

"They can, and do. But this guy seemed so methodical with the first two fires. And we're lucky he's stuck to unoccupied structures so far, Colt. I don't have to tell you what's at stake with his growing number of fires."

"No, you don't. I know he or she is escalating. At least that's what Abi—" Colt pursed his lips, sized up Keith's demeanor. "All right. I'll tell you that she's former FBI. And that her specialty is arson."

"She's just 'former,' huh?" Keith had never seen Colt lie, but people in law enforcement often had to play their cards close. Very close.

"Yes, definitely former. Enough said. Abi has a crap ton of experience in the analysis and psychological profiling of arsonists. And her observations are scaring the crap out of me, Keith."

"How so?"

"We've seen the amping up of the frequency of fires, and the structures are getting more valuable."

Keith had noticed that, too. It was one thing to burn down an old barn that should have been razed years ago, to set fire to it in the dead of night with little or no risk to anyone. But abandoned farm structures like barns and sheds had given way to empty commercial property, to historical homes that were awaiting refurbishment and empty homes like this morning's farmhouse. From uninhabited dwellings to places where people lived or would be able to live soon.

The arsonist *was* escalating, even if it wasn't a straight-line progression.

"What are we going to do about it, Colt?"

Colt's eyes reflected surprise at Keith's admission that they had to work together before he allowed a reluctant grin to cross his face.

"We are going to put our heads together and use every tool we have at our disposal to catch the bastard."

Keith nodded. "What next?"

"Can you spare some time down at police headquarters this morning?"

"Sure. My firefighters are on this, and the station's fully staffed." He referred to the current fire, which his team had already radioed they'd put out. He had his full roster on 24/7 schedules. Thankfully there was no injury or family leave scheduled for the next month. "What time do you need me there?"

"Call Rio and ask him. You'll meet with him and his team."

Colt didn't have to say who was on Rio's team. Keith already knew he'd have to face Abigail Redland for the second time this morning. And while his head knew he should be more detached from her, or even annoyed at her involvement, he couldn't ignore the anticipation he felt at the thought of having another chance to see her

Chapter 2

Abi still wanted to scratch someone's eyes out an hour after leaving the stakeout. An hour after meeting Silver Valley's fire chief. She poured herself a cup of the awful SVPD coffee and waited for the rest of the case team to get their notes together for the wrap-up meeting. And of course they had to wait for the Silver Valley Fire Department officials to show up.

Which would bring her face-to-face with Fire Chief Keith Paruso again.

It'd been a couple of hours since she'd met Keith Paruso and her body had yet to stop humming from the immediate attraction he'd lit in her. It was as real, as strong as her certainty that not only was he a fire chief, he was a dog. As in capital-*H* hound dog. He had the bod and smile to get a lot of women in his bed, for sure. She almost giggled, thinking about how puzzled he'd appeared that she hadn't fawned at his every word.

Focus, focus, focus. She was undercover as a Trail Hiker agent, but outwardly a special advisor to SVPD. That made any kind of romance with other LEA off-limits until this case was solved, especially with another Silver Valley public official who didn't know what she was really doing. Who didn't even know about Trail Hikers. There was at least one if not more arsonists to apprehend. In fact, after today, Abi was certain there was more than one and that the fires were being set individually.

So her love life had to take a backseat—nothing new. The case stretched before her as none other, however. Even with all the twisted cases and sociopaths she'd analyzed for the FBI, she had to admit the Silver Valley fire starter had even her stymied. It was a first for her in a long career of catching arsonists. A career she'd committed to while still in high school, when she'd been brokenhearted at the accidental death of her classmate in a house fire. *Don't go there.* She tore her thoughts from the dark memories.

Making her way through the break room and down the corridor of the medium-size station, she stuck her head in Rio Ortego's office.

"Hey, Rio."

"Abi! Come on in for a bit." He didn't look as tired as she felt, yet he'd been up all night, too.

She sank down in a worn leather chair and took in the framed photo of Rio and his girlfriend, Kayla, that rested near his monitor. Why did everyone but her seem to have a life partner? Would a move to Silver Valley bring her love life back in line? After this case was closed, of course. Not one minute sooner.

She'd been recruited for the secret government shadow agency when she'd left the FBI after ten years of honorable service. The offer had been too good to be true; she'd work contracted missions that paid enough to maintain her Old Town Alexandria town house while traveling the world to complete missions her FBI training seemed perfect for.

Except going "home" to DC had gotten harder. The town house was nice and its location prime—for a commuter, which she no longer was. The days and weeks in between Trail Hiker missions felt longer and, in fact, boring. She'd been toying with making a move to somewhere free of DC's political pressure, away from the abysmal traffic, away from the city life she was ready to leave behind.

"Good work out there this morning, Abi." He didn't look up from the report he studied, and he waved at his coffeepot. "Don't drink that crap from the break room. Have some real joe."

"Thanks, this is fine for now." They had to be in the briefing room in less than twenty minutes and she needed a comfortable spot to sit more than she needed a cup of better brew.

Rio and Abi were the only Trail Hikers on the case at the moment, if she didn't count the police chief. As such, they took pains to keep to the storyline that Abi was a contractor hired to help with the arson cases. Her prior experience as FBI wasn't a secret and served her alibi well, as she posed as simply an arson expert. As the case was almost certainly entwined with the cult, it made her presence more validated. Since the FBI was being called in to work with SVPD to take out the True Believer Cult once and for all, no one questioned Abi's role. And better, no one suspected she was part of anything clandestine.

"Close the door for a minute, will you?" Rio spoke

quietly and she knew he needed to talk about something Trail Hiker–related.

"Sure."

Once the door was closed Rio leaned forward, his forearms on his cluttered desk. "I can't afford for you to be exchanging barbs with Keith Paruso. I'm pretty sure he's aware of Trail Hikers, abstractly, but he doesn't have any official knowledge of the agency. As much as this case may necessitate the need to pull him into TH, with his compliance, we're still obligated to maintain our cover story."

"I get that, Rio." She tried to not let him see how stung she was by his statement. Did he think she was going to jump in the sack with him and tell Keith whom she really worked for? "I understand what a security clearance is."

"It's not about Keith as much as it's about every other officer and firefighter who'll never be part of TH, who don't need to know about Trail Hikers and what we're doing."

"Understood." She dug her bottom teeth into the foam cup. It felt like her father, lecturing her for dating the wrong kind of boy. And she wasn't considering dating Keith Paruso—she didn't know the man.

"Abi, I'm not saying this as any kind of reprimand. You're the perfect Trail Hiker agent—Claudia doesn't hire deadweight." Claudia Michele, the former US Marine Corps General who was the Trail Hiker CEO, had been a tough sell when Abi had reported for her initial interview. Even though Abi had been recruited for the interview by the government shadow agency, she'd still had to prove her worthiness to Claudia, both in the field and at the desk.

"I didn't take your comments personally, Rio. You're not the first alpha male I've worked for, you know."

He smiled. "Alpha male? What the hell does that mean? Is that like some kind of millennial code for 'dickhead'?"

She laughed. "God, I've missed laughing with teammates since I left the FBI. It was the best choice for me, to make a change and come here to Silver Valley, but this kind of camaraderie is rare in the civilian world."

Rio grunted. "I've found it to be nonexistent, frankly. Law enforcement is a family, for sure."

"Working for Colt Todd has to be enjoyable at times, doesn't it?"

Rio's eyes flashed. "Chief Todd's the best, hands-down. And you know he's fully invested with the Trail Hikers, too, but more on a need-to-know basis."

Abi grunted. "From what I've seen, he's more than interested in Claudia."

Rio's eyes sharpened. "Don't be so quick to judge, Abi. All of us in Silver Valley end up working very closely together. It's inevitable that the dangerous circumstances and heroics required to keep Silver Valley safe lead to deeper relationships off the clock."

"Like you and Kayla."

Rio's expression faltered and she saw a red tinge on his cheekbones. He-man, detective and Trail Hiker team lead was blushing over his woman?

"Yes."

"I'm sorry, Rio, I didn't mean to fluster you, for God's sake."

"Save it. You know you fit in almost too well here, don't you, Abi?"

"Maybe. How did you meet Kayla?" Rio's girlfriend was a local florist Abi had met at the SVPD police picnic last week. Before the arson case had escalated.

Rio's smile disappeared and his jaw tensed. "At a murder scene. The second time."

"Oh, God. I'm so sorry, Rio."

"It wasn't a personal friend of either of ours, but by the time we closed the case Kayla had been shot at, more than once."

"She sounds pretty tough."

"That she is." The look of bemusement and absolute adoration that changed Rio's demeanor from grim to grateful shot stabs of jealousy through Abi. Would she ever elicit that kind of emotion from a man?

She sure hadn't in DC; all the more reason to consider her relocation to Silver Valley permanent. As the song said, a change might do her good.

A short rap on Rio's office door interrupted her thoughts and was the only warning they had before the door opened and Keith Paruso entered.

"Hey, Rio, great work —" He cut himself off as he took in Abi's presence. "Abigail."

"I've already told you, Chief, it's 'Abi.'" She stood and held out her hand. "Nice to see you again."

"Right." Despite the doubt in his reply he took her hand, and she had to admit she wasn't impartial to the heat, the damned sexual electricity that she felt engulf her as fully as his hand enveloped hers. "Only if you call me Keith."

"Fine. Keith." She smiled and sat back down. Keith didn't take a seat but stood near Rio's desk as he greeted Rio.

Damp hair and the pungent scent of soap weren't all that told her he'd gone home and had a quick shower. His worn but clean jeans and collared shirt emphasized his broad shoulders and how his torso tapered to the waist of his unbelted jeans, where she noted he had a button fly.

Oh, God, was there anything sexier than a man in button-fly jeans?

Can it, Redland. Rarely had she become involved with a fellow officer or agent on any case. It seldom ended well and, in her case, it had been disastrous. A flash of memory had her in the stifled surroundings where a drug dealer's last stand had cornered her and Frederick. Fred, the one man she'd ever thought she could make a life with...

Until he'd married said drug dealer's daughter, after freeing her from the clutches of the crime ring.

"That's where Abi comes in. Abi?"

"Abigail. You're up." Keith's hand was on her bare forearm, his breath whispering over her cheeks as she looked up at him. She looked at his hand, strong and warm against her skin. His face revealed nothing save professional courtesy and collegial concern. But his eyes flickered with—patronizing glee. Wait, did he think he was doing her a favor by touching her? Did he think she needed the male attention? That she'd react to his touch?

And he'd called her Abigail again, damn it.

"Sorry, my mind wandered. Just piecing together the evidence we have so far." She lifted his hand from her using two fingers and pulled her arm away. She looked at Rio. "I've already told Colt my thoughts."

"Which are?" Keith spoke up, no hint in his tone of the emotion he'd revealed a moment earlier, or of her obvious rebuff of his he-man tactics.

"I don't like how this fire starter has gone from burning down, what, six or seven barns? To all of a sudden move up to larger commercial properties, like the convenience store last month, and before today he aimed at historical landmarks. Today, the run-down farmhouse.

It's not usual, not for a straightforward profile. This isn't someone who gets off on simply lighting fires."

"Tell us something we don't already know." Keith crossed his arms over his chest. So the man had smarts to go with the cocky player attitude. Abi could overlook a sexy man but the sexiest attribute to her was always intelligence. Followed by a sense of humor, which Keith was demonstrating through his obvious need to tease her with his blatant come-on behavior.

Ignoring the way his biceps flexed against his chest, Abi shrugged. "Right. So it's obvious to me that you probably have more than one arsonist. Even though the notes left at the scenes are all the same, from the same paper stock and ink. One person, one entity may be directing several different people to commit the arsons. That's why I'm not convinced these are hard-boiled fire starters."

"I've thought the same thing." Keith looked at Rio. "I told you this three weeks ago, and I mentioned it to Colt this morning. Today's spotting of the suspect makes it three out of a total of eight fires after which we've seen the suspect take off once the engines arrive."

Rio's brow creased and he leaned on his forearms. "Three times none of us caught him, damn it."

"He had an escape vehicle and a driver. There has to have been another vehicle they drove the ATV to. And then, maybe some kind of hidey-hole in the Appalachians. No one disappears this easily without help." Abi stopped before she said anything about the Trail Hikers supersecret command post buried deep behind a cave, which had long ago been sealed from tourists. Keith Paruso wasn't a Trail Hiker.

"What else do you have, Abi?" Keith's voice was like a caress, damn it. It made her thoughts jumble as a guilty heat ran up her chest, her throat, her face. She wasn't sure how, but somehow he knew she'd been thinking of him and not the case. More like he assumed she was thinking of only him. She could practically see the planets revolving around his head—this man really did think it was all about him.

"Nothing that's worth talking about right now." She stood. "I need to get some notes together before the big meeting. I'll meet you both in the briefing room."

"You seem to have Abi riled up but good, Keith. Care to explain?" Rio grinned and all Keith thought about was how pissed his sister Kayla would be if he gave her boyfriend a black eye.

"No, I don't. This morning's the first time I've ever seen her. You never mentioned a contractor working at SVPD before today."

"No reason to bring it up. We have contractors in every now and then. It's not usual, but it happens. This just happens to be a more visible case. And Abi is, well, more visible, too." Keith knew with certainty that Rio's heart was all for Kayla. He never even mentioned that he thought another woman was attractive. As Kayla's brother, Keith was glad, but as a man, the thought of one woman having such control over his emotions made him cringe. "You seem to like what you see. In our contractor." Rio's grin widened.

"You are so damn lucky my sister is in love with you."

"If things go right, we might be brothers, Keith." Rio's expression sobered.

"You're kidding? Does Kayla know?"

"No, and please don't say anything. She doesn't want to hurry our relationship, but, frankly, I've been ready to marry her since we started dating again, when I was still working your case."

Keith nodded. During his "case," he'd been falsely accused of endangering the lives of citizens who'd been in church when it was set on fire. During its most well-attended service of the year—the children's Christmas pageant. The incident and its aftermath had changed his life…and his professional reputation. No matter how much his colleagues claimed it didn't matter, he knew better. It would haunt him until they shattered open the cult.

"Go for it, Rio. You both deserve to be happy."

"Thanks, man."

Rio's bemused expression had Keith smiling in response. He was genuinely happy for Kayla and Rio, maybe even a little jealous. Especially with a woman like Abigail Redland in town.

Hell. He needed to stop this line of thinking before it torched something deeper inside him. He wasn't the type to settle down, not yet. There was the matter of his professional reputation, which he knew would be restored once he caught the arsonist. Nothing else mattered.

Claudia Michele sprayed her silver bob with the expensive hairspray her hairstylist had convinced her would make her thick mane "manageable but still touchable." She didn't know how many times she'd done her hair, put her makeup on, hoping that the men she worked with would notice her as more than a fellow Marine. There'd been a handful through the years that she'd thought would become more than casual relationships, but with the US Marine Corps as her career, the mission had always been her priority and had overshadowed every chance at long-lasting love.

Until she'd retired from the corps and agreed to head up the Trail Hikers. Trail Hikers was her new baby, but she'd made a promise to herself that she'd put her personal life first whenever she could from now on. The chances to have her own children had passed, but she wasn't ready to give up on love. Not completely.

And Colt Todd seemed heaven-sent. The Silver Valley police chief had caught her eye from the first time they'd met. It had been over the True Believer Cult case, which they were still pursuing. Would the degenerate group's evil hold on Silver Valley ever let go?

Her phone vibrated as she picked it up to throw into her Kate Spade tote. One perk of no longer being in uniform and earning a decent paycheck was the fun fashion accessories. She particularly liked this bag because it held her .45 as easily as her Poppy Red lipstick.

"Hi, Colt."

"Claudia." God, she'd never grow tired of his deep voice, the way her stomach tingled each time she heard it. "How are you today?"

"I'm well. On my way in to the office."

"Mine or yours?"

"Mine—I have some message traffic to read. That's email in your lingo. And we're indoctrinating a couple of new agents specifically to aid in the cult takedown."

"Are you allowed to tell me that? About the new agents?"

"You don't officially know who they are or what they're for, but with the need for more manpower to take down the True Believers, I think it's safe to let you in on it."

"I'd rather you let me in on something else."

"Colt…"

"Sorry, sorry. I can't seem to help myself whether I'm next to you or miles away on the phone."

A silence fell between them and images of Colt's lips kissing every inch of her body threatened to weaken her focus on the case. "Thank you for this weekend, Colt. It was lovely."

"Yeah, well, there's more where that came from. As soon as we round up these criminals."

"I agree. I was hoping you had some good news."

"Like that one of our officers happened upon Leonard Wise at the right moment and was able to take them all down? I wish." She heard the ding of a car alarm. "I'm back at the station after spending all morning at the stakeout with the fire department trying to piece together what little evidence we have."

"Any luck? I haven't received a report from Abi or Rio yet." From Colt's tone, she suspected the stakeout had proved fruitless. Colt always took it personally when they didn't get their man or woman after such a concerted effort. It was the mark of a true professional, she thought.

"A little. The bastard got away but we did have eyes on him, and Abi came very close to taking him out."

"What the hell happened?" Abi was one of her recent hires, a secret undercover agent for TH. Former FBI, Abi was one of the most well-trained "new" agents they'd hired to date.

"He had backup and got away."

"I'll be seeing Abi when I get to my office. She's not going to be in a great mood then, I take it."

"Most certainly not. And her run-in with Keith Paruso didn't help."

"Keith?" Claudia laughed. "He strikes me as incredibly personable, especially considering what he's been through since last year."

"Personable to you when he thought you were an admin assistant for the PD's social media, sure. But on the morning after being up all night waiting for a suspected serial arsonist to strike, and then not catching the criminal?"

Colt laughed with her. His laugh reminded her of how he chuckled whenever he visibly aroused her, how his strong profile had been backlit by the sunset this weekend at the shore. When they'd had dessert before dinner and gone to her private back deck to make love before the day was done.

"Claudia?"

"Sorry. I was just thinking about something else."

"I know. Me, too."

Chapter 3

They'd run all around him but never found him. The "rabbit" Mr. Wise had hired, the decoy who made it look like someone else had set the fire, was long gone on the ATV. His back and thighs ached from being in such an uncomfortable position for hours, waiting to verify that the blaze had been set and the message sent to the ignoramuses who were Silver Valley PD and Silver Valley FD. He felt smart, clever that he'd evaded them and was able to get here, to the safe haven Mr. Wise had made for them.

The trailer park looked like any other mobile home neighborhood in America. Neat roads, similarly decorated miniature front yards with flags and animal statues—no silly decorations like gnomes or fairies. Mr. Wise said they were of the devil. But the real difference in their neighborhood was the people. They were all saved from society's ills, all living together in the New Thought community for the same purpose. To save the people of the world from their sins, their evil. Mr. Wise said their job was to warn folks.

"What do you mean he was seen by the police?" Leonard Wise's eyes bulged from red-rimmed sockets and his hands were gnarled balls of flesh and arthritic bone as they rested on the recliner he sat in. They were in the trailer no one was ever allowed in without the escort of Wise's two main brothers. He figured they were like bodyguards, but Mr. Wise was doing what was right for the people of Silver Valley. He needn't fear their wrath or harm from them.

But Lionel feared Mr. Wise right now.

"Sir, I don't mean to alarm you. They got away. The plan went as predicted."

"Predicted?" Spittle flew out of Wise's mouth, and one of the New Thought sisters who stood behind the recliner reached forward and gently dabbed the old man's mouth. He batted her ministrations away. "Leave me, woman! Both of you, go!" The women, no older than Lionel's teenage granddaughters, scuffled out of the room, eyes downcast.

Who was going to wipe Wise's mouth now?

"We don't leave our mission to prediction! I've told you once, I've told you twice, I've told you a million times to eternity, Lionel. When I give you an order it's not for me, for anyone, but for the good of the people! And the evil is rising in Silver Valley. We can't afford any mistakes. And it was a mistake this morning, I say! If the law-enforcement demons got that close to our decoys, you failed! Why didn't you stand up and let them get you while you were at it?"

Sweat that had gathered on his upper lip and in the middle of his back started to bead and drip off him. Lionel fought to retain control of his bowels. Mr. Wise didn't mean…

"Get him out of here! You will repent, Lionel, repent!"

Lionel heard a scream that sounded like a woman in childbirth but also on the brink of death. As the brothers surrounded him and grabbed him by the arms and legs, he realized the sound was coming from him.

"No, no, not the place of peace! Please, I tell you, the operation went fine! Please!" He started to sob but it was too late. In a few short minutes he was shoved into the back of a windowless van and shaken about as it made its way up into the deepest parts of the Appalachian Mountains that surrounded Silver Valley.

Abi was summoned to Trail Hiker headquarters the day after she'd allowed the arsonist to escape. Claudia hadn't seemed upset with her yesterday at SVPD headquarters, but then again, Claudia was a professional. If she were about to reprimand Abi or, worse, fire her, she wouldn't do it in front of anyone else. Especially not at SVPD or anywhere outside of Trail Hiker spaces. After all, it was a secret agency that didn't officially exist.

Inhaling deeply, she steeled herself against self-recrimination and entered her personal code into the outside door lock, after which she entered a very small, confined space in front of the *real* entry. As she peered into the retinal scanner and placed her finger atop the print reader, she tried to convince herself that she wasn't about to get fired. Claudia might be angry at the situation but Abi hadn't been hired so much to apprehend the suspect in the field as to get inside his or her mind.

The door beeped before the loud clicks of several locks opening. When the light panel glowed green, Abi turned the lever handle and opened the twelve-inch-thick steel door into the reception area. She still wasn't used to the plush appointments in the Trail Hikers headquarters office. Located in an office park on the outskirts of Silver Valley, it was minutes from Harrisburg and within twenty miles of several local, private runways. Trail Hiker agents were flown all over the world to participate in time-critical missions. It was far enough from the obvious headquarter sites like New York City and DC to be safe from prying eyes and collateral damage from a terrorist strike, but close enough to get to either place quickly.

Apparently there were a lot of missions at the moment as she felt the practiced, faux-casual glances of several persons seated on the leather chairs in the waiting area. She stepped to the high desk and spoke quietly.

"Hi, Laurel. I'm Claudia's eight o'clock."

"Yes, good morning. She's on the phone. As soon as she's free I'll let you in." Laurel was strikingly beautiful and looked like she could be a supermodel if she wanted to. But Abi suspected she was also trained to handle the worst of situations—all associated with Trail Hikers needed to be able to pull for the team. It was what had appealed to her when Claudia had first approached her for TH work. Abi had been certain she was done with law enforcement but knew she was going to miss the camaraderie she'd come to rely upon in the FBI. And, since her TH work was supposedly part-time, the generous paycheck and benefits allowed her to pursue her other passions as she'd never been able to do as an FBI agent.

Problem was that she had no idea what her passions were. She'd signed up for a yoga class, taken floral arrangement workshops, worked at the local pet rescue, but none of those endeavors had sparked any sense of her true calling.

Not like working for the Trail Hikers did.

"Claudia's ready for you, Abi. Go on in."

"Thanks."

The thick, soundproof doors clicked shut behind her as she entered Claudia's sleekly decorated office. CEO of Trail Hikers, Ltd., and retired US Marine Corps General, Claudia Michele looked ready to take on the biggest shark of Wall Street in her Armani suit and designer pumps. While her shoes weren't five- or even four-inch heels, Claudia wore them better than women decades younger.

"Good morning, Abi. Have a seat."

Claudia's perfectly manicured hand motioned to the chrome-and-leather set of chairs in front of her executive desk. Abi held back a grin. She doubted Claudia's manicurist knew the same hands had probably not only fired deadly weapons but were able to kill without any weapons other than Claudia's skill and quick thinking.

"Thank you. I'll get right to it. Yesterday morning was a bust and it's my fault. I didn't get the guy, and I even had him in my sights. I didn't want to reveal as much at SVPD headquarters yesterday."

"So I've heard. Colt Todd gave me a quick report earlier."

Abi inwardly cringed. Had they discussed how incompetent her actions had been?

"I'm sorry, Claudia. I thought I'd get him—"

Claudia held up a hand. "Stop. He got away. While I'm less than thrilled that it's a negative mark against the Trail Hikers, it happens. If you thought this was going to be like any other case you've worked, this should underscore what we've been dealing with since Leonard Wise and his thugs moved to Silver Valley."

"You are certain the cult is behind the arsons, then?"

Claudia shrugged. "Hell, no. I have no idea, not on all

of the fires. That's why we brought you into this. Your FBI experience is priceless to the team."

"It was worthless yesterday morning."

"You're going to let one slip-up affect your sense of duty, Abi? Really?"

"No, ma'am."

"*Claudia.* We're both civilians here." Claudia was adamant that she was no longer in the military and that they keep to first names only, like other corporations in the business world. It helped prevent breaking the silence on their existence.

"Claudia. No, I've never let a criminal stop me and I'm not starting now. But this fire starter is far more polished than even I expected. He had someone on an ATV waiting for him, at just the right spot that even if I was close enough I couldn't get a clear shot at him. There were too many trees and the ground was too uneven. Everything was in his favor for escape. And we had SVPD, SVFD and TH surrounding him."

"You've already developed a solid profile on him, haven't you?" Claudia's eyes narrowed on her and Abi resisted doing a worm squirm.

"Not on one, but several arsonists. There is no way, in my professional opinion, that these fires were all started by the same person. The notes are all the same, from the same source, giving us a clue as to where the next fire will be. My impression is that there are at least two but probably three or more, working on starting fires in specific locations."

"You think there's a team of them working together?"

Abi shook her head. "Absolutely not. I think they are all reporting to the same entity, be it a person or group, who tells them where and when to set the blazes. They have different methods, different profiles. Each fire starter has used a different accelerant, at least in the first two I've been assigned to. We'll have to wait another week to hear about yesterday's fire, I'm sure."

Claudia shook her head. "No, actually, we already know. This time it was aerosol cooking oil."

"The pressurized can was the explosion I heard, then." She'd thought it was fireworks, but the use of run-of-the-mill cooking spray made more sense.

"We're lucky none of the firefighters had gone in yet." Claudia tapped her pencil on her desk as if in thought but there was no mistaking the direct look she gave Abi.

"It had to stretch them awfully thin, to have so many firefighting teams at the ready in separate locations throughout Silver Valley this morning."

"It did. They called in every department from the county. There were even two from other counties."

"Claudia, don't we risk word getting out about the op against Leonard Wise and the cult with more law-enforcement types?"

"It doesn't matter. As long as Trail Hikers isn't exposed, we're good. In truth, there isn't a law-enforcement department, local, county or state, who isn't aware of what's ongoing. Colt has put feelers out all the way back to where Wise started his evil web, before his long-term imprisonment. The FBI is handling it at the national level, to facilitate the exchange of intel between New York and Pennsylvania."

"I am impressed with Silver Valley PD. They don't leave anything to chance."

Claudia nodded. "Which is why so many of them are also Trail Hiker agents. We can't call on them as often as someone like you, who is able to work for us almost exclusively, but when we do, I never have to concern myself with bringing them up to speed on local ops, as I do the other agents."

"Understood." Abi knew that the vast majority of secret operations didn't occur in Silver Valley, where the TH headquarters was located, but rather wherever they were needed around the globe.

Claudia's pencil stopped. "You didn't mention the Silver Valley Fire Department, Abi. You've been around them enough the past couple of months since you've started. Haven't they impressed you?"

"I haven't had much to do with them, except for my run-in, I mean—"

Claudia laughed. "It's okay to call your unexpected introduction to Keith Paruso what it was. A cluster-frapple."

"That's the cleanest version of that I've ever heard." Abi used the f-bomb frequently in her more difficult cases, and was almost relieved to know that Claudia wouldn't be offended if she were to let one slide out of her mouth during a stressful op.

"It means the same. As for Keith, I think you know what I'm going to have to ask of you."

Abi really wanted to drop the f-bomb now. "Claudia, I don't need his help on this."

"Yes, you do. True, you are the expert at investigating and profiling the arsonist, but Keith has the field practice you don't. He has years, thousands of cases, behind him, Abi."

"That's impossible. He can't be more than two or three years older than me."

"He's two years younger." Claudia's statement made Abi blush. So she was getting turned on by a younger dude? So what? "But he went to firefighting school right out of high school and worked as a volunteer through college. He got an associate's degree in fire science, then went on to get his bachelor's in criminology. After he got his bachelor's degree he took on a paid position with the department. He's been offered state-level positions in law enforcement but turned them down immediately. Keith is a local man who's happiest putting out Silver Valley fires."

"Leonard Wise and his cult aren't just focused on local fires, though, Claudia. Has anyone looked into where these fires are leading? What they're supposed to be accomplishing?"

"That's why I want you to work with Keith, Abi. With your global and his local experiences, you'll be unbeatable. Silver Valley's arson prevention dream team. But keep in mind that he isn't a Trail Hiker and has no need to know about us. Yet."

"You don't think he'll need to know what we're about before this is over?"

"I'm prepared to read him in for informational purposes, but Keith Paruso is a firefighter at heart. His calling is to rescue people, not take out hardened criminals."

"It's just so difficult, working side by side, without being able to totally trust one another." Keith shouldn't trust her, as she wasn't even who she'd said she was.

"I know Keith's an attractive man, Abi, but you've worked through sexual attraction before and not let it disrupt a case, I'm sure."

Abi knew Claudia was trying to lighten the mood but she found nothing casual about working with Keith Paruso. After meeting him only two times she knew that his still waters ran deep. And by her primal reaction to him, she knew that any involvement on her part was going to lead to emotional disaster. Because, unlike Fred, Keith wouldn't break her heart. He'd shatter it.

"This is against my better judgment, Claudia, but you're the boss."

"Thank you, Abi. I knew you'd figure it out."

Abi left, marveling at how getting in and out of the Trail Hiker "corporate" office was more complicated than any FBI facility she'd worked in.

As she sat in her car, contemplating how to contact Keith, she wondered if she had time to run home and freshen up before facing the sexy fire chief. And then she immediately started the car and headed for the fire department. She wasn't in the business of appearing attractive to a man she was about to spend countless work hours with. The sooner she drew the line on her personal boundaries for herself, the better.

Abi didn't date work colleagues. She'd learned the hardest way that it never worked out well.

The next morning Abi parked her car in the small but incredibly functional Silver Valley parking garage. Two stories high, it sat behind the original façade of a general mercantile. According to the historical plaque, the town general store had burned down in the nineteenth century but the façade had remained as a testament to the origins of the town. The parking garage had been erected ten years ago, to keep up with the again bustling nature of the historic downtown.

Walking down the sidewalk it wasn't hard to imagine the concrete under her feet as wooden planks, the sound of horses's hooves and the smell of fresh manure all around. As much as Abi loved nature and the outdoors, she was very happy that she'd been born to enjoy the modern conveniences of the twenty-first century.

Reimer's Real Estate's display of dozens of photos caught her eye and she paused under their green-and-white-striped awning. Several properties were for sale or rent, most in the town itself. An apartment or small house in Silver Valley proper would be nice, and much quieter compared to DC. But if she wanted to live in more of a city atmosphere she'd live in Harrisburg, only fifteen minutes and one quick ride over the Susquehanna River away.

Abi wanted something more rural.

She squared her shoulders and opened the front door of the realtor's office, relishing the jingle of the overhead bell.

An hour later Abi wanted coffee and to share her good news with someone. She grabbed a to-go cappuccino from the coffee trolley in the middle of the square and made the short walk to the town's best florist in less than five minutes.

Kayla Paruso looked up from her screen and smiled when she saw Abi.

"There's our new gal. How are you today, Abi?"

"Great." It felt so damned good to have someone greet her with such warmth, as if she were already a part of this town. "I'm checking things out and well…" She looked at the huge bouquet of pink and white tulips on the counter behind Kayla. "Wow. Those are absolutely stunning."

"They are, aren't they? It's that time of year. We get the cuttings three times a week from Baltimore. Interested in some?"

"Not yet—I'm still in the hotel. That's why I came in here, though. I had to tell someone that I think I've found a great house to rent."

Kayla's eyes crinkled with her wide grin. "Fantastic! I wanted to ask Rio if you'd found anything yet." Kayla was smooth but Abi picked up on the real meaning.

"You mean, am I thinking about settling down here?"

"Yes."

"Maybe. I mean yes, I want to set down roots, start my own business, even. It's just so difficult to know if I'm acting too quickly or too slowly—will I miss the boat on a great deal or am I throwing my money away trying to start a small business? I love police work but it's time to move on and think about something different." Something that would allow her to finally let go of her past and the drive to solve every arson case in her path. Maybe even to be present for a future family, not that she had any delusions that was happening in the *near* future.

Kayla watched her, her bemusement clear. "You know, Abi, Rio doesn't bring work home very much. But he has said that you're an incredible addition to the department. It's not your work skills he was talking about—it's how you've fit in with the other officers, how you seem to enjoy all of the local folks you meet."

Abi grunted. "Rio's my boss on this case we're working, so of course he's going to be nice." Kayla should see what a certain Chief Paruso had to say.

Kayla waved her doubt away with a flick of her callused hand. Floral work had to be incredibly tough on the skin. Abi got it. Handling a weapon, digging through arson scenes—they weren't easy on the hands, either. She took a swig of her drink.

"Have you met anyone else in the area, Abi? Any cute, single guys?"

Abi choked on her coffee. "Jeez, you don't waste any time, do you?" She'd met Kayla at the Silver Valley PD annual fund-raiser when she'd first arrived in town almost three months ago. They'd immediately hit it off, but Abi hadn't taken Kayla up on her offer of friendship. Until this morning.

"Hey, we all need love." Kayla's eyes widened. "Oh,

my God. I hope I haven't offended you, Abi. I'll stop now."

Abi laughed. "I am single, for sure, and I'd love to meet a guy to hang with after this case is done."

"I have a single brother. Wait, you should have met him already. Keith Paruso?"

Blood left Abi's head as she looked at the business card holder near the register. Kayla Paruso, Florist. Oh, no.

"No way." She gulped. "I didn't put it together."

"No reason you should have. And, from your face, I can tell you did meet my brother and let me guess—he was his usual complete butt-headed self?"

Abi's face went hot. "That's not the word I'd use. He's obviously dedicated to his job."

Kayla threw a pair of shears she'd been using to cut florist's tape onto the counter. "He's a damned bastard to women. Did he make a pass at you already?"

"No, no. Nothing like that. At all. God, no."

"He will, trust me. My brother's a bit of a player, I'll admit. I could blame it on recent political events in town, which could have cost him his job, but I'd be lying. He's always been able to make women eat out of the palm of his hand."

"He and Rio get along. Rio doesn't strike me as the kind of guy who'd be more than polite to another man he didn't respect."

Kayla's face got all…mushy. "Rio loves me, so he's going to love anyone related to me. It's how he is. Trust me, though, if Rio thought Keith was a real jerk he'd be protective of me around him. And he's never done that. They've worked together longer than I've known Rio."

"Especially the last few months, I imagine."

"Make it the last year and a half. It's been nuts in this town. You know we lived all over as kids—Belgium, other places. Our parents worked for the government. We were exposed to so much, so young. It doesn't take a lot to faze me. Or my brother. But having the entire town shook up by this crazy quasi-religious group, and Keith being accused of not doing his job right, along with the mayor being fired and a corrupt mayor getting elected before he got arrested, it's been insane. Don't think this is how Silver Valley normally is. We're quiet here."

"I think a lot of towns across Pennsylvania and the US are going through the same thing. Not with a nutso cult, but with drugs, violence. Heroin trafficking, the crimes related to addicts needing money for drugs—it's all mushrooming."

Kayla leveled her gaze on Abi—the same look Keith was fond of shooting at her and she'd only known him for three days so far. Was it usual to see a familial connection so quickly? To feel a sense of knowing these people she'd only just met?

"I know the facts, Abi. I read the paper online, along with other stuff. I really love reading the *New Yorker.* I get it. What's hard is making the transition to the reality that these influences have landed in Silver Valley. Just five years ago it was so much quieter."

It'd always been busy and "insane" in DC, so Abi couldn't relate to that part. The sense of being out of control of her surroundings, of having her quiet world shattered by a freak accident when life had been going so well until then? Yeah, she got that part.

"Hopefully the work we're doing at the station will help put Silver Valley back in the 'sleepy' category." She took a last sip of her coffee before looking around for a waste bin.

"Here." Kayla pointed at the chrome, bullet-shaped container at the end of the counter. "Sleepy sounds good about now." She fiddled with a second tulip arrangement. This one was smaller, almost miniature, with pale peach tulips and daisies. And some other greenery Abi didn't recognize.

"You mentioned starting a small business. What do you have in mind, Abi?"

"I've no earthly idea." Actually, the tiny niggle of an idea had sprouted over the last day or two, but she wasn't ready to commit to it. Commitment regarding anything wasn't viable. Not until they dismantled the cult and Abi was at the epicenter of the takedown ops.

"You'll figure it out. Have you thought of going back to school?"

"I did, but I'm not interested. I've spent enough time in classrooms." And workshops and continuing certification for her weapons handling, physical fitness and knowledge of arson forensics. It made for a great résumé but Abi preferred to be outdoors, with no one grading her actions.

"Understandable." The shop phone rang. Kayla looked at the ID. "I've got to take this, sorry. But I wanted to mention to you that there's a great yoga class every Saturday morning in town. I think you'd enjoy meeting the other women that attend."

"I'll think about it. Take your call—it's okay, I'm on my way out. Thanks for letting me chat."

"Here you go." Kayla handed Abi the peach tulip bouquet, now wrapped in a doily and cellophane and tied with a huge cream ribbon.

"Oh, thank you, Kayla!" Abi's arms instinctively rose to give Kayla a hug but she was already answering the call. Kayla gave her a wink and a wave before giving her total attention to the person on the other end of the line.

Abi left the shop in a bit of a fugue. People being positive and upbeat for apparently no reason. This was what daily happiness was all about. Something that had eluded her during her time with the FBI, save for the brief fling and quick but doomed engagement to Fred.

Yeah, she could get used to a place like Silver Valley. Especially the "belonging" feelings. When she reached her car she dialed Keith's number. He picked up on the second ring, his voice guarded.

But in less than thirty seconds they had scheduled a meet-up.

Chapter 4

Keith waited for Abi at Cumberland Café, Silver Valley's favorite breakfast spot. The place was jumping, as always, be it the Sunday morning after-church crowd or parents who'd stopped to let someone else prepare their breakfast after rushing their gremlins off to school. He kept his focus on the menu, trying like hell to ignore the way his anticipation roiled in his gut. He hadn't looked forward to seeing a woman, professionally or personally, in forever. Or longer. At any rate, *too* long.

The bell above the door perked his attention and he allowed himself the gift of watching Abigail walk into the diner. She wasn't tall but definitely not petite, either. Her figure was athletic, a testament to the chase she'd given the arsonist two days ago. It didn't surprise him that his body responded to her sheer attractiveness, not that he was used to getting erections in public. The scorch of annoyance that he found it difficult to control his baser instincts made him stand and reach out his hand to hers before she was in arm's reach. For crap's sake, he must look like some kind of grade-school kid meeting the babysitter he had a secret crush on.

Her eyes widened fractionally in recognition of him before she walked toward the table. As she neared, her eyes flickered to his outstretched hand and a mocking smile curved her pink-lipsticked mouth. She placed her hand in his. "So nice to see you again, Keith."

"Hello, Abi." He grasped her hand but allowed her to control the shake. One single, firm movement. No up-and-down ritual or enthusiastic pumping. Abigail was a full-fledged professional and had obviously worked in a man's world for a long time. She shook hands like a man.

But her hand didn't feel like anything other than a soft, smooth, feminine asset. Underscored by the flowery scent she gave off. He wondered if it was perfume or if she liked expensive soaps. The thought of soaping her down in a shower...

Son of a whoopie pie.

Abigail Redland was off-limits. Not only because it was good to keep definite boundaries with the people he worked with, but because he wasn't looking for even a short relationship with a woman he knew nothing about. After getting burned by local community members that he'd saved during a fire, trust wasn't his strongest virtue at the moment. He felt safer with casual liaisons that had a preset time limit agreed upon by both parties. There were enough women in Silver Valley who felt the same way. He didn't need to act on his feelings for Abi. Not that he had feelings for her. Feelings were complications he couldn't afford.

"Thanks for saving us a seat." She pulled her hand away and slid into the booth. He liked how she looked around the diner as if it were an artifact in a museum. "I absolutely adore the diners in Silver Valley. When I lived in DC, I got used to a few local places but nothing as fun as a diner. I missed them from when I grew up." She pointed at the menu. "What's the best dish here, in your opinion?"

He slid back into his bench seat. "You must not have been in Silver Valley very long if you don't have your own favorite by now."

"I've been here long enough." She frowned at the list of variations on French toast. "There's not one version I don't want to try. Except maybe for the scrapple."

"Scrapple has its place. Not quite sausage, not quite… grease. Meaty lard. Very tasty."

"Huh. I'll tell you what… I'll bet it was good for the farmers here about two centuries ago, when it was cold out. I'll pass on it for today and go for the carbs. The wild berry French toast looks delicious."

"That's a good choice. They freeze fresh berries in the summer and use them all year."

"How do you know that?"

"I dated a girl in high school whose parents owned a berry farm."

She blinked. "Is that a thing?"

"Of course. There are farms for just about everything. But most do grow a variety of produce. It's hard enough making a living with several different crops."

"I grew up in the city, so farming isn't something I'm familiar with."

Wow, was Abigail Redland admitting she didn't know something? "Are you feeling well, Abi?"

Her eyes were bright, which lent a depth to their chocolate hue he hadn't noticed yet. "What do you mean? I'm fine."

"It's just that I thought FBI types never admitted when they were wrong or didn't know something."

She pursed her lips and raised her brow in mock disapproval. "Very funny, Mr. Who-the-Hell-Are-You-at-My-Fire-Scene."

Abi sat opposite him in a cherry-red wool jacket, and he noticed that the buttons were the shape of little white sheep. Another, softer side of her? As she unwrapped her fuzzy scarf, it snagged on one of the ewe buttons.

"Careful. You're tearing up your scarf." He pointed and she looked down. Her fingers deftly untangled the button and she shrugged out of her coat, revealing a slim-fitting, long-sleeved red top.

"It's okay. I can make another one."

"You made your scarf?" He wasn't any kind of expert but the lacy thing didn't look like anything handmade he'd ever seen before.

She nodded. "And this jacket, actually. It's boiled wool. Felted. Meaning I knitted it about ten sizes too big and then shrunk it in a huge soup pot on my stove. Hot water felts untreated wool."

"You're kidding."

"No, I wish I were. I'm a fiber nerd with a law-enforcement hobby."

"And your favorite color is red?"

"Bingo." She picked the menu back up. "Maybe I'll save the French toast for next time. I can't decide between the gluten-free cherry crepes or the hearty hot cereal."

"Go for the gusto. Their cherry crepes are renowned."

"So you've had them?"

He laughed. "I'm a Silver Valley native and Cumberland Café has been here as long as I remember. My family used to come in here regularly once we settled in the area, when I was still in middle school. So, yes, between family meals and high school dates, I've had just about everything on the menu at least a time or two."

"Only high school dates? Where do people go on adult dates here?" Her expression of sincere curiosity made him smile.

"Oh, we like to go four-wheeling while doing some chew, spitting it out on the way to the firing range."

"I'm not one of the transplants who thinks this is some kind of hick town, Keith." Her eyes softened. "I like it here. A lot."

"Where are you from?" He didn't think it was DC.

And, like that, the sparkle in her eyes was gone. She didn't meet his glance as she sipped her ice water. "Originally? Philadelphia. After I joined the FBI, I worked in a few different places but mostly DC. You? You said your family 'settled' here?"

"Yes, when I was thirteen. My folks were Foreign Service Officers, and my sisters and I lived all over the world. My older sister lives in Ouagadougou, Burkina Faso, with her family—she's working for the State Department, just like Dad did. My other sister lives here in town and owns the local floral shop. Once Dad could retire from the government job, he did, and now my parents still travel as much as they can afford to. And run a gift-shop-slash-international-interior-decorating business in town and online, with treasures they find all over."

"Treasures as in archaeological or more like knick-knacks?"

"Definitely knickknacks. Which is why I have nothing of the sort in my place." Crap—would she think he was hitting on her, suggesting she'd be at his place to see what he had?

The waitress came and took their orders. Abi tilted her head after he placed his.

"You ordered it just because I did?"

"No, I happen to like cherry crepes, too."

Keith studied her and didn't care if it made her uncomfortable or if he was being too forward. "Abi, you didn't answer my question. Tell me more about where you're from. What made you pick the FBI and, more relevant, why arson?"

She remained apparently relaxed as she leaned on her forearms, her hands atop one another. She wasn't at ease, though. The tightening of her fingers around her wrist, the slight jut of her jawbone wouldn't have been noticed by anyone unless they were watching for it. And Keith was watching.

"Full disclosure—I was just at your sister's flower shop. I hadn't put you two together yet. And I really like her."

Unlike you. Keith snorted. "Kayla's got a nice little business going. She might not have the benefits I do working for the town, but she's raking it in now that her shop is well established."

"'Little business'? Would you call this restaurant a 'little' business?"

"Chill. I'm not the jerk you're trying to make me out to be. I'm pro-woman." He gave her his best smile.

Abi raised a brow and motioned at his face. "Really? You think a Cheshire Cat grin is going to change my mind about you?"

Ow. Sucker punch to the ego, that one.

"Back to you, Abi. Tell me why you do what you do."

Her eyes—a man could take a long dip in them. Nothing permanent, of course. But a nice, long, leisurely swim. Naked.

She looked away. "I was always interested in law enforcement, so I had two majors in college—criminal justice and studio art. After I graduated, the FBI was a logical choice." He really wanted to know why she'd picked arson but sensed it wasn't the time to ask. She'd tell him when she was ready.

"I understood that they don't take college grads as agents, that you have to work for a couple of years in the real world first."

She grinned. It warmed her entire face, illuminated her dark eyes and the freckles on her nose. "That's where the studio art major came into play. I managed a large craft store franchise until I was eligible to apply to be an agent. It took me a few times, believe me."

"So why have you quit the FBI? Are you going to sell fabric paint on QVC?"

"How do you know so much about crafting and home television shopping?"

It was his turn to feel interrogated. "I was home a lot last year." He wasn't about to tell her his struggle with the depression he'd slipped into when he'd been falsely accused of wrongdoing. When all he'd ever worked for had been destroyed along with his professional reputation. "It's a long story and nothing for today. Tell me about you, Abi. Why did you leave the FBI?"

Her eyes narrowed and her grin vanished. He'd discovered Abi's line in the sand.

"No one reason. I never really intended for the agency to be a career. It was a chance to gain experience before I…" She stirred her water with the straw, the ice clunking against the plastic glass, and it was as if she were looking into a crystal ball. "I guess I thought I'd end up in local law enforcement or at a fire station like my dad. But I can't say law enforcement's what I plan to do for the rest of my life. I needed a change, that's all."

"So your dad is a firefighter."

"Was."

"I'm sorry."

"No, nothing that awful. He's still alive and still working. He just…he just switched jobs midcareer." With that her eyes clouded and she closed her mouth into a grave line.

He'd expected to be annoyed when she stopped being open to him. Instead he couldn't hide from the sliver of excitement that flipped in his gut. Keith loved a challenge and was finding that, in the short time he'd spent with Abigail Redland, she'd been nothing less than a complex puzzle to figure out. He loved puzzles, complicated problems. Abi fit the bill. So what was with the shaky feeling in his midsection?

Why should he care what the full picture of Abi would reveal?

Abi enjoyed her brunch with Keith but was very aware of his being on edge, or, rather, *at* the edge of asking her more questions. Instead she kept things on the case or on her background, minus the Trail Hikers part. It shouldn't bother her so much to leave out this one part of her job here. She was used to never discussing her work with close friends and colleagues. It was the way of an FBI agent, and it was her way. She'd chosen fire science and arson investigation out of guilt over a teen stunt gone horribly wrong. A decision that had cost her best friend's life and her father's firefighting career.

But here in Silver Valley it felt different. As if she were in a place where no one cared about her past. Or maybe it was Keith. She didn't like admitting it to herself, no more than she enjoyed working with someone when she wasn't being completely truthful. But she had no choice when it came to her Trail Hiker role.

She smiled at Keith.

"Chief Todd and Rio think we need to work closely together. That I need to bring you along with me as I go through each arson site again."

Keith's eyes narrowed and he set his knife and fork down. "Bring me along?"

"I mean, let you know where and when so that you can meet me, if you want to. Although since I plan on hitting each site over the next couple of days, it might be easier to drive together."

He started shoveling his crepes into his mouth again. "That's better," he mumbled around the food, and Abi thought that maybe she wasn't feeling herself. Because the very kind of rude table manners that normally annoyed her seemed…sensual. Manly. For scrapple's sake, Keith Paruso made everything he did appear manly. The guy didn't know how to do anything in a usual, regular guy kind of way.

"So you want to come along with me? Meet me?"

"Either I can pick you up where you live, or you can come get me." He pulled out a business card and quickly wrote on the back. "That's my address and email. The cell number on the front is my only phone." She flipped over the card and noticed the Silver Valley Fire Department seal.

"Thanks. Nice business card. Can you start today?"

"I should be able to. I'll check in with the station when we're done."

Abi was relieved when her phone vibrated. The screen lit up with a text from the real-estate manager she'd been working with for the past two weeks.

"I'm sorry to cut this short, Keith, but I'm going to have to cut out of here a bit sooner than I thought."

"Is it about the case?"

"No." At his unrelenting stare, she capitulated. "I'm on the hunt for a more permanent rental than the business suite I've been staying at. As much as I love the free buffet breakfast every morning, I need more space."

"We're not done, Abi. We need to figure out what role each of us has in this and how we're going to get to the bottom of the arsons." His expression was back to being totally professional without a hint of the genuine interest she'd sensed moments ago.

"Real-estate agents can be tough to pin down and I'd rather not have to reschedule with her." He'd take the hint, surely?

"Does she have a place for you?"

"Looks like it." And it was the rent-to-own situation she'd discovered in the real-estate office window, which she was very excited about. Finally she was thinking about settling down somewhere that wasn't in the middle of a big city. She'd found that living in one could be the loneliest place on the planet when all you did was work, sleep, repeat.

"Where is it, Abi? If you don't mind my asking?"

"Of course not. You just gave me yours. Not that it's like belly buttons or, um, whatever. You know, you show me yours, I'll show you mine." What the hell was wrong with her?

Keith grinned. "I don't think that expression refers to belly buttons."

"Oh." She felt her face redden but Keith's calm expression, the lack of judgment in his eyes, helped her feel safe despite her jumbled simile. Was there anything in her that wasn't shaken up by Keith's presence?

She broke eye contact and gave him her address. Oddly, she didn't mind telling him. She got nothing but healthy, albeit wary, vibes from Keith Paruso. Plus maybe some more intense feelings that could lead to an intimacy she wasn't ready for, might never be ready for. She'd examine those later.

"That's the old Pearson farm, right?"

"I've no idea who owned it before but, yes, it's a couple-of-centuries-old farmhouse, originally." And when she'd scoured the photos and description at the real-estate office it had looked absolutely delicious. Stone walls, dark roof, the rectangular building sat on the highest point of a hill that overlooked Silver Valley. It was in the middle of farm fields all around but the tree line for the Appalachian Trail was visible from the driveway's entrance. The trail had called to her since she'd arrived in Silver Valley. Abi loved hiking and camping.

"You're not worried about living in a farmhouse with the current case?" Keith's brow furrowed and Abi tried to ignore the warm fuzzies that blossomed in her center.

"No. Don't forget, I've been trained by the FBI. And it would be stupid for the arsonists to target me—they'd get caught."

"I like how you think, Abi. I'd like to meet you there. In about ten minutes. That is, if you don't mind?"

"I don't mind."

His face infused with relief. "I've always wanted to get a look inside that house. It was in the same family for so long and they didn't have kids in our generation, so I've never seen it."

"Glad to oblige. We can finish our discussion there." She reached for the check and his hand beat her to it. One instant later and their hands would have collided. Keith's hands felt like he looked. Strong, masculine, sexy. She wished he'd grabbed her hand instead of the check.

"I've got this, Abi. You can buy the next one." His tone was so certain, so sure that there would be a "next" time that she had to resist her natural instinct to buck against his strong will. No one, no man she barely knew, told her what to do or what her future would be. She opened her mouth to tell Keith something to that effect, but he was already at the cash register, his wide grin splitting his handsome face as he spoke with the diner manager.

Keith Paruso was not a man who was easily directed.

Chapter 5

"You'll be able to rent for six to twelve months before you have to make a decision to purchase or not." Diane Murphy, Silver Valley's "premier" real-estate agent, according to the billboard boasting her headshot on Silver Valley Pike, clacked around the empty dining room, her spike heels incongruous with the historical, albeit modernized, home.

Abi stood in front of the wall of windows that had been retrofitted with the farmhouse's most recent upgrade. There were alpaca and sheep grazing in the field just outside the perimeter fence. She knew the animals because whenever she had time off from her Trail Hiker contracts she'd joined some of her college friends and picked back up a hobby she'd once loved: knitting.

Knitting. That could certainly qualify as one of her passions, but not something she wanted to make a living at. Silver Valley already had a local yarn shop. She needed the thrill of physically exerting herself past her limits, like she did when she hiked a rocky trail or climbed an elevation past what she ever thought she could do. Could she make a new career out of her love of the outdoors? A tiny thrill rode up her spine as she envisioned the possibility of shedding the career she'd sought as a grief-stricken adolescent. Arson investigation had been her life but she needed more. Wanted more.

"Isn't the view wonderful? And look at the goats." Diane's words were so enthusiastic Abi didn't have the heart to correct her animal identification skills.

"Is all of this land with the house? How much of the land am I responsible for maintaining?" She didn't own a trowel much less a lawn mower.

"Mmm, let me see…" Diane used her lacquered fingernail as a line marker, running through pages of spreadsheets. "Great news! All of the land, save for what's inside the picket fence and the big red barn, is rented out. The farmers work it for you! Isn't that wonderful?" Her eyelash extensions and heavy makeup were distracting. Abi had seen lighter foundation during a stage production.

"What's good about it is that you won't have to worry about a brush fire, not if the farmers are watering and working the land." Keith had remained quiet throughout the tour, shadowing them from room to room.

"Here, in south central Pennsylvania? Does it ever get that dry?"

"This isn't DC. You've had a lot of rain down there this past year, thanks to El Niño, and we had our share of it, too. But it's not enough to keep the dry spells away. We get long periods of high heat and no precipitation. Add in the winds that come with cold fronts and the jet stream, and it's the ideal mix for forest fires. If farmland goes untended, it becomes the perfect fuel for brush fires."

Abi didn't like looking stupid, especially about anything to do with fires. But her ignorance was real. "I'm from Philly. I just never thought of Pennsylvania as a high-risk area for fires. Other than a home fire."

"It's another reason the Silver Valley Fire Department is stretched so thin as we head into the summer months."

Their gazes met and his bright eyes reflected the knowledge they shared: add in a few arsonists working for a crazed cult and people were going to get killed before the summer was out. The math was pure and simple. There weren't enough SVFD fighters to handle the heavy load.

"Um, guys? I know you're in the fire business and all, Keith, but, really, when's the last time Silver Valley had a grass fire? Truly, Abi, it's not something you should worry about. All of the farmers are local and they'll all be willing to talk to you, I'm sure. Especially if you decide to purchase."

"And I'll deal with you for the entire time I lease?"

"Yes, I'll be your rental agent. I'm the property manager until we sell. The family's decided to split the proceeds after the place sells, and none of the children or grandchildren are interested in the place. It's kind of sad, since it was in the same family for almost a hundred years."

"The Pearsons." Keith ran a hand along the solid cherry-wood balustrade that graced the main staircase. "I heard that this place used to be a tavern before they converted it to a farmhouse."

More scratching of nail against paper as Diane did more searching. "Here!" She flicked at the page. "Look, it's a copy of the paper from last month. They found the remains of a meeting place, or club, that was used by some of the founders."

"Founders?" Abi frowned as she took the paper from Diane. "Oh, my goodness, you mean the Founding Fathers, as in the men who wrote the Bill of Rights!" Abi wanted to put a down payment on the mortgage on the spot. Where else would she ever afford to own a piece of American history?

"I'll leave you with that, and if you even think you'd like to rent this place, Abi, you should jump on it. It won't last long." Diane smiled and stood still in her perfectly tailored Chanel-style suit, living the kind of life Abi couldn't fathom. One without constant danger, fighting nearly demonic forces that seemed to possess the crazy criminals she pursued.

"About that barn…is it empty? A good storage area?"

"It's in perfect condition. You could keep your car in there, and anything else you need to. I wouldn't keep things that the temperature affects, but plastic bins would probably be great."

A storage area for her kayak, paddleboard, skis, tent, backpack. She looked out the front window and noted the rise of the mountains, the bare parts of the rounded mountaintops that indicated ski resorts. If she wanted to make a living in adventure travel, Silver Valley was the perfect spot. Somewhere deep inside her the knot she'd carried since her high school best friend's death started to unfurl.

"I'm in. Where do I sign?"

A half hour later Diane was gone and Abi sat on the front porch stoop with Keith. "I can't believe I'm getting all of this for the same price as a tiny walk-up condo in Alexandria."

"You're renting." He said it like a verdict. His tone said everything his words didn't. *You're not permanent here. You're just passing through. You're not a real resident of Silver Valley.*

"For now." She wasn't about to tell Keith Paruso, a man she hardly knew, all of her plans. Not that she had anything concrete.

"Why settle down here? It'll feel slow after the pace you're used to. And doesn't your family want you closer to Philadelphia?"

What was his freaking problem?

"Let's get one thing straight, Keith. We need to come together on some level to work together and close this case as quickly as we can. I don't want to see your firefighters put in any more danger than they need to be. And I'm going to do everything in my power to get these losers. I can't do it if you're in my way."

"Who said I'm in your way?"

"For starters, you're assuming you know who I am, where I'm from, like when you just said it's quieter here than I'm used to. How do you know what I'm used to? For all you know I spend my off time hiking the Appalachian Trail." Which she did, actually.

"Doubtful. You wouldn't have the experience you do if you hadn't put your whole self into your career. And even though I would have thought our paths would cross before this most recent arson, I'm pretty certain you haven't had much free time since SVPD hired you. Hiking the least challenging parts of the AT takes at least half a day, by the time you drive out there and back." Keith's words rang true. Not the hiking part, but the accurate assessment that she'd put her whole life into her career. To the detriment of her personal life.

"That brings me to my other point, Keith. Our personal lives are off-limits. We're work colleagues. It's none of your business what I do with my personal time."

"It's my business to know you, Abi. You're the one who's going to keep my firefighters from getting hurt. From being sent into a booby trap. And you think I'm going to take your word for it that you know what the hell you're doing?"

"I don't report to you, Keith. If you want professional references, start with Rio or Chief Todd."

The tension between them belied the serenity that practically oozed off the encompassing fields. A bird twittered nearby, as if unsure by the sudden change of energy. Abi could feel Keith's body heat from the nearness of his thigh as they sat next to one another on the stoop. Yet he seemed unperturbed by their words.

Keith sat quietly, staring at the hills of farmland that stretched as far as they could see from the porch. His profile was relaxed but the grim lines around his mouth betrayed the air of nonchalance.

"I don't want to spar with you, Abi. We got off on the wrong foot because we were after the same thing the other morning, and the bad guy got away. We're both professionals, so we were understandably upset. My desire is for us to be on the same page, at least close enough so that the next time one of the creeps runs past us, we catch him."

"I agree." From some unknown pool of sadness, a lump arose in her throat. Keith wasn't her father, but he was a firefighter like her father had been. One of the good guys. She trusted her professional instinct on this. "I'm sorry that I got so wound up. It's been an adjustment, taking work here and now deciding to move here."

"But you're only renting. What will you do when this

case is over? There isn't enough arson work in Silver Valley for the PD to keep you employed."

"I have other options." She couldn't share more with him, certainly nothing about Trail Hikers. Hell, she didn't know what she was going to do after they wrapped up this case. As for her thoughts on starting her own business, they were too fresh to share with anyone, especially the very man she needed to guard from sharing too much with.

It had been just over a week since Abi and Keith parted ways at the farmhouse. He'd said he was going to the fire station and she went to the police station. Abi spent the rest of that day, and all the days in between, poring over Trail Hiker files on the True Believer—aka New Thought—Cult. They were rebranding themselves as the New Thought community but it was the same modus operandi Leonard Wise had used in upstate New York for the True Believers.

Abi would have preferred the quiet and isolation of the Trail Hikers headquarters and its access to more classified files on Wise, but she continued to work at SVPD to maintain her cover as a police contractor.

"Find anything?" Rio slid into the chair across from her in the small conference room where she'd set up shop. His steaming cup of tea reminded her that she hadn't gotten up from her seat since arriving at the station around noontime.

"Nada." She stretched. "I'm looking for any clue as to why the cult, namely Leonard Wise, would want to plague Silver Valley with arson. Torching abandoned buildings can be dramatic, but they don't concern a community until it starts being occupied homes. Even then, it's hard to figure out the arsonist's motive."

"Except you said you believe there's more than one fire starter."

"I do. Claudia agrees, as do I, that our analysts are onto something. If you look at this map, it's clear." She moved her iPad and pointed to a large paper map that was stretched across the table. "The places that have been torched started out on the periphery of town, not far from the trailer park where they're all living. Then they went through town, but still unoccupied structures. Look here—they went out of town to the base of the Appalachians, near the abandoned quarry, and now are coming back up the main pike. If the rate of fires set continues at the same pace, the arsonists will have torched a total of eighteen buildings by next month."

"What does the path of the targets tell us?" Rio stared at the map as if willing an answer to come forth.

"Not much. Until you increase the scale, or zoom out the map. Here." She handed him her iPad where she had the graphic displayed. "Do you see what I do?"

Rio frowned but his downturned mouth curved up as his brow rose and he laughed. "Holy crap, it's in the shape of an arrow."

"Exactly."

"But it's only pointing to a farm field."

"Not any farm field." She expanded the map. "It leads up to the playground of Silver Valley Elementary School."

"No way."

"Of course, it's summertime. Summer break. If anyone tries to set the building on fire, we can be fairly certain no one will be in harm's way. I called the building superintendent and there is only one janitor that goes through the building on a weekly basis. No kids, no adult workshops or what have you. Nothing to worry about, casualty-wise. But the building itself could be at risk."

"Why would they target an elementary school during the summer, then? They're not going to get a lot of press without any kids in there. And not when school's out of session."

"That's the million-dollar question, Detective Ortega. My hunch is that it would be a test run for when school starts."

Keith walked into his station and found a fire hall full of tired, overworked fighters who needed a vacation. He called the team that was on duty together at the large eating table in the commercial-size kitchen.

"Hey, everyone. I'm proud of the work we're doing." Grumbles immediately arose from the men and women who were still peeved about the arsonist getting away from them at the abandoned farmhouse ten days ago. Keith held up his hands, palms out. "Hey, knock it off. No, we didn't get the creep, but that's not our job. Our job is what, folks?"

"Fire suppression."

"Public education."

"EMT services."

Of course the newly fledged officers spoke up first. The long-timers raised eyebrows, took a sip of their coffee, shrugged.

Keith laughed. "All of the above, right? It's whatever we need to do. But nowhere in our job description is 'apprehension of the criminal.' We've held some up, of course, until the police arrived, but that's the exception. I'm asking everyone to take extra care on-scene and make sure, above all else, that you don't mess up the damned evidence."

His phone chimed and he saw the text from the most recent contact he'd entered. Abigail Redland. She'd be pissed off if she knew he'd used her full first name for her contact information.

"Hi, Abi." He kept his eye on his team. While they all acted as if they weren't listening to their boss's conversation, he knew better.

"I've figured something out. Do you have time to come to police headquarters?"

"How soon?"

"Now."

"Give me ten." He disconnected the call and tried to shake the feeling that he'd been with Abi in person. Her voice in his ear, as short as the conversation had been, was nothing less than sexy and familiar.

"New love interest, Chief?" Barrow, the most senior firefighter, teased him. Keith had quite a reputation for his active dating life. Something he hadn't given as much thought to since his career had been shot out from under him last year. When he'd been faced with losing what really mattered to him—putting out fires and saving lives. Firefighting had been his identity and he'd been paralyzed with the fear of never being able to do it again. It had squashed his libido flatter than the station's cement floor. Being reinstated and having his job back had started to breathe life back into him. His zest for not only living but thriving was back. And now with Abi Redland in town…

"Not quite. I'll be at the police department if anyone needs me." He grabbed his jacket and left.

Keith was greeted by Abi and Rio when he walked into SVPD. As soon as he entered the conference room, Abi nodded at another officer. "You can go get Chief Todd now, Nika."

"I'm on it."

"Thanks for coming in, Keith." Abi's glance was professional, but was that a spark of something in her eyes? Interest beyond the professional? Or was he being a self-serving narcissist?

"Glad to be here." Could he sound any lamer?

"I was looking at the maps we've compiled after each arson that we believe to be associated with the cult, and it seems that everything points to one place." Her finger pointed to a familiar spot. Keith's gut dropped.

"The elementary school?"

"Yes. It's a clear line from the first fire at Silver Valley Community Church two Christmases ago to the one from the other day in the abandoned farmhouse."

Keith leaned in and ignored Abi's fresh scent. It was actually on the sweeter side. Like a flower from Kayla's shop.

"You're correct. I didn't think they'd all be so closely related." How had he missed this?

"No harm, no foul. It's easy to miss. Some of the fires were non-starters, stopped by local neighbors before your department was ever called."

Abi's assessment held no professional judgment, no rancor. She understood the fire department wasn't paid to investigate every lead or even track down an arsonist. They were supposed to keep fire damage to a minimum, minimize casualties. Still, the responsibility weighed on him.

"Whatever." Keith didn't want to verbalize what everyone at the table knew: at least one of his men should have put the pieces together. In fact, it was a little unusual that no one had. Firefighters were on the superstitious side of belief and would be quick to notice "coincidences."

"Not 'whatever.' It's not worth getting riled up about. I'm not here to accuse you of not seeing it, Keith. I didn't see it until this morning and I'm an arson expert." Abi's voice was steady, her brown eyes on him, comforting him. Even her gaze felt as though it caressed him.

"I usually notice similarities. The different propellants might be why no one thought the fires could be related." He'd take a hit but his team didn't deserve any blame. They were doing their jobs as best they could.

"Exactly." Colt Todd spoke from the doorway and made his way into the room to take the head seat at the table. "Sit down, everyone. This is going to take a bit, I'm afraid." Under the fluorescent lights Colt's brows were grayer than Keith had noticed, his hair more sparse. Evidently the cult's emergence in Silver Valley was taking its toll. But Colt's eyes were no less bright as they shone with determination.

"First, good job to everyone working on these cases. They all seemed to be individual, random acts of arson, which was making us nuts, trying to track them all. But we've got good reason to believe that instead they're all related. The FBI and our current expert hire, Abi, have pulled together some disparate facts and made a case for us that we can't ignore." As Colt spoke, Claudia walked into the room and sat in the seat nearest the door. Keith thought it interesting that the SVPD's social media "guru" was involved in such a close-held meeting, but maybe she needed to know the facts to ward off any rumors that started.

Colt didn't miss Keith's observation. "Claudia's been taking care of the rumormongers on Facebook and Twitter. They like to blame SVPD and SVFD for everything that goes wrong in Silver Valley. What did you call them, Claudia?"

The silver-haired maven smiled. "The haters. And we're on Snapchat, too."

Colt nodded. "Yeah, the 'haters.' Screw them is my method, but according to Claudia it's important to keep these citizens engaged."

"She's right. The haters are often in the know about who's doing what in town. They could be a source of information, or, even better, witnesses to a crime." Abi spoke with the authority of someone ten years her senior. That sense of camaraderie, connection, flared in Keith's center as he watched her, listened to her. Abi, like him, had been forced to assume professional accountability earlier than most. Being in any kind of public service could do that to a person.

Abi's beauty hadn't been diminished by the weight of her cases, however. He'd seen the ravages of their kind of work on folks; premature wrinkles and early gray hair were the least of the damage. The deeper, more lasting havoc was beneath the surface; like the worst movie you never wanted to ever see again, the images of a botched rescue or failed life-saving mission replayed ad infinitum.

"Keith? Did you catch that?" Rio's deep voice penetrated his thoughts, and the expression on his and everyone else's faces as Keith looked at them indicated he'd missed something critical.

"No, uh, I think I missed it."

"I said we're going to walk through all the scenes together. All the fires from the past two years. I can do it alone if you've changed your mind, but I thought you'd want a representative from your department with me." Abi didn't look at him as she spoke, repeating her request. She thought he'd relent and assign a junior firefighter. He'd thought they'd made some headway about working together. Apparently Abi was the one who'd changed her mind.

"Of course I'm still doing the walk-throughs with you.

I'd rather keep the fighters on watch, and not split up these duties." It would give him more time alone with Abi and by the sharp flare of her small nostrils he knew he'd stymied her attempt to cut him out.

Tough. It was time Abi learned she wasn't the only hard-ass in Silver Valley.

"I plan to start today. I've counted eight fires to date." She met his gaze head-on. "Really, Keith, I don't need an escort if you need the time to arrange watches around the elementary school."

"We do it together." He stared at her, and damn if she didn't blink.

Colt's cough broke the tension.

"It's good to have each of you there. Does anyone have anything else to add? Anything Abi and Keith should be aware of, on the lookout for that we've missed?" Colt's tone was rife with annoyance. He didn't usually need to play referee between two professionals. Keith felt like a dolt.

"I'm not sure what you're hoping to get from these revisits, but I'm here to help. Call me from any site, anytime," Rio said, looking bored and…frustrated. They all were.

The cult had started spreading its fingers into town with that first fire two Christmases ago, Keith was certain of it. The church janitor had acted alone as far as any evidence reflected, but Keith had always felt he'd been egged on by the ugly thoughts and precepts of Leonard Wise. Just as the couple who had accused Keith of negligence had been. But it wasn't anything that could be proved in a court of law. Just a firefighter's hunch.

"Thanks for your support, Chief Todd." Abi's face didn't reflect anything but that of professional interest.

Keith liked it better when she smiled and looked like she'd forgotten what her profession was.

"Abi, can I have a word?" Claudia smiled. She'd waited until everyone had left the conference room to speak.

"Sure. Here okay?"

At Claudia's nod, Abi closed the conference room door. Claudia motioned for her to take a seat and sat in the chair Colt had vacated. Abi didn't miss the natural way Claudia wore her authority. Anyone who walked into the conference room would only see two professional women, and think that the Silver Valley PD social media manager was chatting with the arson specialist contractor. Nothing unusual, per se.

"Abi, you're doing a superlative job."

"Thank you, Claudia."

"And I'm afraid I didn't make the entirety of your Trail Hikers responsibilities clear."

Abi's gut clenched. "Oh?" Was she about to be fired from the first job she'd had outside of the FBI? Right after she'd signed the lease for the house?

"Being a Trail Hiker isn't just about the mission, Abi. I mean, it is, of course, but it's just as important, if not more so, that you have another career. Your main career. Because TH missions aren't full-time for any but the most dedicated, clandestine agents. And you made it clear when I hired you that you'd left the FBI to start a new life, a new career."

Abi heard "youngest" agents in there, unspoken. As agents in any law-enforcement capacity aged, they wanted more than the gritty, life-threatening life of being society's fixers. They wanted the farmhouse, the friends, the family. A spouse.

Are you ready for a family of your own?

"I understand, Claudia." And she did. It was part of the Trail Hikers charter that agents were only part-time, save for a few elite operators. All agents were required to have full-time occupations outside of Trail Hikers activity. Because of its unique capabilities, TH wasn't a job anyone could depend on full-time. And Abi knew she didn't want to be an undercover operative for the rest of her life.

"If you understand, Abi, then please take care of this ASAP. Have you figured out what your new vocation will be? You know you'd be a shoe-in to work here in the station. I'm sure Colt would hire you without blinking."

"No, no, I'm not going to pursue law enforcement. I'm grateful and honored to be able to use the skills the FBI taught me for Trail Hikers cases as needed. Even to help out SVPD and SVFD in future arson cases. That said, Trail Hikers is the extent of law enforcement I want to be involved in for the rest of my career, and only on an occasional basis. If I'd wanted a law-enforcement career I would have stayed in the FBI. I want…" She wasn't certain how to tell a decorated war veteran that she wanted something other than government business. Something more…fun. Adventurous.

"To do something different, right?" Claudia laughed. "Do you think you're the only one? If I were your age I'd jump on the new ways of doing agriculture. My secret passion is hydroponics. I've even started a small greenhouse in my home." Claudia's take-no-prisoners expression softened to that of a child's discovering a flower bud. "I have some cherry tomatoes that are getting ready to be harvested."

"Claudia, I had no idea. Not that I would, since I've been here such a short time. But you always seem so totally immersed in Trail Hikers."

"I am. I love serving the community, whether it's publicly in uniform or behind the scenes. But there's so much more to all of us, Abi. I still have time to explore my passions, but more as hobbies. You have the opportunity to allow your passions to drive your life, your career. You know you can always turn down a TH mission, right?"

"Yes. But I can't foresee ever turning away from solving an arson. It's cliché, I know, but it's in my blood."

Claudia nodded. "Yes. Which is why you're excellent at it. Just don't be afraid to allow real life to come in. On all fronts." Claudia gave her the "don't make me spell it out for you" look that Abi had received from many higher-level FBI agents when she was at the agency. "So, any ideas on your new career?"

"Actually, I do have one."

Chapter 6

Claudia's admonition haunted Abi as she drove through town again. She stopped here and there to note the commercial businesses on Silver Valley's main street, determining which had the best parking spots. She also took her time on the main highway, Silver Valley Pike—it had the most traffic in the area outside of Harrisburg. If she started a business, especially the one she was thinking about, it would need to be easily accessible. Tingles raced around inside her belly. It was exhilarating and terrifying to be able to do whatever the hell she wanted. She'd done her job, her passion, while in the FBI and as a Trail Hiker, but there was always someone senior to her, someone else calling the ultimate shots.

With this new venture she'd be on her own.

It didn't take her long to ascertain that she'd prefer to open a business in the historical part of Silver Valley, but with her limited finances she'd most likely have to settle for a more commercial spot on the main pike. Abi hated settling for anything. Wasn't that what she'd done with Fred? They'd dated on and off for years, whenever their FBI schedules allowed. Work had always come first. It was easy to say she wasn't going to settle for anything anymore, but maybe a compromise would be okay.

Tired of searching for the perfect location for her dream business, she needed a break. Abi double-checked her GPS. She'd entered the address she'd found on the internet for the Silver Threads Yarn Shop exactly as it was listed on the shop's website. The street wasn't familiar, yet the site said the shop was in Silver Valley proper. But she hadn't pulled up to anything that resembled a commercial business. She sat in front of what appeared to be a Victorian home on the edge of the historical residential area. If she wasn't mistaken, the mayor's house was only a block away. It was on the National Historic Registry and this house looked like it could be, too.

She got out of her car and walked up the cobblestone path to the large, wide porch, where she spotted the store's sign. Hand painted and hung from hooks in the porch's roof, it wasn't visible from the street.

Abi peered through the beveled stained-glass front door windows and saw warm lamplight illuminate what appeared to be a front parlor with floor-to-window shelves stocked full of yarn.

She was in the middle of a case and this wasn't the time she'd pick to research her future business ventures. Yet Claudia had encouraged her to and what could it hurt to talk to a local business owner? Just for the sake of it. And if that person owned the knitting shop, the kind of place Abi loved to chill out in, all the better. As she stood on the top step, wondering what to do next, the door opened.

"You here for yarn, honey?" A small, wiry woman with silver corkscrews haloing her elfin features squinted at her over polka-dotted reading glasses.

"Yes." She followed the spritely woman into the shop and looked around her. The woman had led her into what must have been a Victorian library over one hundred years ago. Floor-to-ceiling shelves graced the walls of the round room that rose to a dome painted with cherubs. She couldn't stop the squeal of delight that bubbled when she spied an old-fashioned library ladder that ran on a runner around the room. Vaguely she heard the woman laugh but didn't stop to address it. There was too much to look at, too many colors, too many varieties of fiber to touch. For on each and every shelf was yarn. Skein after skein, with calligraphed names and price labels affixed to the front of each rectangular space. There had to be thousands of different fiber blends in the store. It was fiber nirvana.

Abi reached to squeeze the nearest hank. "Alpaca," she murmured. "Merino. Merino super wash. Ooh, is this cashmere?"

This time the woman's laughter broke her from her junkie haze. Abi turned around. "I'm so sorry, but if this is your shop, and you're a knitter, I know you understand."

"Yes, ma'am, I do." The woman took a step closer. "Are you passing through town? I haven't seen you in here before."

"No, I haven't been here before. And, no, I'm not passing—I have a temporary job but I'm hoping to make my move to Silver Valley permanent." As the words tumbled out she realized that it was true—she wanted to stay there. After she caught the cult's fire starters, after they took down the True Believers. Silver Valley felt like…home.

Keith had nothing to do with it. Really.

"And you're a knitter?"

"Yes. And I crochet, too, though not as often."

"How long have you been here?"

"Close to three months."

"And you didn't look us up until now?"

No, she hadn't. She'd brought enough yarn from her humongous stash that she hadn't needed to purchase new. Not that that had ever stopped her before. "I would have come in sooner but my new job's been kind of crazy."

"Where do you work?"

"Hmm?" She made a pretense of becoming fixated on a variegated wool that would self-stripe as she knit it into the perfect pair of socks for her father. "I'm a contractor for the police department, short-term. I was in law enforcement full-time but really want to do something different."

"And you wanted to open your own yarn shop."

Was she that freaking transparent? "No! I mean, yes, I'm thinking of starting a new business here, but not a yarn shop. Silver Valley certainly doesn't need a new one, not with this wonderful spot. You've done an incredible job with this space." She ran her hand over the walnut shelving with century-old patina that couldn't be replicated. "I'm in need of a business site but I can't say I want the typical kind of storefront. And that seems to be all that's available in the strip malls along the main drag."

"Don't be so hasty. Not every business is on Silver Valley Pike—take this one, for example. I can connect you to the right folks. I've lived in Silver Valley my entire life and served on the Rotary Club board." She held out a slim hand that was bedecked with silver rings, her nails polished a glittery tulip pink. "I'm Esmeralda Fiero."

Abi grasped her hand, appreciating the woman's soft strength. Not unlike the perfect tension in a fiber—soft enough to wear but tough enough to last years. "Nice to meet you."

"Do you have some time? Would you like a bottle of water or a cup of tea?"

"Tea sounds great."

"I've owned this shop for the past thirty years, since I retired from teaching." She laughed at Abi's stunned expression. "I know, I look a lot younger than I am. It's doing what I love that's kept me moving, along with great kids and grandkids. My granddaughter is about to have my first great-grandchildren. Twins!" She stirred a heaping teaspoonful of white sugar into her peppermint tea, dinging a tiny silver spoon against the side of the porcelain mug.

"I bought this house from the original owner, who was using it as an arts and crafts store for all kinds of hobbies. I never liked putting sequins on jeans and such, so when the knitting craze hit I took full advantage. Some years have been leaner than others but I never hoped to make a killing—just enough to not go bankrupt. I figure I have another two to three years before it's time to sell." Esmeralda, who'd told Abi to call her Ezzie, tilted her head. "You're sure you wouldn't be interested in buying the shop, would you?"

Abi grinned. She'd thought her dream was crushed but now it had hope again. "I'm going to start an Appalachian adventure company. I've been a backpacker and camper for years, and I'm happiest on a river in my kayak or on a lake with a paddleboard. I'd love to make the nature surrounding Silver Valley more accessible to locals and tourists alike."

Ezzie clapped her hands together and hooted. "That's perfect! Did you have an office or storefront in mind yet?

There are a couple for sale downtown and, of course, as you said, plenty on the pike."

"I haven't got that far—I won't need much. Most of my resources will be other people. Tour guides, ski instructors. Drivers for picking up the kayakers."

Ezzie leaned forward in a conspiratorial manner. "Did you notice when you walked up that this is a duplex of sorts?"

"I saw that the porch wrapped and the other front door. I thought it was all connected."

"It is, in that I own the entire building, but originally this was the home of twin sisters who settled in Silver Valley after the Civil War drove them north of the Mason-Dixon Line. They were originally from Emmitsburg, Maryland."

"Who lives on the other side?"

"No one at the moment. I live upstairs, over this shop, and the apartment over the shop next door is empty. It used to be a dentist's office. I've had offers from folks who were interested in opening tattoo parlors, hookah bars, bakeries, beauty salons. But their funding never came through." Ezzie leaned over and stared at her. "You have the seed money?"

Abi laughed. "Yes, indeed I do. Financing to start isn't a problem. I've been single forever and have saved a reasonable amount." She was stretching the definition of "reasonable," especially if she hoped to also buy the farmhouse, but optimism was a trait she'd inherited from her mother.

"We can help give your shop a boost by advertising it among our knitting groups. We'll start with Fred."

"Fred?" The familiar name shot a jolt of surprise through her. But, unlike before, when she'd always bemoaned the loss of her last serious boyfriend, she felt more detached from her grief.

Maybe time and distance, and a major job change, *did* heal wounds.

"He's the chef over at Silver Valley Europa Café." Abi knew the place—it was labeled as a café but was more along the lines of a très chic, very expensive European restaurant on the pike. She loved their marinated octopus, a favorite dish she'd first enjoyed when in Italy on an investigation for the FBI.

"He's a knitter, too?"

Ezzie nodded. "He's into Fair Isle and intertarsia." She referred to two complicated methods of working multiple colors into a pattern. "He has so many contacts in this town, it's insane. And quite a devoted following of empty nesters, who are always looking for new things to do. They'll love signing up for your adventure hikes!"

"It's a deal. When can I look at the place next door?"

"Is right now soon enough?"

Abi laughed. "Don't you have to watch your shop?"

Ezzie smiled, obviously enjoying their conversation. "Does it look like I do? Besides, my customers know me and the shop well. If anyone comes in while we're next door, we'll probably hear them, and they'll wait for me. Come on."

Abi followed Ezzie through the back of the shop to where living spaces must have once been but was now stacked with cartons and bagged skeins of yarn. "I can't believe you have inventory back here with all that's out front."

"Most of these are custom orders. I ship all over the world. You saw the website? My granddaughter designed it. She helps me in her spare time." She peered over her glasses at Abi before opening the door to a small hallway that appeared to have one exit to the backyard. "Okay, so don't worry, you will be able to lock your house door just as I do mine."

As Ezzie turned the key in the lock for the empty store's door, Abi felt a sense of déjà vu. She took it as a good omen.

"And here you go." Ezzie stood aside and swept up her arm. "Your new business."

They walked through the space and it was perfect. Between this as her storefront and the barn to store any extra supplies, it was as if she'd planned the entire venture. And she had; she'd been mulling it over for the past couple of months. Claudia's prodding to "get a 'real' job other than Trail Hikers" had pushed her to act.

After they finished the tour she and Ezzie went back to the yarn shop. Abi told Ezzie she was contracted with SVPD and currently in the midst of a big case, so her timeline to actually have a grand opening would have to be flexible.

"Is it okay if I sign now but don't open for a while? I don't know my exact start date. I'll have to talk to the bank, too, for a business loan in case I need it."

"No problemo! Our local credit union is your best bet. I'll give you the loan officer's card that I've used. She's a doll."

"Is there anyone or anything you can't help me with, Ezzie?"

Ezzie ignored the compliment. Abi sensed that Ezzie probably helped everyone out that she crossed paths with.

"So what kind of grand opening do you envision, Abi?" Ezzie poured her more tea and Abi couldn't help wondering if she were sharing tea with some kind of angel. Because she certainly felt as though fairy dust had been sprinkled over her dream.

Silver Valley was interesting, all right. So far not one

person had looked askance at her as the "newcomer."
Except for one.

Keith Paruso.

Abi arrived at the farmhouse as dusk was settling over
the valley. The green grass that had blazed emerald in the
noon sun appeared blue as the sky turned from peach to
violet. She let herself in and dragged along several bags
of housekeeping supplies she'd bought on the way home.
Her furnishings in Alexandria would have to wait until
she had time to set up a move—and put the town house
up for sale. Because even if she didn't stay in Silver Valley, after all—if for some reason adventure tourism didn't
pan out—she wasn't going back to DC.

Pennsylvania was her home state, and being only two
hours from Philly was a nice benefit come holiday time,
when her family threw huge celebrations. Her father had
transitioned from firework to insurance claims after the
debacle when she was in high school. He'd told her time
and again that he'd been planning to leave the firefighting force, anyhow, but Abi had never believed him. He'd
left the department in shame after Abi's classmate and
best friend had died in their family home, at a party Abi
had thrown without her parents' permission.

Abi had worked through the pain, worked through the
guilt over what her mistake had cost her father. Which
was nothing compared to the tragic death of her best
friend. Still, the nagging feelings were always there, be-
rating her to solve the next case.

Enough. She was in Silver Valley to start over, to move
on.

As she blew up the new inflatable mattress with the
battery-operated pump, she was grateful she'd splurged
on the deluxe queen size and new soft organic cotton bed-

ding. It was one thing to sleep on the hard earth while hiking or camping, but this was her first night in her new house. It deserved to be special. In one day she'd gone from being in Silver Valley only because of her Trail Hikers involvement and contractor-for-SVPD cover, to renting a storefront for a business that might turn into her new "vocation," as Claudia had referred to it.

The sun set over the farmlands as she prepared her simple dinner. The alpaca and sheep were gone from the landscape, in for the night in the gray-stone barn she'd driven past on the way in. Would this be her place, where she set down her roots? Would her future children and grandchildren see her as a woman who'd owned an adventure business her entire life, never as the agent she was?

It seemed unfathomable but if luck was on her side, maybe. Maybe Abi would settle down and have a family of her own. Of course, not now and not in the near term. First, she had an arsonist, or two or three, to nab. Second, she didn't have anyone on the horizon to start said family with. Not even a twinkle of a new romance.

Because Keith Paruso wasn't anything resembling a twinkle. More like a lightning bolt—the man was a bull.

Who was she kidding? The dude was getting under her skin. She'd only just met him, yet it felt as if she'd known him much longer. Always the first sign of a crush! Her secret Trail Hikers position meant her feelings, whatever they were for the guy, had to remain secret, as well. Besides, he was so guarded, so very much the professional. Hell, she didn't even know if he'd ever been married or engaged. She'd never thought to ask him.

Now that was a first. Abi never forgot to ask a man or anyone about themselves. And as much as she'd been ready to leave her past behind—she'd resigned from her job at the FBI, after all—she hadn't been as eager to move on and settle into Silver Valley until she'd met its enigmatic fire chief.

Something about Keith Paruso made her want to see how much settling she could do. Who she'd become if she were free of her past and able to follow her heart.

A heart she might be willing to put at risk again. For the right man.

Chapter 7

Keith thought that shadowing Abi as she retraced every fire site was going to be easy—boring, even. He'd never expected to be turned on from watching a trained arson forensic specialist do her job.

"Can I carry anything for you?" he asked her for the sixth time in two hours as she juggled her bag and phone while capturing photos of the dilapidated commercial building they inspected.

Her sharp gaze softened as she stopped and looked up at him from her squat on the cold concrete floor, next to a burned-out wall in a large abandoned warehouse. It had been one of the first fires after the Christmas church blaze.

"I'm sorry, Keith. I tend to go into a kind of trance when I do this work."

"I understand." He stepped forward and reached for her shoulder bag on the floor next to her. "Which is why

I'm happy to let you work away as I go over everything I remember from each fire. I've brought all of my original written notes and printed the computer files. Let me get this out of your way and take some notes. Between the two of us, we might come up with something."

"You were at each and every fire?"

"Yes."

"I thought you were on administrative leave for several months?"

"True. And, officially, I didn't step foot near a Silver Valley blaze during that time." He waited for her eyes to again seek his. Even in the pale light that slanted through the shredded roof, he saw the spark of light that was uniquely Abi. "Unofficially…"

She laughed. "I'd have done the same."

"Would you?" He leaned over to see what exactly she was taking photos of. Shards of glass, wood?

"If it were my territory and I felt I'd been wrongly removed from duty, absolutely. I'd make sure I didn't put anyone or any evidence at risk. And I'd probably not draw attention to myself." Her gloved fingers plucked up what she'd been photographing and she placed it in one of the plastic evidence bags that seemed to grow out of her pockets. "I'm thinking that maybe you weren't so big on the 'staying in the shadows' part?" She stood and drew to her full height. In running shoes and blue jeans she was a full head shorter than he was, but her aura seemed to fill the huge space. What was it about Abi?

She coaxed a laugh out of him. Since he'd met her, his chest felt as if it had expanded from the way she made his sense of humor come to life. It'd been too long.

"I didn't get caught. Colt saw me a few times at a scene but pretended he didn't. The town, my friends, they all knew it had been some kind of a setup—the charges against me."

She considered him, her dark eyes missing nothing. "Why don't we take a break? I've got ice water in my car, and I think I might still have some coffee in my thermos." She pulled off her latex gloves and shoved them in her jacket pockets. They walked side by side to her car where she opened up the back door and pulled out two water bottles. "I usually use refillable only but I keep spares for when I'm going to be traveling all day."

He took the bottle, wet from the cooler she'd kept it in. "Thanks." After they gulped for a few minutes, Abi leaned against her car and shielded her eyes from the sun as she looked at him.

"Tell me what happened last year, Keith."

For the first time ever, besides talking to his sister or Rio when he was investigating the case, Keith opened up.

"You've read the reports. The Silver Valley Community Church was set on fire a year and a half ago, right during their biggest event of the year."

"Yes, the Christmas pageant. Is it true they even had real farm animals?"

"Yes. That sounds strange to you, I'm sure, since you've lived your life in cities. But out here, folks wait all year to bring in their farm animals. Just like the Bible story, there were oxen and donkeys and a goose or two."

"I'll have to make it a point to see that this year." She laughed and took another sip of her water. "Go on."

"We put the blaze out. There was a big brouhaha afterward, even though SVPD caught the arsonist red-handed after he'd tried to kill more than one person. It's natural for a community to inquire about how such a potentially catastrophic incident could occur in the first place. Understandable. Expected."

"But?"

"At the same time, Silver Valley was going through political upheaval. The mayor was indicted for felony charges of embezzlement and it allowed an outsider to slime into the campaign and get elected. The outsider, as I'm sure you've read, was an embezzler and possible front man of the cult."

"I read that." She listened without any hint of judgment, simply taking in his words as if he held the answer to the entire case. Keith loved how Abi gave her total attention to the job at hand, and liked it even more when that attention was on him.

"Out of the blue, a couple who were long-time members of Silver Valley Community Church filed charges against Silver Valley, the fire department and, in turn, me. They had survived the fire, as had every other church member. They hadn't sustained any injuries, either. Their claims of my negligence were patently false, and the couple clearly had been coached."

"As if a special-interest group or lobbyist had got to them?"

"Exactly. But this isn't the nation's capital, and I'm not some representative whose constituents want answers. I'm a paid Silver Valley employee, and the lawsuit mandated that the town had to place me on administrative leave."

"Which was later rescinded when the couple dropped the suit."

"Yes, but…" How could he tell her what it had really cost him?

Abi nodded. "But the damage was done. To your reputation. Even though the paper ran those feel-good articles on you. And the local television station did an exposé on the out-of-town mayor. People hear what they want to hear."

His stomach sank. "You looked me up online." He felt like a damned fool. "You've just played me when you already knew the story? When you'd said you'd read about it, I thought you meant in the police reports or the local paper's archives."

"Give me some credit, Keith. I'm former FBI, and I'm still in investigator mode working this case. Of course I looked you up."

"Colt or Rio vouching for me wasn't enough?" He didn't really know if they'd done more than confirming his identity, but they were his friends. Rio seemed destined to become his brother-in-law. He sure as hell hoped they'd stood up for him.

She tugged at her blond ponytail. "Of course they're supportive of you. Neither of them told me one iota about what you've been through with your job and the false charges."

Satisfaction wormed its way back into his self-esteem. Rio had the right to tell anyone he wanted to about the case; he'd been the one to get the charges against Keith dropped.

"I'm being a bit defensive, I suppose, but can you explain to me why we're having this conversation? It seems you've already made your mind up about me."

"Chill out, dude. I hardly know you. You sure as hell don't know me. I get the feeling you're used to women falling all over you. I imagine my lack of interest is annoying." Only when she looked at him did he see the humor in her eyes.

"My ego's not that easily bruised, trust me."

She toed the graveled parking lot in between sprouting weeds. "From what I read, you took a sucker punch for the team."

"I had no choice."

"You did. You could have countersued the town and taken the couple who charged you to court. They lied under oath. That's perjury, Keith."

"And slander. But all's well that ends well." It didn't sit well in his gut, but that was his problem.

"You just let that couple go free, no repercussions for what they'd done?" Her perplexity was palpable.

"They weren't mine to prosecute, charge or set free. The city and county could follow through, and in fact the county pressed charges. The couple agreed to share what the cult had told them if the county dropped the charges, so they settled out of court. They said they'd been brainwashed but there wasn't any substantial evidence or proof. It doesn't matter. They were crazy, hoodwinked by the cult. That's pretty clear. The True Believers, New Thought, whatever their name is today, wants nothing less than to destroy the nature of a place like Silver Valley. The members have to buy into the fact that the local community—in our case, Silver Valley—is doomed. Planting an awful mayor, targeting the LGBT club at the high school, starting fires—it's all part of the plan to control folks with fear. Leonard Wise is a megalomaniac waiting to implode. Fortunately SVPD and the FBI are standing by to move in the minute he makes a misstep."

She slowly shook her head. "It's not fair that you were a target, that anyone has to suffer because of people like Leonard Wise. And local government should have protected you from all of it."

"Look, I know you used to work for the Department of Justice, and that you probably think every case has a right or wrong, a definitive line that proves who wins or loses. But Silver Valley isn't DC, Abi. I know and have lifelong relationships with the people I work with. To file against Silver Valley or the county would be like suing my own family. I trusted SVPD to get to the bottom of it, and I was right to trust them."

She pushed off the car, bringing her a half step closer to him. Her hips were within reach of his hands and if she upturned her face one more inch, it'd be easy to think they were any old couple standing on a driveway next to a car.

"Trust all you want, Keith. Good on you that it's worked for you in the past." She pointed at her chest. "Me, I'm going to trust *after* I get all of the facts."

"That makes no sense, Abi." Neither did the way being this close to her was making him hard.

"Sure, it does. Are you going to just trust that the original investigative work on all of the arsons in Silver Valley over the past year and a half was done correctly? That no smidgen of evidence was overlooked?"

"SVPD has one of the top forensic teams in the state. We've worked hand-in-hand through many fires and emergency situations. I have complete trust in them."

"Don't be so defensive. I'm not poking holes at SVPD or Silver Valley in general. This is a great place—you saw me sign a rent-to-own lease! I'm on your side." She paused, eyes reflecting the morning light, as if thinking about what she'd just said. "As far as the case goes."

He drank the remaining water in his bottle before crushing it. "Are you saving this to recycle or do you want me to?"

"I'll take it." She tossed both of their empty bottles into the backseat of her car, where he noted several large bags that appeared stuffed with clothes.

"Run out of moving boxes?"

"What? Oh, those aren't clothes." She hit the lock on her key fob and smiled. "Let's get back to work, Keith."

* * *

She didn't care if Keith thought she was some kind of hoarder. He said nothing more about her huge black plastic bags. They filled her trunk, too. Since she'd only just started to realize that she might want to explore making a living out of her love of being outdoors, she wasn't ready to share with him or anyone else what was in the bags, or that she'd gone back to Alexandria on a quick day trip to get what was turning out to be the tools of her new trade.

All kinds of camping, hiking, rappelling gear filled the bags. Scuba and snorkeling equipment, several sleeping bags and cushions. She'd already moved her two kayaks and paddleboard to the barn last weekend. She needed to order more equipment for the business but there wasn't time. Not yet.

When she and Keith finally finished with the third and last warehouse of the day, they agreed to meet again in the morning at the first of five abandoned residences the arsonist had torched.

As she drove through central Silver Valley she smiled. She had another hour to work on what might be the next step in her staying in this town permanently. Her new business.

Her head wanted her to believe it was only her new business, but her heart was the wiser. She couldn't keep from smiling as she thought of Keith's expression when she'd told him she was thinking of staying in Silver Valley. As if it mattered to him, too.

When Saturday morning dawned on the first weekend Abi didn't have to go to her place in Alexandria, she decided to take Kayla up on her invitation to early morning yoga class. She'd agreed to meet Keith later, at noon, to walk through another site or two. It was work, nothing more, but she couldn't escape the giddy feelings akin to knowing the man you cared about was coming to take you on a date. And Keith was becoming more than a date or romantic interest. It seemed impossible in the short time she'd known him, but it also felt as if he'd always been a part of her life.

She should be scared at the enormity of her emotions but instead was buoyed by them.

Claudia and Colt had encouraged her to take the weekend off but she couldn't. Not when the arsonist was still out there.

The yoga studio door chimed like a gong as she opened it. Long chains of brass bells and glass beads hung from the door and windows, soothing her eyes in the early hour. She smelled jasmine incense and immediately thought of the backyard she'd played in as a kid in Philadelphia. Small, closer to tiny, by central Pennsylvania standards, but her mother had used every square inch to grow flowers.

"Hi. I'm Charlotte. Welcome." A spritely woman with curlicued hair smiled as Abi signed in and paid.

"Thank you. I hope it's okay that I've never taken a class before."

Charlotte shook her head. "No problem. I'll show modifications for each pose, so just do what your body tells you to. There are mats in the corner, next to the cubbies and hooks."

"Thanks." Abi had meant to get her own yoga mat but had forgotten as she'd been more focused on finding a mattress to sleep on and soap.

"Abi?"

She turned toward the voice and saw that Kayla had a mat laid out in the center of the studio. "Hi, Kayla!

Nice to see you here. I decided to take you up on your suggestion."

"I'm surprised you're awake this early. Rio wouldn't even budge this morning. Here." Kayla patted the ground next to her mat. Abi unrolled a mat from the bin next to Kayla. "A word of warning—don't follow my moves. Charlotte will keep you on track. I'm more of a walker or runner."

"Will do. I'm sure I'll find this challenging. I've never done this before." She stretched by touching her toes as Kayla was doing. "I'm not surprised Rio's sleeping in. He's been really busy." They'd stayed late at the station last night, trying to predict when the arsons would next hit. The past two weeks had remained quiet after the house fire where she'd met Keith.

Had it only been two weeks?

"You all have been busy. It's nice that you're taking some time for yourself, and a yoga class is perfect. It must drive you nuts to have to work with all those men. You're going to love this class. We all go out for coffee afterward, if you're interested. Or tea—Charlotte docsn't drink coffee."

"That sounds really nice! I haven't had much time to get to know anyone here yet. As for guys at the station, I don't mind working with men, not at all. I'm kind of used to it."

"From the FBI?" Kayla lowered her voice as if it were classified that Abi had worked for the government; it wasn't. So Rio had told his girlfriend where she'd worked before. Nothing classified in that; the Trail Hikers was far more secretive. And her FBI background added to her cover of being an investigative contractor with the police department.

"No, more from how I grew up. My dad was a firefighter and I was always around him and his department, from the time I was very young."

Kayla nodded. "I get it."

"How's the flower business?"

Kayla's eyes lit up. "Wonderful! We're headed into the busiest season with all the proms, weddings and graduations. As crazy busy as it gets, I've no complaints. I love the fact that I get to make people happy with something as simple as flowers. How about you? Are you enjoying the contract work with SVPD?" Kayla's eyes reflected innocence but Abi had a feeling Kayla knew damned well she wasn't just a contractor. Rio and Kayla had worked together on a case involving the criminal mayor and Kayla had helped bring down a small part of the cult's initial dealings in Silver Valley. Abi had read the reports.

"It's fine, but I think I may be onto something more along the lines of a career change."

"Really?" Kayla's eyes grew big. "Care to share?"

Abi wanted to tell Kayla, as she was very excited about her new business, but Charlotte walked to the front of the studio class.

"Time to get settled, everybody." Charlotte's voice ended their conversation. For the next hour Abi found herself in positions she didn't know she was capable of. She had solid core strength and any move requiring muscle wasn't a problem. Trying to "ease" into any move wasn't natural for her, as her FBI and Trail Hikers training had been physically robust and encouraged heavy exertion. Still, she gave it her best shot.

The class came to an end and she had almost two hours before she had to run home, grab a quick shower and then meet Keith at the next arson site on their list. Definitely enough time for coffee with Kayla and the girls. As she shrugged her sweatshirt over her tank top, her phone alerted her.

Keith Paruso.

"Good morning, Chief." She was half teasing him, as he'd repeatedly told her to call him "Keith."

"Abi, we've got a problem." Humor was crushed by the gravity of his tone. "We had a fire overnight at the elementary school."

Children. They'd done the practice run as she'd predicted, and the next time school could be in session.

"Where are you?"

"At the school."

"I'll be there in five."

Chapter 8

The elementary school building appeared intact as she drove up the wide road to the front, but when she turned into the back parking lot she was greeted by one large fire engine and a group of firefighters in various states of taking off their gear. Two SVPD units were near the fire truck and she caught sight of a few officers stranding crime scene tape around the back entrance to the building. She parked her car and ran up to Keith, who stood with one man off to the side.

"Chief Paruso." He turned and looked over his shoulder.

"Abi." As soon as she was even with him and the other firefighter, he nodded. "Tiger, this is Abigail Redland, with SVPD. Abi, this is Andy Gregory. We call him Tiger for short." Both men laughed before Tiger turned incredibly turquoise eyes on her.

"Weren't you at the fire the other day? On Wertzville Road?"

She looked at Tiger, then Keith. Abi didn't want to say too much. "Yes, I was there."

"You weren't in uniform then, either."

"I'm not SVPD. I'm a private contractor working on these arson cases with them."

"Abi, Tiger's my assistant fire chief. He ran the department while I was on administrative leave last year. I trust him with my life, needless to say."

"I'm sure you trust all of your fighters with your life. Isn't that part of the job?"

"What I mean is, Tiger knows what's going on with the arsons in detail. I went over what we've found so far."

"Oh." Abi wasn't sure whether to smack Keith upside his head now or to wait for privacy. What was he thinking, telling someone else about the case particulars?

"Abi?" Keith stared at her, his genial expression morphing into concern.

"I'll, um, talk to you later, boss. Nice to meet you, Abigail—Ms. Redland." Tiger gave a quick hand salute and walked away.

"Abi, what's this all about? I think you've scared Tiger away."

"Scared Tiger away? No, I didn't do that. You did. You are the reason I'm ready to clock someone."

"As long as it's not me. Why are you so upset?"

He stood in the morning sun, bright blue sky and white puffy clouds framing his face as she looked up at him. The man looked genuinely puzzled. "What is it, Abi? Say something."

"Call me after you've dealt with whatever's happened here." She waved at the school building. "You haven't even told me what's going on—and want to explain to me how anyone got past our watch?" Between SVPD and the fire department splitting duties and patrols, they were supposed to be closely monitoring the elementary school. "And you've discussed a very sensitive case with one of your team. All of the Silver Valley Police Department doesn't know the details of the arson cases!"

Comprehension flashed into anger in his eyes. "Are you questioning my judgment, Abi? Because I've been in Silver Valley a hell of a lot longer than you have. If anyone needs to be vetted, it's *you*. How the hell do I, or Tiger, or Rio, or Colt, or anyone, know that you're trustworthy, save for your résumé? It's my understanding that FBI agents don't just 'leave.' Were you asked to leave? Fired?"

"Are you freaking kidding me? I don't work for you, remember? You've been at the arson sites when I go through them at *my* invitation. It's not your right to be anywhere except putting out a fire!" She tried to force her breath to slow down with no luck. The last time she'd been this steamed… She'd caught Fred in bed with another woman.

Great. Freaking great. She was acting like Keith was a personal acquaintance instead of purely a professional one. While she tried to get her thoughts together and put her personal thoughts about Keith back in their box, Keith stared at her like she was a woman possessed.

"I didn't have time to reach you. I asked SVPD to contact you as soon as I heard. When you didn't show up, I called you, personally, as soon as I had a spare moment."

Her phone. She'd turned the ringer off during yoga, and at some point it had ended up on the studio floor under her sweatshirt, which was why she'd noticed Keith's last call—she'd just uncovered the phone at that point and saw his call light up the screen in the dark studio.

Abi swallowed. "You might be right. I may have missed some calls earlier, before your last call."

"As for the more important point, whomever I deem

worthy of my trust is good enough. Is that clear? I don't report to you or SVPD or even the goddamned FBI!" As he spoke he kept his hands on his hips, his arms still. Everything he needed to say, he did with his voice and his eyes. His eyes were on fire, his focus so totally on her. Where was the usual fire she should be digging deep for to hurl at him? Where was her mettle?

It'd migrated south, apparently. Because she was at once so contrite yet so hot for Keith. He was everything she usually avoided—too muscular, too bold, too confident, bordering on arrogant. Yet on Keith, it was a potent mix. A great mix.

She broke eye contact and looked over his shoulder. "I'm sorry about my phone. I won't miss another call. Want to fill me in on what happened?"

Keith continued to stare at her. Obviously he'd expected more of a fight from her.

But as she looked at the remaining crew, her thoughts honed in on the case. There had been a fire in the elementary school this morning. Thank God it was Saturday during summer break.

"Let me talk you through what my fighters and I found when we got here. I was here while it was still smoking pretty bad, right after they put the flames out. It caused a lot of smoke, but fortunately the fire wasn't an issue.

"It ended up being a very amateur fire, probably intentionally so, set in a metal wastepaper basket and placed atop a stone countertop in the art room. It was meant to burn out, but it was enough to set off the sprinklers and alarm."

"Art room? Near paints and other combustibles?"

"Yeah, but like I said, they'd made sure it was going to burn out quickly. What I'd be more concerned about if

I were working this from the police angle is how the hell they got into the building without an alarm going off."

"Show me where."

She followed Keith through the entrance doors, noting the digital keypad to the right of the entry. "Do all faculty need a key to enter?"

"Yes, they all have to swipe their fob each morning, whether the janitor has unlocked the doors already or not. This being a Saturday, the doors were locked. Whoever broke in had to have a key fob."

"No signs of B and E? Broken windows, door frames?"

Keith raised a brow at her. "I know what breaking and entering is, Abi." He paused in front of what she saw were the cafeteria doors. "Are you okay, Abi? You really flew off the handle there."

"I'm fine. Let's stick to the case right now, okay?"

"Whatever you want." He led her to the art room, where the SVPD forensic team still worked. Rio stood in the midst of it all, taking notes.

"Hey, Rio."

"Abi! I just spoke to Kayla. She said you were on your way."

"I'm sorry I turned off my phone and missed your initial calls. Thanks for being persistent." For not giving up on her.

"It's not a problem. This was still going to be here when you got done. Did you enjoy your class?"

She felt Keith's gaze on her.

"Yes, it was a very welcoming group."

Rio shook his head. "I have no idea how Kayla wakes up for it on a Saturday. She has to get up so early for her flower orders in Baltimore during the week that you'd think she'd want to sleep in. She's devoted to Charlotte's class."

"She's not the only one. The studio was full." She looked around the scene. Trash can, blackened on the inside and slightly along the rim. The scent of recently burned paper and gasoline. A dark shadow of where flames had singed the ceiling looked down at them. A shudder ran through Abi. "That could have sparked the entire building."

"It could have, but the sprinklers went off in time." Keith spoke, the resonance of his voice familiar to her after working with him a few short weeks. "Plus the alarms sounded much sooner, from the smoke and fumes. They're super-sensitive, so much so that we do a lot of runs out here for false alarms when school's in session."

"What sets them off? Rubber cement?"

Keith shook his head. "The kids don't use any of the adhesives that we did, except for plain white liquid glue, no fumes. But the paint removers the teacher uses can set off the alarms. As can the off-glazing of the kiln, depending upon the type of paint they use on the ceramics. And last year we had a false alarm from a scented candle the art teacher burned during a faculty potluck after school."

"We'd rather have the false alarms." Rio interrupted Keith. "It's good practice for the faculty and students to evacuate the building, too."

"Yeah, we want it to be automatic in case there is ever a real event." Keith spoke as he looked around at the classroom. "We were lucky today on so many fronts. The kids aren't here, school isn't in session and the bastard who started it knew enough to make sure it would burn out before the building caught fire."

"But they almost blew that, right?" Abi pointed at the singed ceiling.

Keith's eyes were bright but the lines around his mouth deepened. This really bothered him, having a lunatic loose in his fire jurisdiction. Abi understood. "They most certainly did. God, if I ever get my hands on these sneaky creeps, I can't be held responsible for what I want to do to them."

"You get a hold of them, Keith, and that's all we'll need to get a conviction." Rio put a hand on Keith's shoulder. "We're collecting evidence from all across the county, right, Abi? We're going to let them walk right into their own trap. Sooner or later one of them has to make a mistake and leave the wrong kind of evidence behind, or be caught in the act."

"How did he get past SVPD patrol?" She didn't want to sound so accusing, but the nod from Rio indicated he felt the same frustration.

"They had to be waiting, probably in one of the back-yards or even houses that surround the school. We've got several officers knocking on doors, asking questions. And they got in from the back somehow. We're thinking maybe by climbing up the roof from the loading dock. The roof trap was smashed open."

"My department would be happy to help with the watch duty, Rio."

Rio shook his head. "That's SVPD jurisdiction and you know it. I'm sorry we were outwitted but it's not the fire department's job to run stakeouts." The tension between the men was palpable and Abi knew from experience that diffusing it before it got too crazy was more important than her inner desire to scream in frustration that SVPD had let the bad guy sneak in.

"Rio's right. So are you, Keith. We're lucky no kids were here." Although she thought that maybe one of the arsonists being utilized by Leonard Wise could be a youngster. It certainly made sense to her as an outsider. She pulled on a pair of latex gloves. "Can I take a look?"

Rio raised his hand toward the wastebasket. "Go right ahead. You know as well as the forensics team what you're doing. Any objections, Keith?"

"I've got none."

"Then I'll leave you two alone to work your magic. I hope you find more than we did. Abi, report back to the station when you're done here."

"Will do."

Keith knew Abi Redland ran deep, but had never expected the outburst that came after she'd found out that she'd been notified of the school fire near the end of the active firefighting. He was certain SVPD contacted her—it was up to her to pick up her damned phone or not.

So why did he have the niggle of guilt in his gut? She wasn't his responsibility. Hell, she worked for SVPD, not for him. And he certainly didn't report to her.

The classroom seemed smaller with just the two of them than it had with half a dozen forensic and firefighting officers prowling about. Something about the air—it had to be from the leftover burned smell, not from being in the same room alone with Abi. It wasn't as if he hadn't been alone with a woman before.

"Anything stand out to you?"

Abi didn't answer him. She had her head inside the trash can, and it looked like she was inhaling the air. He cleared his throat and raised his voice. "Can you really tell what burned with your nose?"

"Can't you? You're as much of a fire expert as I am." Her voice echoed in the tin can. She didn't look at him as she straightened and slowly walked around the room. Looking for what, he had no idea.

"Sometimes, but this looks pretty straightforward. Lighter fluid and matches. All I smell is burned paper."

"And no one found an empty container?"

"Of lighter fluid? No. But we found a half-used book of matches on the floor."

She stopped in front of him. "Where is it?"

"Forensics took it. They're not reporting to you now, are they?" He couldn't help it. She had that smug "I'm the expert here" look on her face again.

"Drop it, Chief." Ouch.

You're starting to give a damn, Paruso.

Chapter 9

God, not now. Not during this case, the case that was the cornerstone of clearing his name. Not with Abi, a woman too complex and full of contradictions. He wanted a woman who was simple. Easygoing.

Someone needed to tell that to his dick.

Hopefully, Abi hadn't noticed his boner. This was a moment worthy of the record books—the first time he didn't want a woman to know how much she aroused him.

"Did anyone figure out what was in the waste can for sure?"

He shrugged. "Paper, as far as it appears. Nothing unusual there."

"But school's not in session. Wouldn't the janitor have emptied the baskets before the weekend?" She held up bits of charred paper that surrounded the bin. She pulled out her phone and dialed a number. "Hey, it's Abi. Did you guys get samples of the paper burned in the waste bin?" He saw her shake her leg in impatience. "What about the paper on the floor around the counter? I'll get whatever else I see." She shoved her phone into her jacket pocket and bent over to pick up a piece of copy paper that was under a worktable next to the counter. It gave him an incredibly advantageous view of her luscious bottom, the multicolored striped yoga pants that were incongruous with her formal detective manner. Did she have any idea how freaking sexy she was?

She straightened and because his attraction to her kept him focused on her curves a beat too long, she caught him red-handed. Staring at her with what was no doubt pure lust radiating off him.

Abi was watching him with her wide eyes, her expression guarded. She felt this, too, this tug that existed since they'd met in the field around the old house. She had to. And yet she still didn't trust him. Fine.

"What do you think that piece of paper is going to tell you?" It came out rougher than he'd meant. No wonder she didn't want to trust him—he sounded like a jerk.

She raised her gloved hand, holding up the sheet of white paper with text printed on one side. "This could lead to a lot, or nothing. But one thing's certain." She placed the paper on a worktable, pulling an evidence bag from her jacket pocket. He should have turned away, apologized for leering at her, or not taken the bait.

"What's that?"

"You, Chief Paruso, were just staring at my ass. Correct?"

Was it possible for a grown man to blush like a complete nerd?

"Guilty as charged."

Haughtiness, feigned superiority, all melted away and what was left on Abi's face was clear. Pure interest. It was in the way her eyes lit, like they did when she thought she found something significant at a fire scene. The way she tilted her head, very slightly, barely perceptible. But he noticed it because he'd been watching her so closely over the past few days. A feeling he wasn't overly familiar with splattered open in his chest.

The deadliest signal from Abi was her smile. It mesmerized as she walked toward him, the piece of paper momentarily forgotten. She stopped a foot from him and damned if he didn't feel his heart fight to keep from exploding.

"Keith, you're a great catch for Silver Valley, I'm sure. But we're both professionals, and we both know the long hours and intensity this case is going to require. Hanky-panky isn't on the docket."

He choked and coughed, and it wasn't from the fire residue. "Did you just say 'hanky-panky'? Are you, like, ninety?"

"I did. And we're adults. Let's get it out in the open so that we can let it go."

Her words made sense, they really did. And he wasn't one who was used to working for affection from women. He liked to be with women who wanted him as much as he did them.

"Like hell."

Abi didn't resist as he grasped her upper arms and pulled her body up against his. The scents of charred paper and rubber cement yielded to Keith's musk, definite and uniquely his.

"I'm sure all the girls like this Neanderthal move. It's quite slick, actually. Do you practice—"

Keith planted a firm kiss on her lips. No tongue, no seductive caresses. Just pure lip-lock. He didn't even close his eyes. She knew, because hers were still open.

Abi shoved against his chest. "Really? Is that all you've got?" As she challenged him she fought the warmth that blazed from her lips, tingling after such an awful first kiss, to her midsection, tightening her nipples along the way.

"You've no idea, Abi," he growled and his eyes even looked leonine as he stared at her.

"At least do it right." She wrapped her arms around his neck, stood on tiptoe and pressed her lips to his. Gently at first, she kissed and nibbled along his mouth, delighting in the sheer physicality of being this close to him. It was too easy to shove back all of her protesting thoughts, all the reasons she had to not get this close to this man.

It was when she outlined his lips with her tongue that the controlled strength reverberating through every inch of his most muscular frame let loose.

Keith took over their embrace with the finesse she'd normally associate with a ballet dancer, not a firefighter. But the heat in his hands as they cupped her ass and drew her to him, the deft licks of his tongue into her mouth— they were unmistakably full of Keith's fire.

They gasped and laughed and groped as the kiss continued. Abi couldn't get enough of his hands on her, and with a deep yearning not unlike that with a first teen love, she wanted to be naked, Keith inside her. Before her thoughts started to intrude she hooked a leg over his hip, and Keith not only lifted it higher, he bent over and grasped her other leg, forcing her to lock her feet behind him. The powerful press of his erection against her softest spot with only his jeans and her yoga pants between them made her dizzy with need.

"Oh, my, oh, my, don't stop. Don't stop." She ran her

fingers over his crew cut and pressed his face to hers, needing her lips against his, their tongues intertwined. No kiss had ever felt this incredible.

"Is this how you like it, babe?" He thrust his pelvis up, making her dangerously close to begging him to take her right there, in the art room.

The school classroom.

She was in an elementary school classroom.

Son of a whoopie pie.

"Keith." He didn't open his eyes but kept trying to kiss her, his tongue precariously close to forcing her to throw caution to the wind and ignore who she was. What she was—a Trail Hikers agent. "*Keith.*"

He slowly opened his eyes—blue orbs cloudy with lust—and considered her, his breath hitching in his chest the same as hers. "Hell." He dropped his hold on her legs and she unceremoniously dropped to the floor, her hold on his shirt all that kept her upright.

"I didn't mean just drop me on the floor, for heaven's sake!"

He ran his hand over his head, scratched the back of his neck. The same neck she'd had her lips and tongue on. "This wasn't very gentlemanly of me, Abi. Sorry."

"I don't give a flying flip about manners, Keith. I do care about our professional relationship." The words spilled out as they were—practiced phrases and beliefs from her FBI time. They were still relevant because as a Trail Hiker her mission came first. Had to come first.

But all at once she didn't see why being in the Trail Hikers while having the most spectacular sex of her life had to be an oxymoron.

Keith looked down and his silence made her as crazy as when he was trying to tell her how to do her job, or when he acted like the skirt-chaser he had the reputation of being. It was as if he wanted to make sure his words would be the right words. As if…as if Keith cared.

"Keith, we're not kids. This was a one-time little thing. It doesn't and won't affect how we go forward."

He kept his gaze on the floor, still silent.

"Keith, please say something. I'm sorry that I took advantage of the situation."

He took two steps to where she'd left the paper in the evidence bag and crouched down. She watched his strong hands as he donned gloves. When he stood again, he held a business card in his hand, which he read. "Check this out, Abi. I think we might have our first big break."

She walked over to him and took a look, not touching it so as not to get her prints on it. She again noted the incongruity of such a big, physical man being so detailed and adroit, of how his attention to detail had led to him spotting the card.

"Dennis Taylor, US Department of Defense. Army War College, Carlisle, Pennsylvania." She stared at the raised font on the creamy, expensive card stock. "This could be a parent's card. Or maybe the art teacher's husband."

"The art teacher is Scott MacKenzie. He's married to Adam Colby, one of my firefighters. And, yes, this could be a parent's business card, or any other person's. But my bet's on something else."

Abi looked around the room, at the floor that was spotless except for where the shower had left it slick and the few random ashes from the fire had landed. "The janitor cleaned this room on Friday. During summer break he cleans once per week." The chairs were still upside down on the tables.

"He wouldn't have missed this area." Keith motioned to where he'd spotted the card.

"I'll check it out." She took another evidence bag out of her pocket and held it, open, toward him. Keith dropped the card between her hands and she sealed the bag. They did work very well together and she was relieved to be back on neutral emotional territory. "I'm going to head to SVPD. I'll make sure you're informed about whatever we find out. I think we're going to have to wait to do our walk-throughs of the other fire sites." She put both evidence bags in her tote and walked toward the classroom door. She needed space, time away from Keith. Before she made another stupid move. What was she, fourteen with raging hormones?

"No problem. One more thing—you should come to the fire department and make sure you're on a first-name basis with everyone. Unfortunately, I think we'll have more instances of you working around us."

Wow. It had to have cost Keith hugely to offer her a tour of his turf.

"That'd be great. I'd appreciate it."

"We'll set up a time soon. And, Abi?"

His voice reached out to her just as she hit the threshold. Not trusting herself to turn fully around, she looked over her shoulder. He stood in the middle of the classroom, his stance relaxed, a lazy grin on his face. "Yeah?"

"That was a great way to blow off some steam."

The next week, Keith made good on his promise to call Abi to set up a tour of the fire department. She drove up to the front of the building, parking on Silver Valley's main street. The façade was over a century old and had been maintained to keep its National Historical Site certification. She'd expected maybe one engine, maybe an EMT vehicle. Pressing the buzzer on the left side of the entrance door, she spoke into the intercom that was similar to the security setup at the police station. "This is Abi Redland. Chief Paruso is expecting me."

"Be out in a minute, ma'am." The deep voice wasn't Keith's but still sounded familiar. A large figure loomed behind the frosted glass of the entrance door and she came face-to-face with Tiger when he opened the door.

"Tiger. Nice to see you."

"Abi. Come on in. The chief's in his office. He had some business to take care of." Tiger wore a smirk on his face and Abi assumed he and Keith must be friends outside of work.

"So you don't buzz folks in like they do at the police station? Don't you have a security camera on the door?"

Tiger walked gracefully for such a muscular man. She was figuring out that firefighters had to be just as physically fit as she had while an FBI agent, or as much as a police officer. They also had to be quick and graceful, which often came out in their stride. Tiger's stride was smooth, his demeanor almost charming.

"There's a camera on the door and all other parts of the station, 24/7. We've had our share of solicitors lately, so we've taken to opening the door only for pre-approved guests. That includes any firefighter on duty or off, and their spouses. Some of the girlfriends, too. As you can see for yourself." He shot her a grin and motioned at an open office door.

Three women, all young and attractive, were jammed into a small, wood-paneled room. Their focus was clearly on the fire chief. Keith sat at his desk and appeared decidedly uncomfortable with the attention. Not like the playboy persona he'd initially projected when she'd met him that first day at the farmhouse arson.

Stop thinking you're changing him. That would only lead to heartbreak.

"You have to stop bringing me doughnuts, Angie. And Vicki, I'm going to have to freeze your peanut butter cookies and share them with the department later."

"That's why I brought you the fruit plate, Keith." The woman on the right spoke up.

Abi allowed herself the privilege of rolling her eyes before she rapped on the threshold. Three sets of eyes were on her, and she didn't think she'd felt more scrutinized when she'd gone through the obstacle course at Quantico.

"I'm here for my appointment with Chief Paruso."

Keith's gaze found hers and he quickly stood. His smile reflected interest and relief. "Abi! Come on in."

Abi gave him the same smirk Tiger had flashed at her only moments before. "Take your time. I can wait in the hall."

"Thank you, ladies, for the treats. The department and I appreciate them. I need to get back to business now."

Taking Keith's cue, the women filed out of Keith's office. "Bye, Chief."

"See you next week."

"Let me know if you'd rather have my brownies next time."

"Bye, ladies." Keith scratched his head and gave Abi a devastating smile. A smile that said he was glad to see her. "Come on in."

"I'm afraid I don't have any baked goods for you. I had no idea you had such a sweet tooth."

He lowered himself into an old, squeaky chair and motioned at the overstuffed chair in front of his desk. Abi sat.

"I got a reputation for eating up all of the sweets in the station kitchen when I was a young firefighter. I had the metabolism and the time for daily double workouts to burn it all off. Now, I watch the refined stuff. I still love a good doughnut, but lately I've developed a taste for spicier fare." He leveled his gaze on her, raising his brow. Damn it but she wanted to believe he only flirted with her. It was too easy to believe it, when he'd been so aboveboard with the women who'd just left.

"You look ridiculous. I'm sure your tactics work for the other ladies, but you forget, I've worked with mostly men for all of my career."

He had the humility to appear embarrassed. Slightly. "That's okay, Abi. You're helping me up my game."

"Give me a break, Chief."

"As for the women? They're all either married to, engaged to or dating my firefighters. They like to have a little friendly banter about baking me treats. But really, the sweets go out in the kitchen for everyone and they know that."

"Methinks the man doth protest too much. How about the tour you promised?"

Chapter 10

Keith kept any response to Abi's Shakespeare reference he'd thought of to himself. Let her think he was a simple man whose daily highlight was flirting with the significant others of his firefighters. Keith loved it when an opponent underestimated him.

And he liked showing his department to her, more than he'd expected. It was a kick how Abi's eyes lit up at the more minute details of the station's history. "That's the original fire pole?" She pointed at the brass fixture in the center of the garage, and as she did a woman slid down it with practiced ease.

"Hey, Johnson, I told you not to do that unless you absolutely had to."

The woman landed softly and turned to face Keith and Abi. "Sorry, Chief, I couldn't resist it."

"Abi, this is Colleen, our toughest and most adroit firefighter. She was an award-winning gymnast in college, in case you couldn't tell."

"Hi." Colleen held out her hand and Abi took it.

"Nice to meet you. How many women are in the department?"

"Two." Keith and Colleen answered in unison.

"Is that typical?" When her father fought fires there hadn't been any women.

"It's average." Colleen spoke up. "About the same percentage as when I went through school. I'm told it varies."

"Colleen's correct. We have more female firefighters each year but proportionally the numbers have remained the same in our department for the last five years or so."

"Thanks." Abi nodded at the other woman and Keith couldn't help comparing her to Colleen Johnson. Women in male-dominated fields always seemed to have a shared sense of struggle and accomplishment.

"You two are a lot alike, having to prove yourselves in a tough field."

"Passing firefighting and FBI obstacle courses are hard, no matter who you are, right, Colleen?" The young woman smiled at Abi and Keith hid a grin.

"And, yes, to answer your question." He slapped the gleaming pole. "This, along with the garage and the part of the building where my office is, are all original to the Silver Valley's first fire department. Upstairs is the bunkhouse where the folks on watch sleep, and out back, where we're going now, is the newer part of the building."

"Enjoy your tour, Abi." Colleen nodded and headed toward the door.

"Follow me." He turned when he really wanted to grab Abi's hand and lead her around the station. It was odd, this feeling of possessiveness. Had to be something primal, as he'd not experienced it in a very long time. Keith was more of a one-date-per-woman man and he made sure that he hooked up with women who had the same expectations. It was less messy that way.

He heard her intake of breath when they entered the new part of the building.

"It's like *Back to the Future*." She looked at the top-shelf technology at the main desk, where an operator sat monitoring the feeds from the county Emergency Management Services.

"Hey, Lisa, this is Abi. She's working with SVPD as an arson investigator. You'll be seeing her around more."

"Hi, Abi." The young woman was as friendly as Colleen had been, and Keith saw the way Abi visibly relaxed. "Hey."

"Let's head into the engine bay." They took the back way into the garage, whose modernity was mammoth when compared to the antiquity of the original building. "As you can see, we have two engines, and there's also an SUV that I use. It's set up for comms and coordination."

He called to the guys washing down the engine they'd pulled out onto the driveway and introduced Abi.

"You'll see her at future calls, so heads up. Give her right of way and any equipment she might need." He looked at Abi. Were her brown eyes ever *not* looking right through him?

"Have you gone through firefighting training?"

Abi nodded. "Not as much as you, of course, not at all. Enough to know what different blazes feel like and what you're up against with them."

"Do you know how to use a respirator?"

"I was trained to use one, yes. If I had to I could, but I'd be better off if someone walked me through it again."

He appreciated her frankness. "If it's up to me, you won't need one while you're here. It's our job to put the fires out—you get the information after it's safe. But just in case, I'll walk you through our equipment before we leave today."

"You don't have to, Keith. I wanted to see the department and meet your team. Your time is better spent doing your work here. I don't want to interfere with that."

"Trust me, I'll tell you when you're interfering." He nodded toward the break room. "Let's go get a morning snack."

"Do you usually have this whole kitchen to yourself?" Abi bit into one of the special muffins one of the spouses had baked and any remaining snark she had about grown women fawning over Keith evaporated. "Oh. My. Gosh. This is the most amazing lemon poppy seed muffin I've ever had."

Keith stretched his legs out from the head seat of the huge commercial cafeteria table, so that they were next to Abi as she sat on one side. She ignored the blatantly possessive move. And was happy to have her hands full of a muffin so that if she were tempted to reach over and touch his thigh, which she wasn't, she couldn't.

"Told you. Those must be Melody's. She's dating one of the guys." He chugged water from a glass bottle with "Chief" emblazoned on its silicone holder. Abi acted like she was focused on her muffin, but really, would any breathing woman ignore the way his Adam's apple moved up and down his chiseled throat?

Keith lowered the bottle and his gaze held hers. "I think I've caught you this time, Abi."

No words were needed. He was referring to when she'd called him on checking out her ass.

"Not going to defend yourself?" He looked so damn smug.

"Nothing to explain. You run an equal-opportunity

operation here. What's good for the gander is just as enjoyable for the goose."

"Too hot under your collar to quote Shakespeare this time?"

"Very good, Chief. I was afraid your reading was limited to the Sunday comics."

"Ah, no. Sorry to disappoint you."

She looked at him. Was he perturbed? "What made you want to do this?"

"Be a firefighter?" Keith ran his finger along the side of his water bottle. It had started to sweat and the moisture gathered on his fingertip. He wiped his hands on his pants. If he was *her* significant other, she might think of more unconventional ways to take the moisture off his finger.

She licked her lips. "Yes. Why not move like you were used to, or go into a business that involved overseas travel?"

"I still love to travel but Silver Valley is my home. I've been here long enough to know it's the best place for me. Firefighting is something I've wanted since I was a tot living in Europe with my folks. Most kids outgrow the need to be in charge of a huge engine and run a hose. I never did." She watched him closely and expected him to make a sexual innuendo out of the hose comment. But his face was somber, his eyes clear and on her. "I'm where I belong, Abi. Have you ever felt a sense of belonging?"

"I've felt that I was in the right place for now, but no, I've never felt 'this is it,' as in 'I'm not going to do anything else.'"

"You're in the midst of changing careers now, aren't you?"

"Pretty much, yes."

Keith rapped his knuckles on the table. "Let's finish

this up. You've got to interview the dude from the business card, don't you? Mr. Taylor?"

Again, he caught her with her guard down. She'd learned her lesson: Keith Paruso's mind was as tight and as sharp as his way with women was smooth and practiced. Abi realized she'd been wrong. The man wasn't a bull—he was a shark.

"How long have you worked for the Department of Defense, Mr. Taylor?" Abi smiled what she hoped was congenially at the man who sat across from her and Rio in the US Army War College's student library. The base was only fifteen minutes from Silver Valley and Abi wanted to keep appearances of the interview being perfunctory, merely routine.

"Sixteen years." Dennis Taylor didn't smile. He seemed to be distracted, as if he had somewhere else to be.

That was about the right time frame. To be considered for attendance as a student to the War College as a US government employee, he would need to be at least at the civilian equivalent of a midrange military officer. The officers at the Army War College were mostly O-5s, which were commanders or colonels, depending upon the service. The civilian equal was a GS-14 and it normally took the better part of two decades to attain it. "How have you liked being an Army War College student so far?"

"It's fine. Pardon me... Ms. Redland, did you say?" He looked at Rio as he spoke, showing complete disrespect for Abi. She watched him closely as he acted like an ass. She'd interviewed suspects like this before, and even if Dennis didn't end up being involved in the elementary school fire she'd bet her bottom dollar all was not aboveboard with him. "I have a class in ten minutes. What is the real purpose of this meeting?"

"As Ms. Redland told you, we're here to close the loop on an incident at your child's elementary school. Have you heard about it?"

"Is this about the fire in the art room? Yes, my wife said something about it." He casually smoothed his suit jacket sleeves.

"How many of your children are enrolled in Silver Valley Elementary School?" Abi kept at it, enjoying how she and Rio worked to basically tag-team their suspect. Without the constant tension she struggled against as she worked alongside Keith. The constant awareness. She needed all of her energy on the suspect, not a hot fire chief. Of course Dennis wasn't an official suspect. Yet.

"Two. Our daughter is in fourth grade and our son is in kindergarten." His affectation of boredom was getting on Abi's nerves.

"And are they happy there?"

He shrugged. "Sure. As happy as any kids that age are to go to school."

"You told us you live in Silver Valley, yet most of the students here at the War College live in Carlisle or on base. Why did you pick Silver Valley?" Rio took over the questioning and Abi was relieved. The guy didn't respect women, that much was clear. She'd rather observe Rio work the interview than deal with such a turd.

"My wife is a full-time mother and we thought the community in Silver Valley was better suited to our views on how to raise a family."

"What kind of views would that be? You see, I'm looking to find a place to buy a house for my girlfriend and me, so I'm genuinely curious as to why you picked Silver Valley instead of Carlisle." Rio was smooth. Abi wanted to high-five him for his superior performance as the "good cop."

Dennis leaned in, both elbows on his thighs as he spoke to Rio. Abi used the time to study him. If the bastard didn't want to look at her or acknowledge her, fine. It gave her carte blanche to analyze him, his body language. "Silver Valley has a more traditional feel. A friend of ours told me about it, that I should check it out, before we made our move from the DC area."

"DC? I just moved here from there myself. Whereabouts did you live?" Abi couldn't resist.

"Fairfax County." He gave her the quickest of glances before pointedly turning his attention back to Rio.

"Your wife was okay with the move for such a short course? You're only here ten months, barely a school year, right?" Ooh, Rio was going in for the kill. Abi loved it. The master's degree Dennis was taking was an intense ten-month course, designed for mid-to-senior-level military officers and government employees. Many students who lived two hours or more away opted to live in apartments that surrounded the base and commute home on the weekends. It provided minimal disruption to their families.

Dennis blinked. Once. "My wife does what's best for our family."

"And who was the friend who recommended Silver Valley?" Rio wrote in his notepad, apparently asking the question in the most casual manner. Abi knew differently.

"I don't remember, actually. We had a lot of friends in our church community in northern Virginia."

Abi wished she could meet Dennis's wife and see what her thoughts were. But since they'd only found a business card, they'd be out of bounds questioning his wife unless he proved to be a valid suspect.

"Do you have any more questions, Abi?" Rio deferred to her, much to the jerk's consternation.

"No, not at the moment. Thank you for your time, Mr. Taylor."

"Have a good day." He stood and walked away without shaking either of their hands.

Abi waited until they were in the police vehicle driving off base to voice her opinion on their suspect.

"He was an odd duck."

"Creep is more like it." Rio eased the sedan into traffic on the main pike. "I know what you're thinking, Abi, and I agree."

"That we may have just met the newest member of the True Believers?"

Rio laughed. "You got it. Did you hear him use the word 'community' more than once?"

"And he made it clear he runs the show, not his wife. And since when does Silver Valley have more community-minded people than Carlisle? Both places are great to raise kids." She'd only been here a few months but that was clear enough to her.

"We'll keep an eye on him if we need to. This is getting us to the point where we need eyes in the cult."

"You mean like Nika did at Christmastime?" Police Officer Nika Pasczenko had managed to get inside a True Believer cult meeting, and identified several members. It was a stroke of luck that had yielded a few leads but so far no arrests.

Rio nodded. "Yes. But it needs to be someone the cult isn't familiar with—"

Whatever he was going to say was interrupted by his phone, which was on speaker, hands-free.

"Rio." Rio looked at Abi and smiled. "Hey, Colt…Yes, we did. Abi's with me now…He wasn't budging. Was a complete jerk, actually, which affirms for me that he might have ties with the cult."

Rio motioned at the dashboard, silently asking if Abi wanted to talk to Colt. She shook her head. She'd fill Colt in later, after she wrote her report.

"What's that?" Chief Todd's voice was breaking up. Rio looked at her, his expression grim.

"There's a fire. Keith's already on the scene." Abi understood that much of Colt's words.

"Where?" Rio accelerated in the direction of Silver Valley.

"It's the warehouse district. You and Abi take it easy when you get there." The thread of trepidation in Colt's voice was unusual and Abi's gut twisted.

"Got it." Rio looked at her as the comms with Colt ended. "You up for this?"

"You know it."

Chapter 11

Keith let his team take the lead into the fire, confident in their abilities but also taking the chance to survey the area surrounding the warehouse. SVPD was handling the traffic along the pike, keeping all except emergency vehicles away from the distribution district. Of all of the logistic facilities, this was the worst the arsonist could have picked.

The fifty-dock warehouse was the North American headquarters for Amoeba, the leading online store for all science-related toys. Amoeba sold chemistry, biology, astronomy, engineering kits and more for ages newborn and up, and had hit the *Fortune* 100 last year. It'd made a big splash not only in Silver Valley and central Pennsylvania, but nationwide, as well. It was the epitome of hometown-girl-hits-it-big, as the founder and CEO was a thirty-something single mother who'd grown up in the area. Everyone knew Cassie Hudson. So this arson was very personal to Silver Valley.

Keith scanned the other distribution warehouses within sight of Amoeba. None appeared to be fazed by the fire going on here.

"Chief, it's getting too hot in here. I'm sending the team out." Tiger's voice was in his ear on the mic system.

"Get them out." He waited for six fighters to emerge from the loading dock they'd entered at the back of the building. He counted three, then five. No Tiger. He approached the team. "Hey, Bill, where's Tiger?"

Bill took his helmet and self-contained breathing apparatus off, sweat running down his face and the back of his neck. "He was right behind me."

A bang sounded, followed by a billow of black smoke pouring from the open bay door.

"Give me that." Keith was already in firefighting gear but had left his helmet near the engine when he'd started his walkabout. He grabbed Bill's helmet, an SCBA from the backup pile, and ran toward the black smoke.

He crawled into the building below the smoke layer, looking for the source of the blaze and, more importantly, Tiger. Row upon row of metal shelving was ablaze, the previous contents barely recognizable with the strength of the flames. He rose and ran through the wide berth between the aisles, where normally forklifts operated. His apprehension grew as he went by each row, looking for a body. At the middle of the warehouse he saw what had caused the noise that preceded the dark fumes: two of the huge shelving units had collapsed onto each other, their spilled contents combining into a huge fireball. From the smell and fumes he knew the merchandise had to be plastics. His time was running out; the heat of the blaze narrowed his window to find Tiger.

Come on, Tiger. Where the hell are you, buddy?

Fear that he'd have to turn back toward the loading

dock propelled him forward, praying to find Tiger. He scanned the area where the shelving had collapsed and, through the smoke and rising flames, spotted a familiar lump. Tiger lay on the concrete floor fifty yards from him, only inches from the burning metal shelves.

The air was thick and his breathing labored, even with his SCBA. If Keith lost consciousness, he'd be no good to either of them. He slammed down onto his knees and crawled to Tiger's inert form. He had seconds to get him out of there, before having his team come in for both of them put too many lives at risk.

"I've got Tiger, bringing him out. Stay out of the building. Repeat, stay out of the building." He reached Tiger and grabbed his shoulders. "Tiger, are you with me, man?" It was hard to shout with so little oxygen.

Tiger's slight nod was all he needed to get his own adrenaline pumping. Tiger was alive—they both had a chance. Keith knew that the chances of him making it all the way from here to the dock door without collapsing were slim, and impossible if he stood and inhaled the fumes, even with his SCBA. The air at floor level was manageable.

"Trust me, Tiger. I'm going to get us out of here." He wrapped his harness straps around Tiger's massive chest and shoulders, and began to crab-walk them both out of the aisle. He heard pops and booms and crackles all around them and knew he had a minute, maybe two, to get out of the warehouse. The thought of thousands of tons of steel collapsing on him and Tiger clawed at his awareness but he pushed it away.

He counted the crawling steps in his mind, saving each breath for the oxygen his muscles needed to do the job. Tiger would be a heavy load on a clear day with perfect weather; inside the burning, smoke-filled warehouse, it felt impossible to move his large form. It took several seconds for Keith to feel his rhythm kick in, but when it did he focused entirely on maintaining forward motion. After what seemed like hours but had to have been only a minute, they reached the larger aisle that led to the loading dock.

"Chief, do you want backup?" Colleen's voice in his earpiece.

"No, no backup. Not yet." The words required herculean effort as he kept moving. His muscles were starting to protest and he feared it wasn't from exertion as much as lack of air. It would be so much faster to lift Tiger on his shoulders and make a run for it, but the fumes would kill them both.

His vision started to blur and he would have cursed had he the energy. All he could do was focus on the open door.

Gravel spewed up onto the police vehicle's body as Rio skidded to a halt near the row of three fire engines. They'd passed two others on the way in, and their loud sirens sounded behind them as Abi got out of the car.

"Where's Chief Paruso?" she questioned Colleen, the first firefighter she came to. There were only one or two around the engines, working the hoses. The rest were in a semicircle around the loading dock they'd driven up to. The other bay doors were randomly closed and the open doors had smoke coming out of them, huge billows of charcoal clouds that were beyond frightening.

"He's inside—we're waiting for him to come out with Tiger." Colleen adjusted hose pressure as she shouted above the din. "We're putting as much water and chemicals as we can on it and it's still not slowing down."

Raw fear froze Abi on the spot. Keith was inside that

building. With his firefighter Tiger, the man he'd introduced her to at the elementary school.

Keith.

"Don't even think about it." Rio was next to her, watching the action.

"There's nothing I can do, even if I wanted to run in there." No use arguing what he insinuated. It was true—if she thought for one moment she could go in there and save Keith and Tiger, she would.

But she was an arson forensics expert. Not a firefighter.

"You can pray, Abi." Rio shielded his eyes from the sun. "This is the largest fire I've ever witnessed, that's for goddamned sure."

Abi couldn't just stand there. She left Rio without a word and ran up to the firefighters that arced water over the roof of the long, rectangular building.

"Any word on Chief Paruso?" She spotted another familiar face from her tour of the department.

"He's in there, getting Tiger out. The fumes are the worst and Chief's SCBA probably can't keep up with it all, so it's slowing him down. He'll be out."

The SCBA wasn't able to give him enough oxygen? That would be like her going into a stakeout without her weapon.

She watched in what felt like slow motion as the water rained down on the building, pouring over the cement loading dock and obscuring the entrance. A loud cheer went up and she wasn't sure why; she couldn't make out anything. Until the hose was pointed away long enough to allow two figures to crawl onto the dock. She recognized the large shape of Tiger, on the ground. And Keith, next to him. Right before Keith crashed to the concrete slab, inert.

"Keith!" She heard a woman's scream and felt strong arms around her waist. As she fought off her attacker she stilled and blinked. Rio. It had been *her* scream.

"I told you, Abi, don't even think about it."

Keith pushed away the ministrations from the EMTs but didn't make a move to remove the oxygen mask they'd slapped on him. Not yet. His lungs were on fire and he was only beginning to feel like himself.

"Sir, you need to let me examine you." A no-nonsense EMT glared at him but her tone was patient, practiced. He didn't recognize her—she had to be from another township. All of the county response teams had been called to the fire.

"Okay. But I'm fine, really. How's Tiger?" Except for the sharp stabbing spasms in his lower back, but he'd had them before, after hauling someone out of a burning building or heavy lifting. It came with the territory. As the EMT went back to work taking his vitals, he spotted Abi talking to Rio in the small gathering around the ambulance.

"Your colleague is being treated. He'll be okay."

Thank God. He'd thought that he might fail Tiger in there and leave the poor dude to die on that godforsaken floor. No one had been more relieved than he had been when they'd made it to the loading dock. Keith had known his department and several others would be waiting for their exit, intent on having them out of the way safely, and putting the fire out. What he hadn't expected was that he'd see Abi in that group of firefighters, Rio holding her back.

Sheer relief had permeated his every muscle.

What is she running to? It had been his last thought before a back spasm hit him and his knees had buckled, forcing him to lie on the dock. The EMTs must have thought he'd passed out but it had been his damned muscles that had given out.

"Can I talk to him?" Abi's voice cut through as she interrogated the EMT. Had he noticed how sweet it sounded? How a sense of peace settled on him when he heard her?

"In a minute, ma'am."

Abi's eyes sought his and he couldn't figure out the emotion screaming out of their brown depths. Was Abi furious or amused? He must have looked like he was in distress because the EMT was patting his forearm. "It's okay, Chief, just keep taking deep breaths and relax. You're fine. Your lungs might be a little sore but you'll be okay."

"Tell that to my back." His voice sounded so damn weak and he started hacking before he got "back" all the way out. Abi's eyes grew wide.

"Stop…" He held up a hand but had to cover his mouth again as another spasm hit him.

"Don't talk now. Wait until you catch your breath." Abi's voice, her breath near his ear. He opened his eyes to see hers locked on his. "Unless you saw something you think Rio and I need for the case."

"Ma'am, I'm going to have to ask you to step back." The EMT wasn't pleased.

"No." He reached for Abi, tried to grab her hand. But she was closer than he'd judged and he grabbed a handful of breast instead. Abi squeaked and straightened quickly as the EMT frowned down at him. "Didn't mean…" *Cough, cough, cough.* His hand slid down her side, found hers. He entwined his fingers with hers and tugged. Abi leaned down, blocking the onlookers.

"Shh. Just play along with the EMT like a good boy and we'll spring you out of here." She stood back up but kept hold of his hand, and he saw her smile at the EMT. "I'm okay here, right?"

"Whatever." The EMT wasn't happy but with Rio standing next to Abi and Abi alongside Keith, what was she going to do?

Abi knew it was most unprofessional to keep holding Keith's hand but extraordinary circumstances and all. She turned to Rio as Keith got poked and prodded and kept refusing to go to the ER.

"As soon as he's up to it, maybe he can tell us something."

Rio's mouth was a grim line. "Unlikely. It's going to take hours to put this out." Which meant that much longer to figure out the cause and if it was related to their case.

"Is it just me or does it feel the least little bit personal, after we interviewed Dennis Taylor?"

Rio chewed on his lip. "No way of telling. Yes, it seems a crazy coincidence, and no, I don't really believe in coincidence, especially when we're talking about fires so close together and now this one so big. But until we have evidence, we wait."

"Right." She shifted her weight, her hand sweaty in Keith's. "And, um, Rio?"

"Yeah?"

"Thanks for having my six." She used the military idiom, adopted by LEAs, that referred to covering for one's backside. "I don't know what I was thinking back there. When I tried to go to the dock."

Rio looked at her over his shades and then at her

hand in Keith's. "I have every idea what you were thinking."

Unfortunately so did she.

"What's the scoop?" Colt walked up to the group, and the firefighters that surrounded the ambulance at a respectful distance from where Keith was being treated parted, letting the chief of police in.

"Keith here took a bit of a hit when he dragged Tiger out of the warehouse. Tiger was knocked out when shelves collapsed, regained consciousness before the EMTs got to him but they sent him to the hospital right away. No update yet, but my guess is a concussion." Rio spat out the updates as Abi used the time to take stock of the action around her.

She squeezed Keith's hand one more time before letting it go. "I need to do a walk-around." Keith started to protest and she placed her hand firmly on his shoulder. "Take it easy. I'm not going into the warehouse, for God's sake. But a walk around the area might yield something, right?" Before he could complain any more, she walked over to Colt.

"I need to get my bearings and see the different points of entry on this property. Stay with Keith?"

Both men nodded, waved her off. She took a last look at Keith and smiled as Colt and Rio stood on either side of the gurney, protective of their injured teammate.

Abi approached the building and spoke to the firefighters still battling the blaze, hoses sweeping the building and fire methodically. She flashed her ID. "I'm going to take a look at the property around the warehouse. Okay?"

"Don't go any closer than we are right now, ma'am."

"I won't."

She started with the area nearest the loading dock first. The firefighters were getting closer, and she thought that within five to ten minutes they'd be able to direct the water spray directly into the warehouse. They were going to need chemicals to smother the burning plastics. The fumes were pretty intense and she was twenty-five yards from the building.

The concrete dock was almost five feet off the ground but certainly scalable by a physically fit person. The arsonist she'd spotted at the house fire had been young and slender, and fast enough to outrun her, which said a lot. She wasn't Olympic material but had always been a decent sprinter.

Ignoring the anxiety wrought by the image burned into her consciousness of Keith collapsing on the same dock, she started to walk the perimeter of the building. About half of the loading dock doors, scroll-type garage contraptions, were closed tight. The rest were open, the air feeding the fire. The one on the end where more smoke billowed out, on this side of the building, was directly opposite the dock Keith had collapsed on. She was going to have to interview the general manager of the warehouse to find out if they'd had any deliveries today. There were no trailers at the docks on the firefighting side but when she walked around to the other side of the immense building, six of twelve bays had trailers attached. She took photos of each one and their license plates.

The lone cry of a hawk caught her attention and she looked up. It'd come out of the dense forest that started not far from a nearby chain-link fence that separated the warehouse property from thickets and fields that backed up against the woods. After she finished inspecting and photographing each loading dock, Abi walked to the fence and started her investigation of its integrity. Within two minutes she hit pay dirt. The fence was split wide open, enough to allow a man through.

Son of a shoo-fly pie. She snapped photos, noting the places where the steel wire splits were smooth—this had been deliberately cut. No rust, either, making it fresh.

A rustle in the thickets that grew up to the fence from the tree line raised the hair on the back of her neck. She pocketed her phone and drew her weapon in one move, all of her muscles tense and on alert.

Come out wherever you are, you mother—

A flurry of shaking branches to her right was followed by a very large groundhog parting the bush with his rotund shape. She stared down the interloper, still holding her weapon in front of her with both hands. Silence surrounded her, pierced only by the low roar of the water hitting the roof of the warehouse from the other side where the firefighters worked. And the sound of Punxsutawney Phil's nose twitching.

She holstered her weapon. "It's just me and you, dude, huh?" The oversize rodent immediately turned and scurried away, his toffee fur catching the sunlight as his body undulated with his laborious movement. So it was true about the local groundhogs. They really didn't have a fear of humans. He'd sure had her hackles up.

Lionel's heart pounded and he kept both hands over his mouth to keep his laughter silent. That had been close! The bitch had almost caught him. He huddled under the fir tree, knowing his smarts had saved him again. Brother Wise was going to be very, very pleased. Maybe he'd even promote him to be his right-hand man.

Because he was ready. Brother Wise had said to set a small fire at the big sign outside the entrance gate to the warehouse. To warn the stupid woman who ran the sinful toy business based on man's science that her profit was made on the blood of people like him and his New Thought family. That it had to stop.

And now he had something better, something more precious. He'd been able to go into the warehouse, start the fire there. He had been videotaping the fire ever since and had a great shot of the one firefighter collapsing after he dragged one out that Lionel hoped was dead by now. Silver Valley needed to heed Leonard Wise's prophecy. The True Believers were the only way out of sinful living.

When the bitch had started to walk around the perimeter of the building, he'd had to run and use the way he'd come in earlier. It had been so exciting, carrying the backpack with the explosives, he'd almost been unable to cut the fence his hands had been shaking so badly.

She'd gotten too close and he'd have lost a lot if he'd been caught by her or one of her bullets. Although he doubted the bitch could shoot. Women weren't designed to fire guns. They were made by the Creator of earth to bear fruit in their wombs. That was what Brother Wise reminded them every night at their prayer gatherings.

But she hadn't caught him—he'd caught her, on tape, and he'd taken a few stills of her, too. With any luck he'd have perfect profiles of her to share with Brother Wise so that she could be brought to real justice. Her ID had been clipped to her bulletproof vest, too, and he hoped it showed him what he really wanted. Her name. He wasn't going to tell Brother Wise or anyone about that yet, though. Not until he had the real McCoy to bring to the New Thought founder.

* * *

"Have a seat, everyone." Keith walked slowly into his townhome and nodded toward the living room as he, Abi and Rio entered. Abi took in her surroundings and immediately decided she'd underestimated Keith. While his place had a bachelor pad stamp on it, with a few obvious things like a Kegerator, Xbox game console with fancy remotes and the largest flat-screen she'd ever seen in a residential home, it was purposefully decorated. Contemporary hound dog with touches of genuine domesticity.

"Is that parsley on your sink windowsill?" Sprays of herbs grew from utilitarian terra-cotta pots.

"What, you don't think Neanderthals can sprout seeds?" Keith was in pain, his back sore, but his humor was intact. Abi smiled.

"Enough. Abi, make us a pot of coffee. Or tea. Or water. Keith, sit your ass down and take a load off." Rio was all cop, his orders in the form of barks. It was easy to forget that Rio had almost lost a friend today, too.

Abi tried to shove down her embarrassment. She felt every bit the fool she'd been since she'd met Keith. It was clear to Rio that she cared a little more than one usually did for a work partner. Offering comfort to Keith after his near-death event was one thing, but continuing to hold his hand through the next several minutes? Flirting with him just now? Probably a bit too much.

She filled the carafe with tap water and routed in the cupboards for a coffee filter and a bag of beans. Keith had a grinder on the counter and she made short work of the hand-roasted blend, purchased from a local gourmet coffee shop according to the label. She would have pegged Keith for more of a Folgers dude.

"Come on out, Abi." Rio called her from the living room.

"Just a sec." She set the pot on and brought out water glasses she'd filled for all of them. "Keith, this is most important for you, as the hospital was most adamant about your hydration."

"Yes, ma'am."

They all looked at one another, appreciating the quiet and calm after the deadly chaos.

Then they got to work.

Chapter 12

Abi spent the next few days completing her investigative work at the remaining arson sites. Her methods didn't change but her overall comfort level was much less as she missed having Keith with her. He needed daily physical therapy to get his back right, and he had his own work to see to, especially after the warehouse fire.

Face it, you miss him.

She did miss Keith, but it wasn't the time to muddy up the waters of the investigation with a relationship. Especially one that would risk her blowing her cover. Keith wasn't the kind of man to take anything at half measure. Which made her imagine exactly what kind of measures he'd take with her body.

"Hey, Abi." Rio's voice startled her. He sat across from her in the small office the station had allocated her for the time she worked on the arson cases. "Figure out anything more?"

"No. Any word on the security tapes from Amoeba's warehouse security?"

"That's what I came in to tell you. We're bringing in an employee who was caught using his forklift to load flammables into the explosives area of the warehouse. It's all on tape. I'm going to handle that, but I want you to speak to Cassandra Hudson and get her take on this employee."

"No problem. Do you want me to go to her?"

"No, have her come in here. She already gave a statement the day of the fire but now that she thinks she knows who was responsible she may have more light to shed on it."

"Fine, but I'm a little confused, Rio. Wouldn't there be several layers of management between her and a forklift driver?"

"The term in distribution circles is 'put-away drivers.'" Rio grinned. "It sounds so basic, doesn't it? But it's a tough job and the local warehouses have a difficult time keeping qualified employees hired. It's high burnout and requires a knack for depth and space perception."

"How do you know this?"

"I worked at a warehouse the summer after college, before I got accepted into the police academy. Good pay, long hours and I'm grateful I'm a cop. Anyway, Cassie is infamous for her involvement in every aspect of her business, to include the warehouse. I guarantee you that she knows this operator by name and probably his family's deal, too. She's hands-on. It's part of what made her so successful."

"Good to know. She sounds like the perfect witness. I'll call her."

"Thanks, Abi."

Rio stood. "By the way, Keith is back at work. In

case you didn't already know." He left and she was glad he didn't see her blush, as she was sure she was doing.

Keith hadn't made contact with her and she felt a familiar squeeze of discomfort in her middle. She'd wrestled with her embarrassment for being so demonstrative when he'd been injured. Holding his hand at the scene, really?

She put the call into Cassandra Hudson and focused on preparing for the interview. It was better than beating herself up over something so trivial in the big picture.

And kept her from brooding over the fact that Keith hadn't made an attempt to contact her since the warehouse fire. Not even for work. Not that she expected him to call her socially, but more to ask how the investigation was going.

Abi stared at her desk as her heart dropped. She was willing to let go of her past, start over in Silver Valley. Somehow that had become synonymous with having Keith in her life, and not just as a work colleague.

Was there any chance that Keith had come to the same conclusion about her?

Cassandra Hudson was tall, with long red hair that framed her intelligent eyes. Eyes that looked at Abi with a sense of purpose. Abi liked her immediately. In no way did Cassandra exude a diva attitude or give off the sense that she thought she was better than anyone else because she was one of the top CEOs in the world. If Abi didn't know it, she'd think Cassandra Hudson was any other Silver Valley woman. She had a sense of complete ease as she sat in the chair Abi offered, and helped herself to a bottle of water set out on a tray with store-bought cookies.

"Please, call me Cassie. Everyone here does." She

downed half the bottle of water. "Sorry, but I've been working at the warehouse 'round the clock since the fire, trying to salvage what we can."

"Were you able to salvage any of your inventory?" Abi watched Cassie as she answered questions. Body language revealed more about a person than their words.

"We're not sure yet. The smoke damage has just about wiped our inventory out. To be honest, now that I'm over the shock of losing it all, it's okay. I know it will be okay. We can always have more manufactured. Our customers are willing to wait for our products, and the wait won't be that long. I consider my company, myself, very, very lucky that no one was hurt."

"Except for two firefighters."

"Oh, my gosh, yes, of course. I wasn't forgetting that. They saved my employees who would have been stuck in that part of the warehouse. Keith and Tiger are great guys."

"Yes, they are. So, you've had a chance to look at the security tapes?"

Cassie nodded. "Yes. It was clear to me that the person responsible for the fire was Ethan McSherry, but it sure surprised me. I mean, he's been one of my most valuable employees at that level of operations. Never late, never missed work."

"Why are you sure he's responsible, Cassie?"

Cassie's eyes widened. "For one, he was caught on tape loading dangerous materials—chemistry kits and such—alongside cleaning supplies. We don't store cleaning supplies in the actual warehouse where we store merchandise. They're kept in a separate part of the building. Second, he got the load of bleach and ammonia from separate trailers, which means he had to purposefully place them alongside the flammable kits we have for older children. This isn't something that can be done by accident, even if you tried. The fact that he timed the placement of the cleaning supplies within hours of when the fire was started is pretty damning. I mean, I'm no police officer or detective like you, but I know my products, my warehouse."

"Tell me what you know about Mr. McSherry."

"Ethan came to work for us three years ago. He's a high school graduate who wanted a better paying job than flipping burgers. With no specific skills, the warehouse was the perfect environment for him. He always seemed upbeat, happy to be at work, to have a job. He used to show me pictures of his kids on his phone during his breaks." Cassie trailed off, her gaze looking over Abi's shoulder as she thought. "You know, now I remember seeing his wife at the family picnic and fun day we have every August. They were newlyweds when he started with us but already she was pregnant, and it turned out to be twins. They've had two more kids since the twins— they were all at the last picnic."

"Anything unusual about his wife? Have you met her?"

"Yes, and she was very shy but nice and friendly the first couple of times. This last time I remember in particular because she got into an altercation with another worker's husband. It was about him being married to another man—she had strong feelings about that." Cassie shuddered. "It was truly awful. My company is founded on equal opportunity and tolerance. It's a toy company— we pride ourselves on diversity. Ethan's wife was spewing some hateful stuff. Fortunately the other employee's husband walked away and chalked it up to plain old ugly bigotry." Cassie took another sip of water. "I was horrified and apologized to both the spouse and my employee."

"Did you say anything to Ethan?"

"No, actually that time I let my general manager of the warehouse handle it. There wasn't anything to say, really, because it wasn't one employee going after another. If it had been Ethan, I would have fired him on the spot. He'd never given any indication of being anything more than a dedicated associate. None of the other workers have ever complained about him."

"You seem to know your employees well."

"It's a small operation, all told. Amazing, isn't it? With a global reach. Technology and the internet have made it globally successful. I've always believed that knowing my employees and treating them like family is key to a thriving business." Cassie blinked, her eyes pooling with tears. "That's what makes this so hard. Amoeba is a huge financial plus for Silver Valley and the entire region. It boosts the economy, and we contribute to many local charities. To have a local commit such an act of brutal violence, starting a fire..." She wiped her tears with her fingers. "All I can say is that you won't catch the bastards soon enough for me."

Abi liked Cassie. A lot. "We're on it. Thank you for your time and for coming in again today. I know you've got your work cut out for you with rebuilding."

Cassie shook her head. "It's nothing, really. What the firefighters did, what you're doing—you've got the tough job. Thank you."

"You're welcome, but thank me after we close the loop on the folks who burned down your warehouse."

Nothing new had crossed Abi's desk in the week after she'd interviewed Cassandra Hudson. She used the time to secure a small business loan for her shop, after she'd made sure there were no similar businesses in the area. A plus to the case slowdown was that she found herself at home more in the evenings. Abi was grateful for the lull in the case the past week had offered as she sipped her jasmine tea and watched the sunset from the bay window the previous owners, the Pearsons, had installed in a back living room. It was more of a great room, an addition that added almost a thousand square feet of living space that was equally perfect for holiday gatherings and quiet alone times. She'd flipped the gas fireplace on to chase the cold chill the rain had brought, and ate her dinner in front of the warmth as the natural light faded. Finally the skies were clearing, allowing for spectacular shades of peach and violet to frame the mountain ridge. When she'd lived in DC, it had been a rare evening on which she'd caught the sun setting over the Potomac. Yes, Abi definitely liked it here.

Her phone buzzed and she contemplated ignoring it. They hadn't had a break in the arson and cult case since the arrest of Ethan McSherry. The problem was that he wasn't talking a whole hell of a lot. Not enough to incriminate the real source of the criminal activity: Leonard Wise. And they couldn't prove either Ethan or his wife was involved in the cult, not yet anyhow.

She relented and looked at her caller ID. "Abi, here."

"How are you?" She closed her eyes at Keith's voice, wishing again she could replay those moments next to him while the EMTs tended to his injuries. Why did she have to go all girly?

"I'm fine, Keith. What can I do for you?"

"I was hoping we could get together. To talk. About the case." He'd left a pause between his statements that was long enough to give her too much room to imagine.

"Right now? Can it wait until the morning?" As much as she'd love to see him, she couldn't trust that she'd keep things professional. That her hands wouldn't grab him, touch him, run her fingers through his hair.

"I'd rather clear the air now." Keith's voice convinced her to ignore her concerns.

She looked at her watch. "Where do you want to meet and when?"

"Are you home?"

"I am."

"I'll come to you."

"Okay." She spoke to the empty room as Keith had already disconnected. A quick glance at her empty plate and another empty mug from this morning motivated her to start a quick cleanup. Not that she cared if Keith thought she was a slob.

As she walked from the living room to the renovated kitchen, she heard a scraping noise and froze. Complete silence enveloped her and, after a few moments, she figured it had to be a critter, maybe an opossum in the basement or a groundhog against the house foundation. The yoga girls had told her that it was common to find all kinds of mammals in the crooks and crannies of an old farmhouse this time of year, when the temperatures could still dip uncomfortably low.

Stacking the dishes in the sink, she reached to turn on the hot water to rinse them and heard it again. *Scratch, scratch, scratch.* Followed by a click.

The back door.

Dropping to the floor, she crawled to the kitchen table where she'd dropped her purse and holster. Abi took out her weapon and held it in front of her, posing in a catlike crouch. She made out the outline of a tall man through the white, eyelet-trimmed curtains that obscured the window on the kitchen door, which had been opened a crack. A light flared and illuminated his profile more but before she could react he pushed the door all the way open and threw an object into the house.

Glass crashed and she smelled gasoline.

"Freeze!"

The man's face reflected stunned surprise. Recognition dawned with a jolt. Mr. Taylor! Hadn't he noticed her vehicle outside? He had a baseball bat in his hand and, after a quick meeting of their eyes, he turned and fled.

Abi began pursuit. She jumped over the back porch railing as his form headed for the fields surrounding her house. He was aiming for the cornfield that had just started its rapid growth. Once he reached it, she'd be hard-pressed to find him.

"Taylor, stop or I will shoot!" She forced the words out as she ran, full-bore, at the man. He showed no sign of wavering, no movement that indicated he was going to turn back or stop.

They were twenty yards from the cornfield.

Abi used her training to dig deep and call upon the sprinter she'd once been. She thanked God for all the hours at the track when she reached the suspect. Grabbing his shoulder, she forced him to spin around. Abi kicked his groin and shoved against his face, making him drop to his knees and then into a fetal position.

Her weapon trained on him, she watched the groaning man while slowly doing a visual sweep of the area. "Are you alone?"

He continued to groan.

"Answer me!"

"Yes. I'm alone." This through clenched teeth.

She got close enough to make out his face for the second time. "Mr. Taylor, want to explain to me what the hell you're doing?"

Keith pulled up to Abi's house, ready to do battle with the toughest woman he'd ever met. Also the woman he'd been most attracted to in his lifetime. Which he had to admit said a lot; he'd never claimed he was a monk.

The front of the house was unassuming in the growing dusk but he anticipated the welcoming warmth inside. Heat that had nothing to do with Abi's fireplace. He walked up to the front door and pressed the doorbell. As he waited, he looked around. He smelled the distinct odor of something burning. Was Abi grilling outside?

After ringing the bell twice and knocking once, he figured she might very well be around back and walked through the damp grass to the side of the house. A flash of light in the window off the kitchen shocked him into action. Flames were clearly visible in her kitchen. He ran to the back door and up the steps, hoping like hell Abi was okay.

"Abi!" he called into the kitchen with no luck. A narrow line of flames was licking across the hardwood floor and inches from the walls. He knew from the smell that gasoline was involved, so he didn't waste time with water. He grabbed the nearest kitchen towel and started stomping out the fire. As soon as he was level with the sink, he took a small kitchen rug and threw it on the flames, smothering them. He ran back to the open door and hoisted an entrance mat, using it to finish off the flames that had started to climb up the wall. The smoke became thick and heavy as the rugs killed the fire.

"Abi!" Damn it, where was she? As he searched he hit autodial on his cell and alerted his department of the blaze. "I've put it out but it needs double-checking." He disconnected and called out again for Abi.

"Back here. Outside." Her voice was unmistakable. He must have missed her in his focus to get to the flames.

"Where?" He burst through the kitchen door and scanned the yard.

"Just around the right side of the house, by the corn-field," she shouted and he followed her voice, running again at full tilt. Until he spotted her.

Keith stopped in his tracks. Abi stood over a prone body, her weapon trained on it.

"Will you call SVPD for me? I take it you've already called the fire department."

Chapter 13

Colt and Claudia arrived together at Abi's house, while Rio showed up with the forensics team.

"Claudia's here to make sure nothing gets out on social media that isn't accurate." Colt stood before Keith.

"Good idea. We don't need any public speculation right now." Keith went and joined his firefighters. He'd overseen SVFD's walk-through of the farmhouse to make sure he'd put the fire out completely, and wanted to thank them for their efforts. Hardwood embers could smolder for a long time, breaking into a deadly fire with little warning.

Dennis Taylor was taken away in an ambulance, under 24/7 surveillance of two SVPD officers. The arson team gathered in Abi's living room. After what felt like days but in reality had been less than two hours, it was quiet again.

"There's stronger stuff if anyone wants it. I have wine and a nice bottle of vodka in the freezer. Normally I'd have more to offer, including cookies, but I've just moved in."

No one made a move for the booze. There was too

much work to do, too much thinking to cloud it with alcohol. Abi had made a pot of coffee and boiled water for the tea drinkers. She had to find extra mugs in the box she'd hauled from DC, as her cupboards were still pretty bare.

"I thought an intelligent man like Dennis Taylor would have made sure you weren't home before he torched your place." Rio sat near the gas fireplace, his expression grim.

"I pulled into the barn when I got home, and I didn't have any lights on yet. I was eating dinner in here and enjoying the sunset. I can see how he didn't think anyone was home. But he had a baseball bat with him—I guess he thought he'd take me out one way or the other."

"My concern is how the hell he knew where you lived. It's clear he knows what you're doing on the case, too." Keith's anger boiled in every word. He was sitting in an easy chair she'd had delivered only yesterday, along with the sofa that Colt and Claudia sat on. Abi was sitting on the hearthstone, near Rio.

Abi waved her hand in front of her face in surrender. "It's my fault. I know exactly how he got it. I had my badge on at the warehouse fire. Anyone could have snapped a photo of it then. Normally I don't wear it outside of SVPD, but since I was working with firefighters I wanted full access. I was being sloppy."

"We've not made it a secret that we have an arson expert contracted with SVPD." Colt looked at Claudia. "It's impossible to keep every fact about a case confidential."

Abi looked from Colt to Claudia and noticed the understanding that passed between them. Colt was referring to the Trail Hikers. He couldn't come out and say it with Keith sitting right there, but his concern was evident.

Had outsiders penetrated the Trail Hikers? Did they know the agency existed, and if they did, were they targeting Abi because of her status as an agent?

Claudia shook her head. "No one knows anything we don't expect them to." She looked at Abi. "And you've been making a lot of friends in the community, right? Didn't I overhear that you've attended classes at the yoga studio?"

Guilt hit a sucker punch to Abi. And she had nothing to feel guilty about—did she? She'd been following Claudia's orders to try to find her purpose outside of law enforcement.

"Yes, I've been getting to know a lot of folks. The yarn shop owner, for one."

"That's Cassandra Hudson's mother." Colt looked up from the fire.

"That's interesting, but I can't see either of them being involved with the cult. They're both self-starters, women with a strong sense of their own power." Abi thought the connection interesting. And liked that so many women she'd met in Silver Valley ran their own businesses.

"You're right." Claudia put her mug down on the makeshift coffee table—an overturned packing box. "Neither Cassie nor her mother is suspicious, but we can't overlook people who work for them. Obviously."

They all nodded or grunted in agreement. Cassie ran an impeccable business yet she had one bad egg—Mc-Sherry—who'd helped bring her entire corporation to a halt.

"And then there are all of the people who have helped me get settled. My real-estate agent, the contractors I'm hiring for my shop, the farmers who rent the land that comes with this house if indeed I opt to purchase instead of just renting."

Silence, then everyone spoke at once.

"You're opening a shop?"

"What kind of business?"

"Where is the shop?"

Abi held up her hands. "Whoa, one at a time. I've leased half of the house that Ezzie has the yarn shop in. Ezzie owns the building, or now that you've told me she's Cassie's mother, maybe it's Cassie's house. At any rate, she was looking to rent it out to another small business, and it's perfect for mine."

"Which is?" Keith spoke up, his gaze wary. What was he so damned afraid of?

Abi inhaled deeply. It was one thing to put the wheels in motion to open her own business; it was far more permanent once she spoke it aloud to the group who'd known her best during her few short months in Silver Valley.

"I'm opening a sporting adventure shop. My mission is to provide outdoor, back-to-nature experiences to locals and tourists alike, in and around Silver Valley. I'll have kayaking, hiking, camping and several other outdoor activities. It's going to depend upon who I can hire initially, but after it's up and running for a year or two, I hope to add in a type of recreational theme park on the land that abuts the base of the mountains behind this farmhouse."

"So you're planning on staying in Silver Valley?" Claudia's delight was evident.

Abi slowly nodded. "Yes. For now. Of course, I'm not really getting into this business too deeply. Not until we close this case."

"You shouldn't put your new career on hold, Abi. Not when it looks like this case might go on longer than we expected." Keith looked at her with a strange expression. Why was her personal life so important to him?

"Keith's right, to a point. We can't afford to lose you at SVPD right now, but as there are lulls in the case, you should feel free to pursue this." Colt looked around the room. "Although I think we can all agree we haven't had too much downtime with this string of fires."

Abi knew she had to speak up. "There won't be a lull from here on out. Leonard Wise is on a roll, and now that we've all but determined that one of his cult members, or at least someone who's attended the meetings, is behind two of the fires, he's going to ramp it up, right? Isn't that what he's done in the past—tried to agitate the community with crimes committed by others?"

Claudia nodded. "Yes. He was quick to move into the churchgoing population by reaching out to members of Silver Valley Community Church two Christmases ago, then he had the mayor thrown out on trumped-up charges. The replacement mayor was a nightmare and Silver Valley is still licking its wounds over that one."

"And don't forget how he used his members to threaten the high school this past Christmas." Rio was scrolling through notes on his phone. "Nika did a great job bringing that to a halt."

"He's not above drawing from the darkest, most close-minded parts of our town, that's for sure." Abi couldn't take her words back. Silver Valley did feel like her home. "I need to take a look at the statements from everyone we've interviewed and arrested in the past two weeks. Maybe there's something we've missed. This has to be part of a bigger plan. As much as I love arson forensics, I'm still betting that all of these fires are a means to an end."

Claudia started to speak but a brief touch of Colt's hand to her wrist left her silent. Abi looked at Keith. He'd noticed.

"I agree. Rio?"

Rio nodded at Colt. "Yes, sir. Well, we all know what we have to do. Abi, do you feel safe here tonight?"

"I'm fine." Especially now that the creep was locked up.

"I'll stay here with her for a while." Keith stood and walked to the picture window. "Although I dare say Abi's a much better shot than I am."

They all laughed.

Once everyone except Keith had left, they went into the kitchen, where Abi stared at the fire-damaged mess left behind by the Molotov cocktail.

"I can't thank you enough, Keith. You saved my house."

"You would have put it out once the police arrived and had control of Taylor."

"No, I wouldn't have made it in here in time. No way. I had to keep him under watch until SVPD arrived. You definitely knew what you were doing. Obviously." She blushed. How stupid could she sound?

"It's okay, Abi." He put his arm around her shoulders. "Luck and timing were on both our sides."

"How's your back feeling?"

"It's good. Much better." He smiled and she thought, hoped, he might lean in.

Instead he dropped his arm and she immediately missed his warmth.

"I'm just relieved that I finally caught a suspect. If I'd been three for three, it would have been hard showing my face at the station."

Keith chuckled. "No one expects you to do police work, per se. You're at SVPD as an arson expert, more of a profiler, right?"

Guilt tugged on her conscience. "Yes, something like that." She couldn't get too close to Keith, not while she was working as a Trail Hikers agent. And yet he was six inches from her, his masculine energy palpable in her small kitchen. Making her knees feel like slush.

He lifted her chin with his finger. "Abi, we need to talk about the other day. At the warehouse."

"I'm sorry about that, Keith. You were injured, on a gurney, and I tend to be too much of a caretaker when it comes to my colleagues. You didn't need me in there, making everyone else think that...that..." She couldn't say it, wasn't sure what to say.

"That we're a couple?" He leaned in and kissed her. Unlike the hormone-fueled kiss in the elementary school art room, this was a more thoughtful gesture. His lips were warm on hers and when she thought, hoped, *prayed* he'd deepen the kiss, he outlined her lips with his tongue and then pulled back.

"I'm not sure what's going on between us, Abi, and from the dazed look in your eyes, you aren't, either. Maybe we need to start over, take things a little slower?"

"Or not at all?" She let the words go, expecting he'd drop his hand from her chin, back up, leave. Instead he put his hands on her shoulders and pulled her in. For a hug.

Wanting so much more, she took the affectionate gesture.

"It's too late for that, babe." He pressed her head against his chest. "Relax. I'm not going to try to get into your panties tonight."

Damn. She giggled.

"Let me hold you for a few minutes. It's been a rough day for both of us." Abi relented and allowed her cheek to press against his chest, his T-shirt under her cheek, his heart thumping against her hand. She closed her eyes and let it be just the two of them, Abi and Keith. No secret agent and fire chief, no law-enforcement officers, no thought of the case. Just this moment, with Keith.

He couldn't believe it. He was the picture of domesticity, standing in the burned-out kitchen of an old farmhouse, holding a sweet woman in his arms. It was a far cry from the Harrisburg nightclubs he'd frequented for years, or the New York City bar scene he'd partaken of on his free weekends.

And it scared him.

He dropped his hands from her shoulders and took a step back. "We're going to have to work well together to bring down the cult. Silver Valley needs all of us, especially you with your expertise. I can put out fires, but I'm not much of a criminal detective."

Abi sighed and he loved how her small mouth opened, her lips rosy against her smooth skin. "Yes, we do need to work together. You have practical knowledge of the area I can't learn from maps or the internet or reading old case files."

"And you can get into an arsonist's mind. I have some experience there, and I can guess at motives, but you have a gift with it, Abi."

"Thanks, but it's all in the genes." She looked around the kitchen. There was at least two weekends' worth of work to repair the fire and smoke damage. He wished he could snap his fingers and fix it for her. "I can't deal with this right now."

"May I suggest that we take a break? What's on your schedule tomorrow?"

"Tomorrow? I still have stacks of papers I have to read, countless reports that are on the SVPD system that I want to go back over. There's so much to get through—"

"It'll still be there on Monday. Let's take the day off together. Go somewhere fun. You're opening a nature tourism and adventure business? How much do you know about the Appalachian Trail?"

"Enough to know that Pennsylvania's considered one of the toughest spots for it."

"Yes, and we have several access points right here in Silver Valley. Have you checked any of them out?"

"In the past few months? No. I've been too swamped with the case." And she hadn't mentioned if she wanted to live here permanently yet. But he wasn't going to ask her—he couldn't. He still wasn't sure how he felt about Abi staying in Silver Valley. Not after his initial shock and elation at her business announcement.

"Let me show you a favorite hike of mine. It's about three hours total—two hours up the mountain, one down. We'll leave early enough that you'll still have a good part of the day to yourself once we get back."

Her hesitation didn't bother him; he understood how difficult it was to take a break from an ongoing case. Especially one of this magnitude. What bugged him was the wariness in her eyes. As if she was weighing his offer. As if maybe she didn't trust him, not completely.

"Are you up to a hike after hurting your back at the Amoeba fire?"

"You are a caretaker extraordinaire, aren't you?"

"I told you no different, buddy."

"Yes, I'm good to go. It's better for me to walk than sit around. It hurts less, and the moving will help as long as we take it easy."

"I don't plan on rappelling." Her dry tone and timing was perfect. He laughed.

"I'll pick you up at seven or so?"

Their gazes met. Abi's eyes were deep pools of mystery to him, as much a mystery to him as she was. How was it that they'd only met less than a month ago and yet he felt he'd known her much longer? As in, forever?

"Seven sounds good. I'll bring the water and I can pack us a light meal for when we hit the top of the hill. Is it Darlington Shelter?"

"Yes. You've been looking at the topography maps?"

"Yes. It's my job to know every day hike within a thirty-mile radius, if I want to run my business well. I saw it and wondered how it would be getting up there. Parts of it look pretty steep."

"It is, but nothing too rough. You won't need hiking poles, unless you prefer to hike with them."

"Sounds good. See you at seven, then?" She looked at him and he saw so much in her eyes. Intelligence, warmth and maybe—hope?

"Yes. I'll pick you up. Lock up after I leave."

Abi woke at least six times in the night, a holdover from standing long watches at the Bureau but also mostly from having a Molotov cocktail thrown through her kitchen door and a break-in. This was part of what she thought she'd be escaping by leaving the FBI. Working for the Trail Hikers was something she did because Claudia had recruited her expertise for rare cases like this. It wasn't her goal to stay as a permanent agent.

Still, she loved a good fight and Silver Valley was worth protecting, at all costs. She thought about this as she made a cup of tea and some toast—keeping her breakfast light with a long hike ahead. The town was a true slice of Americana, and diversified at that. The thought of anyone wanting to threaten what freedom meant to her and the folks of Silver Valley was enough to make her think about signing on as an SVPD officer. If she hadn't already started on her new life.

The beckon of a new start as a regular civilian running her own small business gave her pure elation. The bubbles of excitement in her belly outcrowded the knots of dread that had kept her up all night.

A quick knock at her kitchen door followed by Keith's voice shook her out of her thoughts.

"Coming, coming." She made sure it was him first and then unlocked the door. "Good morning."

"Good morning to you." His eyes were on her, assessing, before he nodded at the doorjamb. "You've got to get this lock replaced and add a dead bolt. I'm surprised no one ever did that before."

"I'm not. This is Silver Valley—you know better than I do how trusting everyone is around here. Until relatively recently this was a farmhouse and the Pearsons worked the entire land, right? Come on in." She walked into the kitchen and flipped the kettle on. "Cup of tea? Or I can brew you come coffee, but it'll take longer."

"Tea's fine. We've got time—it won't get too warm today for our hike."

"Does it ever get that warm here?"

"Don't let this cool summer fool you. We hit the nineties by June sometimes, and with equal humidity it feels like the tropics. You had it in Philly growing up, didn't you?"

"Yes, it was pretty steamy. But always a breeze, since it's so close to the ocean. I suppose the Susquehanna River doesn't offer the same kind of relief?" She handed him a cup of English Breakfast tea. "Sugar or milk?"

"Nope—but I'll have some of that lemon."

"Sure." She cut a slice for each of them, then added a dab of honey to her mug. "Here, have a seat." They sat at the small but sturdy Colonial-style table that the previous owners had left.

Keith looked around the room. "Yeah, it took a hit last night but at least you can still function in it."

"Again, thanks to you." She sipped her tea and watched him. It wasn't as if she'd never shared a morning beverage with a man, but Keith was different. He wasn't someone she'd enjoyed a round in the sheets with and then parted amicably from. Nor was he a long-term boyfriend who she'd grown tired of, and he of her.

Morning sunlight reflected in his gaze. "You're thinking too hard. Today's supposed to be a day of relaxation. A total break from the case."

"Hmm."

"I mean it. I'm not going to show you all my secret places on the trail if you don't agree."

"Secret places?"

"My parents used to take us hiking all over, no matter where we lived. I grew up partly overseas, with my dad and then later my mom, working for the Foreign Service. The best way to get to know an area is to walk through it—not only the towns and cities but the countryside, too. We griped as kids, but then my sisters and I started making up our own stories on the long walks. In Germany they call them *volksmarches* and they're pretty cool, especially in the winter with packed snow under your feet. They have hot-chocolate stops and warm rolls with butter. As a kid, it doesn't get much better."

He looked out the kitchen window at the sky, but she knew he was seeing childhood memories. "When we moved here, we discovered the Appalachian Trail and, of course, we had to hike it. We were getting into our teenage years then and not so keen on being with our parents that much. So we'd run ahead of them and find all kinds of hidey-holes just off the beaten path. Sometimes it was cool, like a small cave or abandoned bear's den. Other times it wasn't so great." Keith paused, then began to laugh. When he caught his breath, he looked at her. "One time we happened upon a bear cub. We were mesmerized by it, until we heard our parents yelling for us—they had spotted the mama bear and she was headed our way."

"Oh, my gosh. What did you do?"

"We got lucky is what. We backed away from that cub and hid behind a boulder. The mother grabbed it and ran away. You know she knew we were there, but maybe finding her cub was more important than having us for lunch. We never went off the path after that."

"Are there still a lot of bears around here?"

"There weren't for a long while but they seem to be making a comeback. Only on this side of the river and this side of the turnpike. It's interesting how man-made structures like a highway have a way of dividing up nature. Not that it's all bad, because in this case it keeps all of us from waking up to bears in our backyards."

"I'm not used to hiking with a weapon—do you think we need one?"

"No. Absolutely not. No one has been attacked by a bear or any other creature on the AT that cuts through Silver Valley. Except for the various human-on-human assaults, which I'm confident we're well protected from. I'd say we're good to go, but you be your own judge."

Her weapon had been an extension of her for so long, ever since she'd become an FBI agent. And working for the Trail Hikers, it was required. Which reminded her— she had to carry her weapon 24/7 as long as she was employed in a mission for TH. It was part of her contract.

She'd put it in the small backpack she was carrying.

"You're wandering away again, Abi."

Those baby blues were on her again and, dang it, the man didn't miss a thing. "I'm overthinking everything. Part of the fallout of being an analyst for so long."

"Will you be able to leave that life behind for good?"

"I'm counting on it. It would be a damn shame for the fate of Silver Valley Adventures if I can't."

His smile was wide. "You've decided on a name for your business."

"Yes. Just now. It has a nice ring, doesn't it?" As she returned his smile she hoped his obvious happiness at her proclamation wasn't just because she'd picked a good moniker for an outdoor travel business.

Her heart hoped that Keith wanted her to stay in Silver Valley.

Chapter 14

"This is beautiful, Keith." Abi took in the canopy of deciduous trees that protected them from the morning sun, relishing the sound of frogs near the stream they were crossing. She loved walking across running water, atop rocks.

"Glad you like it. You're good at navigating the tough spots so far."

"The academy at Quantico trained me well. I'm sure you feel the same way about firefighter training."

Abi walked in front of Keith, aware of his breadth and long strides behind her. They were at the base of the mountain Keith had chosen for their day hike, a path Abi hadn't been on yet, part of the Appalachian Trail.

"Firefighter training was tough, but I was prepared for it. It's nothing like what you went through down there, I'm sure."

Abi paused as the path started to ascend steeply.

"Training is training. It's the experience that makes a firefighter or agent."

"True."

Their glances caught and Abi acknowledged a feeling of warmth and camaraderie as they stood a few feet apart, alone in the woods on a cool summer morning. "Thanks again for offering to do this, and showing me the AT. As much as I love hiking and nature, I've never been on the AT in Pennsylvania before."

Keith's smile widened to a grin. "Whoa. You mean this is a first for you, Ms. I-Know-It-All-Just-Ask-Me?"

"I'm not a know-it-all. I always ask questions about things I don't understand."

"Uh-huh." His eyes were so blue against the greens of the forest. She heard birds and wildlife scuttling around in the underbrush, felt the cool breeze that was reluctant to let go. It all faded to background noise as her focus narrowed to Keith. To her breath, heavier than it should be for the brief hiking they'd done so far. Keith's nearness did that to her.

Keith took his hat off and played with it, casting his gaze downward. "What about two of the most unlikely people finding out that they're getting along all too well?"

Abi knew it was dangerous to allow his flirting, no matter how lighthearted, to lift her spirits as if she were about to fly. Because when it came down to it, they were flirting. Doing the same kind of mating dance the birds were. Yet she didn't want to play the shy ingénue. Abi wasn't afraid to take what she wanted, and she wanted Keith.

"I don't know the answer to that one, Keith. What do you think?"

He placed his hat back on, hoisted his small backpack higher. "I think that too much thinking about anything isn't good for the soul. We're out here to decompress, let our minds wander, right? If we can let go of it even for a few hours, we can hopefully figure out what's next in the case."

"Maybe you should be the one starting the nature adventure business."

"Oh, no. I'm a firefighter through and through. When I was a kid, it's all I ever wanted to be and I never outgrew it."

"I understand." And she did, but how much, she didn't want to tell him. Not yet.

They spent the next ninety minutes climbing the side of the mountain. Abi had been all over the world and had hiked in many places. Out west this would be considered nothing more than a small hill—they were only climbing a little over one thousand feet in elevation. Still, her heart rate rose with the exertion and her leg muscles let her know they were getting a workout. They hiked in silence, pausing to look out at the valley spread before them or at a couple of skunks that appeared oblivious to their presence. Abi was relieved when the furry black-and-white creatures disappeared from sight.

They got to a tricky part of the path, near the top, as Abi could see the sky through the trees. But they had to climb a steep rock right before the trail flattened out.

"Let's take a break here." Keith pointed to a huge rock outcropping. They made their way onto it and Abi lowered to her knees as she crawled out to the edge. "This looks scarier than it is."

"Yeah, it does, but you still don't want to fall off it. This is called Hawk Rock." Keith eased himself next to her, both their legs dangling from the smooth edge as if they sat on a park bench. "Look over there." He pointed to two hawks that circled in the distance. Before Abi had time to blink, they were at eye level, only yards from them.

"Wow. We're at their cruising altitude."

"Isn't it fantastic?" Keith's profile was as rugged as the rock they sat on, and she had no doubt this was a man to be trusted. A solid individual. A man of integrity.

Like Dad.

As if he sensed her thoughts, Keith looked at her and then covered her hand with his, giving her a gentle squeeze. "Let it go, Abi. Whatever's eating at you."

"Nothing's eating at me. I was comparing you to my father."

Keith tilted his head toward her. "Oh?"

"My father is—was a firefighter. He dedicated his whole life to it."

"Your father did what I do?" Understanding, then suspicion, then disbelief ran across his face.

"Yes. He was even the chief of a department, like you."

"Is he still working?"

"Yes—no, not firefighting. He's getting ready to retire." She fiddled with a strap on her small pack. "He left firefighting years ago, when I was a teenager. It was my fault."

Silence stretched and Abi kicked her feet in the air for nothing else to do. It was time to tell Keith her background—all of it. "In the interest of getting to know one another, and being able to trust each other, I owe you this, Keith." She couldn't tell him she was a Trail Hiker, but she could tell Keith who Abi Redland really was, down deep.

"My parents went to Atlantic City to celebrate the New Year with two other couples they're still friends with. I asked to stay home to make money babysitting for the neighbors. I was seventeen and full of myself. My parents were pretty lenient with me, as I always got straight As and never caused trouble like my older brothers had. And they weren't really trouble, thinking about it now, just typical boys being boys and all.

"The kids I was supposed to watch got the flu, so their parents canceled their plans. I was home alone for the holiday, with my older brothers already out of the house, either living on their own or away at college. But no one was there that night. So I did what I thought would be the most fun—I had a party that my parents had expressly forbidden. They wouldn't have minded if I'd had girlfriends over to watch chick flicks, or whatever, but I did what I knew I wasn't allowed to. I invited everyone I knew and they all brought an extra kid or two.

"By midnight the house was packed, the beer flowing, and everyone was having a good time. Until I smelled pot coming out of the bathroom in the basement, I thought I was going to pull it off—have a big party, clean up the next day, and my parents would be none the wiser."

"And?"

"And it didn't work out that way. By the time I smelled the pot—I was upstairs flirting with a boy I'd had a crush on all year—a fire had been started in the basement fireplace. You know how those old row houses are built? Ours had a full kitchen downstairs for when it was too hot to cook in the summer. My grandfather had put in a fireplace for the winter months when he wanted some alone time from my grandmother. This was all before I was born. When my dad married my mother, and they bought the place, Dad had the fireplace closed up but left it for aesthetic value. Can you imagine, a built-in fireplace in a basement? Anyhow, the drunk kids in the basement started the fire with newspaper, not knowing that the flue was permanently shut."

"Shoot."

"The smoke was intense and there were old *Life* and *National Geographic* magazines stacked in boxes near the fireplace."

She stopped. Keith kept his hand on hers, waiting for her to finish. He already knew part of the ending; he just didn't know how many.

Abi sniffed. "Everyone got out. We all got out onto the front lawn. Except for Donna. She was my best friend, Keith. And she'd gotten so stoned on the pot that the guy I'd been flirting with brought that she wasn't thinking straight. There was only one way out, up the stairs—we lived in an older home. She tripped on a throw rug we had down there, under the stairs, which is where the bathroom was. Everyone else had made it upstairs and outside and thought she'd already gotten out. It was confusing and the smoke was dense.

"Once we were on the lawn I counted the kids—I had already called 9-1-1. I realized that Donna was missing and ran to go back in, but the police department arrived ahead of the fire engines and a cop held me back. I screamed at him and told him I had to go, or he did, to get my friend. He didn't believe me that I could do it. I was the fire chief's daughter. I knew how to crawl under the smoke!"

Her shoulders shuddered and she wiped at her cheeks.

"Abi, I'm so sorry."

"You can guess the rest. You do this for a living. Donna was found by the fire department within the next five minutes, but it was too late. She'd inhaled too much smoke. She never regained consciousness."

Keith knew that there was nothing he could say: no

gesture of compassion would be enough. Abi had lived through every parent's worst nightmare and lived with not only her own survivor's guilt but also her parents' disappointment. So he continued to sit, and hoped by staying next to her she'd understand that, as awful and horrific a result of a decision she'd made as a teen was, it didn't change who Abi was. A passionate, honest, *real* woman that he cared a hell of a lot for.

Too much so.

"I haven't told you this to make you pity me, Keith." Her eyes were on him.

"I don't pity you, Abi." It was on the tip of his tongue to tell her how he really felt. But he was only beginning to accept how deeply he felt about her. What those emotions might lead to.

"I picked fire science and forensics as a way to give back, to somehow pay back for what happened to Donna." She drew a finger through the dirt. "It's taken me this long to realize I'll never pay it back, and that I also don't have to go on beating myself up for the rest of my life. It's time to go forward."

"Are you still harboring guilt for your dad's career break?"

She sighed. "No. At least, I don't think so."

Keith watched her profile. What a brave woman his Abi was.

Abi wasn't sure how long they sat on Hawk's Rock but judging from how sore her butt was when she stood, it had been close to an hour.

"I'm sorry, Keith. I don't want to ruin our day with such a downer story, but you deserve to know who you're working with. And I owed you this much, after putting you in an awkward place at the warehouse."

"I didn't have a problem with it, Abi. You're the one who's wrapped around the axle about it." He hopped to his feet with surprising agility for a man with a back injury.

"How can you do that after straining your back less than a week ago?"

"Practice. And lots and lots of core work. If I didn't work out, I could never do my job."

"It's the same for me. Or was. And will be, with this new business." They were several feet from the ledge, the wind cool and pine scent heavy on the air. As the sun rose to midday, the area was out of shadow. Except for the brim of Keith's hat, which gave his eyes enough protection that they were fully open as he looked at her.

"You have the bluest eyes I've ever seen." Her voice was a whisper. She reached up and placed her hand on his chest as if under a trance. But it wasn't Keith's spell, or her desires, that compelled her movement. It was what they shared—the charged connection that wouldn't let up.

He grasped her hand and lifted it to his mouth, placing an openmouthed, moist kiss on her palm. She groaned, squeezing her thighs together against the heat that pooled between her legs. "Oh, boy."

Keith smiled, her hand still in his. "'Oh, boy, that was weird' or 'Oh, boy, that was hot, do it again'?"

She grasped the bottom of his shirt with her free hand and tugged him to her, farther from the edge to a small copse of trees hidden from the trail. "Again. And this time, don't stop."

Keith took over from there, holding her hand and leading her to a more secluded area that appeared to be part of the rock outcropping but the flip side. Not a cave, per se, but a sheltered area with pine needles as cushion and tree trunks, bushes and ferns as protection from unwanted eyes. Not all of the summer foliage was in full bloom yet but there was enough to feel safe. Keith's arms did the rest.

"Come here, Abi." He sat on the ground with his back against the stone, his legs stretched in front of him.

She hesitated. "Are you sure your back can handle this?"

He didn't answer until she was seated on his thighs, which forced her to wrap her arms around his thick neck for balance. The heat and strength of his quads under her ass was beyond arousing. "My back will be fine, Abi. I'm not going to make love to you for the first time, not here. But we're going to have some fun with a little old-fashioned necking."

"'Necking'? I haven't heard that since my grandmother told me she and Grandpa used to neck in the back of his Oldsmobile when they took drives in the country."

"Stop talking, Abi."

Their mouths met with equal hunger and insistence. Keith's kiss was expert; his hands had to have a certification for the way he stroked her back, her ass, her breasts. And his lips were the pure definition of firmness meeting sensuality. When their tongues touched, Abi squirmed with want. If there wasn't a rock wall behind Keith, she would have pushed him backward; to hell with not making love out here for their first time.

Keith couldn't get enough of the woman in his arms. He wished they were naked in his bed instead of fully clothed on a public hiking trail. "Abi, you're so damned beautiful." He kissed her throat, her chest, cupped her breasts in his hands. "Your breasts are amazing."

"I thought you said to stop talking." She tugged on his earlobe with her teeth and his erection verged on painful.

"It's time to start talking again or we'll both be naked on the AT."

"So?"

He reluctantly lifted his face from hers, cupping her head in his hands. "I told you, I want you in my bed, your bed, any damned bed, the first time we make love. I don't want to have to worry about bruising you, or having you get Lyme disease from a damned tick."

"Bruises? Are you trying to tell me something? You don't have a special room in your place, do you?"

He grinned. "I don't need a special place. I've got my hands, babe. And, for the record, no, I'm not into the kink stuff so much. I'm just letting you know now that we've waited so long to finally give in to our attraction that I can't promise to go slow or be gentle the first several times."

"I'm not some feeble maiden, Keith. I can handle whatever you're up for."

Her eyes were pools of sinful chocolate and he loved that she was so totally focused on him. As he was on her. It was rare, for them to have a time when work faded away and they were faced with only each other. He loved it.

"Keith? You're drifting." She sat up and turned to face him, kneeling carefully on the hard ground. She took his hands. "What are you thinking about?"

"You have to ask?" His cargo pants had a freaking tent at the crotch. He felt like he looked—as if he were seventeen and his hottest fantasy had come to life.

She reddened, already flushed from their kisses.

"You're something, Abi. You are the toughest person I know, but you're also so sexy and feminine. Is it okay that I say that?"

"Why wouldn't it be?" She looked genuinely puzzled.

"Do you think I check my girly-ness at the door when I go in to the station?"

"You kind of have to, don't you?"

"I never stop being a woman, Keith. Do you stop being a man when you walk into a female-dominated space, like a lingerie shop?" She blushed and he couldn't stop his grin.

"Not at all. Point taken." He licked her earlobe and she arched against him before pulling away.

"Abi, stop fighting it. Or at least tell me why you're holding back."

"I wouldn't call letting you kiss me like that 'holding back.'"

"Hey, you were kissing me just as hard. And that's not what I meant. Sometimes it's like you've got something more to tell me. I could never know enough about you." He knew he was pushing her but he found that the more he was around Abi, the more he wanted.

She stood and offered her hand, which he ignored, preferring to get back on his feet on his own steam.

Abi's eyes were bright as she looked up at him. "There's always something people don't tell each other, isn't there? Otherwise, what's the point in being together, trying to figure each other out?"

"You've got a lot to learn, Abigail."

She watched Keith head toward the trail and followed him out of the place she'd forever remember as the hottest make-out location in Silver Valley. The same man she'd had that instant physical attraction to, the man who'd saved his teammate and her house, had held her in his arms and kissed her as if she was the only woman in the world.

"There are some things that couples don't have to discuss, Keith." Had she just called them a couple?

"Leave it for now, Abi."

His tone was firm but he didn't deny her "couple" comment and she fell into step behind him for the last few turns of the trail before they reached the top of the mountain. The freedom and pure enjoyment of the last moments were shattered by her guilt. There was no way to be completely honest with Keith. Not unless she was done being a Trail Hiker.

And duty trumped her desires.

They ate their packed lunch on a battered but sturdy picnic table not far from the trail shelter that had bunks for hikers who needed a place to overnight. Halfway through, both of them received texts from Rio.

New intel. Team meeting at 2pm.

"It's ten o'clock now. We'll make it back in good time, right?"

Keith put his phone away. "Yeah. It'll only take about an hour to get down. You want to go in earlier?"

"Yes." Abi wanted to check out any information Claudia had from Trail Hikers. Another reminder of the gap between her and Keith.

"Any idea what it's about?" Keith looked at her with trust. Guilt raised its ugly head.

"No, but I'm guessing it's about where they think the cult will strike next. They know we're onto their track, and we've arrested enough suspects to keep the county jail busy for a while."

Keith nodded. "Where do you think they'll hit next?"

"I have no idea. That's why I'm up here with you, remember? To let my brain rest." But while she was taking a break someone had beat her to the punch, apparently. And for the first time in her professional career it didn't bother her. Her competitive edge was still there, she wanted to be the best at what she did, but she no longer had to have all the answers.

"What? You look like you've seen a ghost." Keith wrapped his napkin and lunch crumbs into a tight ball, which he put in his pack. A big rule on the Appalachian Trail was to leave no sign you'd been there. Hikers were supposed to take out whatever they brought in, including waste when possible.

Abi thought about what he said, about how her life seemed to have changed overnight. Certainly her priorities were in upheaval. "Not a ghost, so much. More like a flash of my future."

"And you find it scary?"

"No. Maybe too good to be true."

Keith didn't reply and they hiked down the mountain in shared silence. Abi knew her thoughts needed to refocus on the case, but her heart relished the intimacy of being in such profound natural beauty with Keith. As if she'd traded in her FBI badge and agent persona for a woman falling in love.

Another first.

Chapter 15

Colt walked into Trail Hikers headquarters ten minutes after Claudia called—she never called him from her secret job unless it was urgent. He was granted access and ushered into her office with no fanfare and no argument, a testament to how important it was that she see him.

She looked up from her desk and stood as he walked toward her, the thick, heavy door clicking shut behind him as her receptionist left them alone. Worry lines were evident in her usually smooth forehead, and her mouth had only a hint of the usual smile she gave him. Her eyes betrayed her joy at seeing him, and he hated to admit it but he was relieved. Her feelings for him hadn't changed.

"I came as quickly as I could."

"Thank you. I'm so sorry to be so abrupt on the phone, but you know the reason."

"I do."

"Sit." He eased into the comfortable chair in front of her desk and leaned forward.

"What have you found out?"

Claudia rapped an unsharpened pencil against her desk, a habit he'd noticed when he'd first met her. "There's intel from our sources and others that Taylor isn't the only guy who's been in touch with the True Believers."

"That isn't surprising, is it? There's an element of any society that is attracted to the kind of evil rhetoric spouted by Wise and his cronies. The military is a microcosm of that—there were bound to be more, Claudia. The Army War College is no exception."

"Yes, but this time they're foreign. And have direct links to a terrorist organization." When she didn't name one specifically, he knew that she couldn't. And he didn't need to know, frankly.

"So they're students there?"

She shook her head. "No. You're aware of the annual summit that's held at the Army War College on international relations? We have good reason to believe there are imposters coming from at least three different countries, posing as delegates to the conference."

"Then let FBI head them off at the pass and arrest them when they arrive. You do know when they're arriving, right?" Colt couldn't take on more than necessary. SVPD was strained with their current caseload.

"That's the problem. They obtained visas to come to the summit, which isn't until next month. They left early and…it appears they're already here. They've been here for three months."

Colt's stomach sank. "Do we know where they are? Do you think they're sleepers?"

"No, and yes. That's my biggest issue right now. They are 'en route,' yet no one has seen them since they touched down at JFK this winter."

"Have you told Rio this yet?"

"No, of course not—I wanted to talk to you first. Why?"

"He's called a big meeting of everyone on the arson team for two o'clock today. We've had this lull over the past couple of weeks, and I wanted everyone rested while they could. But our vacation from the cult appears to be over."

"I got the same text. Has he told you what it's about?"

"Yeah. It's what I think you've already figured out, and where I think we're headed with this op." Their eyes met. Claudia was so much more to him than a retired Marine Corps General or the CEO of a top-secret government shadow agency. She was the damned love of his life.

"Colt, we can't let our personal life get in the middle here."

"We can't ignore it, either, Claudia. I'm not asking you to quit your job or to blow off this mission."

"But will you let me do what's needed, for the good of Silver Valley and most likely our nation?" Claudia knew what she asked of him. To allow her to do what she had to do, regardless of the risk. And she called upon his most basic instincts, the reason he was in law enforcement.

She drove a hard bargain, his woman.

"What do you need from me? From the police department?"

"SVPD and the entire county are going to have to go on full alert, the length of time unspecified. And I'm going to read Keith Paruso into Trail Hikers. He has to know what's coming next."

"You're not doing it because you think there's something between him and Abi?"

"Are you questioning how I run my shop, Chief Todd?"

"No, ma'am. But we've all seen the way they are around one another."

"It takes one to know one." Their gazes collided and Colt wished like hell they weren't in her office.

"Indeed it does."

Abi sat at the conference table as the officers working the case piled into the room, filling the folding seats set up against the back wall. She hadn't seen Keith since he'd dropped her at her house, agreeing to meet her here. He'd gotten a text and told her he had to stop somewhere before the meeting, but didn't specify where.

Colt walked in, followed immediately by Claudia and Keith. Claudia slid into an open chair at the table, while Keith opted to stand at the side of the room. As she looked at them, Abi wished Claudia would read Keith into Trail Hikers. Then she could come clean about what she was doing here—it was purely selfish on her part. But it wasn't her call.

And even if she could tell him, what difference would it make? It wasn't going to make their budding relationship last any longer than the few additional weeks she expected this case to last. Keith was an avowed player and showed no indications of being ready to quit the hound-dog show. She wasn't ready to make any kind of big commitment, but she didn't want to get seriously involved with a player, either. And her first choice would never be a firefighter. It was too close to her deepest, most awful memories. She'd shared the worst with Keith, yet she knew she'd never be able to let go of how she'd ruined her best friend's life and her father's career.

Colt cleared his throat and the room went silent.

"Thanks for coming in, everybody. Rio's about to brief us all on the latest developments in the True Believers case and, more specifically, what the arsons have all been about and what we think they're leading up to. Let me say that we wouldn't be here without the hard work of Abi, and the support we've had from Keith and his department these last several months.

"As you all know, the cult's arrival into our town, when it started to cause trouble, began earlier than we first thought, as far back as the Silver Valley Community Church fire two Christmases ago. There isn't time to run down the list of all you have accomplished since." Colt paused long enough to make eye contact with each officer present. "You've made a big difference. I couldn't be prouder at how we've attacked this issue. But there's more ahead, probably the worst of it, over the next week or so. It's easy to be anxious to get it all done, and quickly. But I don't want any heroics out there. All levels of enforcement from local to national are involved at this point. We will give deference to whomever gets it, no backwash. Got it?"

A few groans, a shuffle of feet, but nothing hostile against the Feds coming in. Abi had never been prouder to be working with SVPD. Like the man in charge of it, the department was a class act.

Colt went on to explain a few more details and tactics, then turned it over to Rio.

"After looking at the locations of the last several fires, and combining that with intelligence we've received from several sources, it's come to our attention that the cult is somehow trying to target TMI."

The room was as silent as Abi had ever heard it. Everyone in the room knew what TMI meant: Three Mile Island—the nuclear reactor plant that provided electricity for the entire surrounding area that included Silver Valley. It had been made famous due to an almost-nuclear accident in the late seventies. As with all nuclear power plants, it was always a concern, security-wise.

"We think that Wise is somehow expecting to successfully break into the facility or, at the very least, stage some kind of explosion outside of it, to gain national media attention. So far we've kept him off the airwaves by apprehending suspects as the crimes occur, and the media has been cooperative in emphasizing his history and criminal record, not bringing his current rhetoric into the spotlight."

What Rio wasn't mentioning was that no cult member had come forward from Silver Valley to tell what happened in the True Believer/New Thought meetings. The New Thought meetings took place exclusively in the trailer home compound Wise had purchased for the sole intent to house his community of brainwashed converts. SVPD had managed to infiltrate the meetings last Christmas, but that was it. It had been too risky to send anyone else in since. He placed his hands on his hips as he continued. "I'm confident that TMI can and will handle its own security, with help from federal agencies. We'll go in only as requested, of course. I don't want us underestimating the cult, but let's face it, they're not going to get into the nuclear facility proper. There are too many tripwires. They may want to get caught, and that would make our job easier." A wave of soft laughter, then more silence. "We're on a 24/7 watch schedule, beginning at eighteen hundred hours tonight. Let your families know that you're on call for the foreseeable future. The FBI, ATF and others have their best people on this, folks. Hopefully our job will be limited to surveillance and apprehension, but be prepared for anything. I don't want anyone going anywhere without full body armor. Chief

Paruso and his department will keep doing what they're best at—putting out fires. Any questions?"

Rio approached her after he adjourned the meeting. "Abi, stay here for a minute."

"Sure." She sat back down and noticed that Keith had sat beside her. Claudia and Colt remained in the room, too. After the last officer filed out, Rio shut and locked the door.

"The good news, folks, is that we're close to ending this and getting Leonard Wise locked up for the rest of his life."

"The bad?" Abi couldn't resist.

"That we're going to have to figure out a way to infiltrate the cult starting now. We need to find out if international terrorists have joined Wise at the compound."

"Let me fill you in," Claudia spoke. "For the record, Abi, Keith is now one of us. He was read into Trail Hikers before the meeting. He doesn't have the training you do but needed to be in on the intelligence we have."

Keith was a Trail Hiker. Abi looked at him and saw his guarded expression. As she expected, she didn't feel as relieved as she'd once thought she would. Abi wished they were alone, that she could find out what he was thinking. She was more confused about her feelings for him than ever.

"We have reason to believe that three international terrorists are living on the lam in Silver Valley. We think they found out that Wise is planning his big TMI take-down, and are hoping to get in on it for their own reasons."

Abi waited for Claudia to say more. Claudia looked like she was steeling herself for a big statement. "I've looked at Abi's reports, which by the way, Abi, far surpass anything we've ever had for such a case. Your thoroughness and attention to the minutest detail in the evidence reports are what led us to the international link in the first place."

"How so?" It bothered her that Claudia hadn't told her before now but she also understood that everything handled at such a sensitive intelligence level had to be compartmentalized, for good reason.

"At the elementary school fire, you found Taylor's business card. You also inadvertently discovered the residue from matches on the charred paper you collected—matches that were made overseas, in the Mid-East."

"Actually, Keith found the business card." She nodded at him but Keith's focus remained on Claudia. Hell, was he angry with her for not telling him she was a Trail Hiker? He had just been read in—he had to understand that she couldn't possibly have told him.

"Yes, well, now we combine that with the fact that three men from high-threat nations obtained visas to attend the international symposium at the War College next month. But they then forged their dates and arrived early."

"Wait a minute. They got through airport security and customs and then disappeared?" Keith sounded incredulous and it hit a vein of annoyance in Abi.

"If you had any idea how many suspects we stop on a daily, hourly basis, you might appreciate that sometimes people slip through the cracks. No system is one-hundred-percent foolproof, Keith." What the hell was she doing, getting angry at Keith like this? Did she think it would hurt less when he told her he didn't want to see her anymore?

"I'm aware of that." He dismissed her as if she were a rookie. "Claudia, why are you so sure the terrorists are with the cult?"

"We're not, but since there appears to be a connection

between Taylor and them, it makes sense. He was also on travel to the same country six months ago."

"We have a spy, then. A traitor." Abi spoke, needing the confirmation.

Claudia nodded. "We're not working that angle, though—NSA and FBI have it. If those men are going to attempt a takedown, it's more likely to be a cyber attack combined with a physical breach. Too much for one agency, even a powerful one like TH, to handle. We have to focus on the cult and its local operations."

"And SVPD will be backing up this the most, since we've been in it since the start." Rio spoke from his seat. "We've been stopping them at each escalation on their part, we can handle this last part."

"This 'last part' is going to require infiltrating the cult again, much like Nika did, but for longer. Until the end." Claudia's tone made Abi take notice.

"Use me, Claudia. I'm the most likely person to go into the cult. No one in town knows me that well yet." Abi had worked mostly at a desk while in the FBI but she had been trained for all kinds of work, including undercover.

"No. I'm going in." Claudia spoke with authority as if daring anyone to contradict her. Abi felt sorry for the person who tried.

"What? That's not realistic, Claudia." Colt's personal emotions erupted. "Put one of my people in there, or two. I've got a few officers who go home after work and spend all night on those damned video games. They don't get out much and there's little chance anyone in the cult knows them."

"No way, Colt. All of the SVPD officers work traffic and criminal beats. They all run the risk of being identified as police. I'm the best shot. Besides, I've got a secret weapon none of you know about."

Abi held her breath. Why did this feel like some kind of *X-Files* episode?

"I'm the granddaughter of an Appalachian preacher. I've seen it all, from people speaking in tongues to snake dances. There's not a sermon on earth that would surprise me, for good or evil. And I know how to play the demure, quiet church mouse."

Rio coughed in an obvious attempt to cover a laugh. "No offense, Claudia, but I can't picture you as demure anything."

Claudia smiled demurely. "Why, Rio, ye of little faith. How do you think I bamboozled my folks into letting me take the SAT and apply to the Naval Academy? They never thought I'd make it, never thought I'd get in. If they'd thought for one minute that I'd go in the military, they wouldn't have allowed me to try. But they thought they were teaching me a lesson about where women belonged. So I played their game, and worked out after school when they thought I was at Bible study. I passed all the entrance exams with flying colors, and went on to enjoy a good career in the Corps after I was in one of the first classes of female graduates."

Only Claudia Michele would deem being one of the first women to graduate from a centuries-old male bastion of bigotry, and then over thirty years in the Marine Corps where she made general, "good."

They all digested what Claudia proposed.

"What can I add to this, Claudia? I've analyzed every bit of evidence and all the reports to date." Abi had to help more directly. She was in it too deep not to.

Claudia nodded. "I need you to shadow Keith's call-ins, be on scene at any fire that is related. And, most important, I want to know the ins and outs of Three Mile Island. Abi, you'll work on that, along with going in as Rio tells you to. Rio, you're in charge of the surveillance team. We're placing watch teams in expanding rings around the site, above and beyond the regular security, which is very tight."

"Will do."

"Keith, you'll run your department as usual, but I also want you in direct comms with Rio and the TMI fire department."

"Done. I've trained with them before."

"I understand that. This is more than concern over a nuclear meltdown, if you can believe it. We don't want a cult using the reactor site for any kind of propaganda, and we don't want international agents of any kind figuring out how the security plays out. I'm more concerned about the terrorists gaining intelligence on the site than I am about them trying to actually blow it up."

Abi wasn't so sure. They lived in days of extremist action and abhorrent violence. A nuclear power plant was exactly what a terrorist wanted to attack. As well as a deranged cult leader—it would enable Wise to hold millions of people hostage to his sick message.

Over the next hour they planned the next steps to dismantle the cult. Abi heard it all but her mind was reeling with the reality that terrorism was knocking on the door of Silver Valley, of all places. Her arson work had morphed into an antiterrorism campaign. She knew from training and life that no location was safe; anyone could become a target at any time. But she'd found her own kind of peace of mind here. Even with her tumultuous emotions surrounding Keith.

"You don't believe the terrorists are going to let a chance to blow up Three Mile Island get past them, do you, Claudia?"

"Of course they won't, Abi. But it's our job to make sure they don't even get close."

She found Keith in the reception area on his way out of the building. Abi had to half jog to keep up with him.

"Why aren't you talking to me?"

"Not here, Abi." His voice was a controlled growl. She followed him out of the building and into the parking lot, the amiable mood of their hike long forgotten. Had it only been this morning?

She jumped in front of him and planted her feet, hands on her hips. "Okay, how about here?"

He stopped short of running into her.

"Damn it, Abi." He looked into the distance, his tension visible in the tight lines around his mouth. "My car."

"Fine."

"Waiting on you."

"Okay." She stood still, not sure of where to go. "Where did you park?"

He sighed and jerked his thumb to the right. "Back lot."

Once in his car they sat in the front seats, staring out at the white-brick wall of the station.

"Are you going to tell me what's bothering you?"

"What's to say, Abi? That I feel as though you've played me for a fool?"

"How do you figure that?"

He slammed his hands on his steering wheel. "It's my pride, if you want to know the truth. I totally get that you couldn't tell me who you really were, but it still stings."

"But I did tell you who I really am, Keith. None of what I said about my family was untrue. And I have been working as an arson forensics analyst here—the only thing I had to hold back was my work as a Trail Hiker."

"Let me show you who *I* am, Abi." He reached for her and she didn't hesitate to go into his arms and answer his greedy kiss with her own. They didn't break apart until they were both near the edge of letting go completely.

"We've fogged up your windows." She loved how their breaths intermingled, how their hearts felt as though they pounded together.

"Babe, it doesn't matter who you are, who I am. What matters is what we are *together*. Do you feel it, too? Tell me you do, Abi."

She couldn't promise him anything, but she could answer this one question truthfully.

"I do."

Abi worked long into the evening after she left Keith's car. Since they'd addressed the constant tension between them and her secret work, she'd had a hard time getting emotionally settled again. She'd told herself that being undercover was the real reason she'd kept him at arm's length. Now, she didn't have that excuse. Didn't want any excuse to stop another searing kiss. She groaned over the maps she was studying on her screen. The mere memory of his lips on hers made her want to chuck it all—her contractor job, this case, law enforcement in general—and go to him. Screw his brains out.

Her sense of duty was too strong, her need to not make a decision about Keith equally so. She really wasn't sure if that was good or bad.

Enlarging a satellite photo of the area where she thought the cult might have set up some kind of hideaway, Abi looked for anything that looked different from a photo of the same area two weeks ago. If anyone from the station walked in on her, she'd claim the shots were from FBI-ordered intelligence. But they were shots Claudia had signed off on, and the request to have the entire region monitored had gone into effect almost a month ago.

It was at a high cost to taxpayers, and Abi wanted to make sure the dollars were well spent. A tiny dot caught her eye and as she enlarged it she thought it might be an ATV. Maybe the same one that had aided in the escape of the first arsonist?

"Any luck?" Rio spoke quietly behind her.

"Jeez, I didn't notice you coming in."

"Sure you did. You just knew you could trust me."

"Maybe. And, no, nothing yet. I'm going to keep superimposing the sat images with the topography and hiking charts. At some point they're going to overlap."

"And then TH will have to go in there and take them out." Rio's weariness reflected in the way he cracked his knuckles. "But my guess is that it'll be FBI who gets that job."

"I don't know, Rio. It will all depend upon when the fires and explosions start again, if they do."

"I hate not knowing when."

"Don't we all."

Chapter 16

Lionel tried to keep his groans as quiet as possible as he approached the meeting center. Brother Wise was waiting to talk to him and it wasn't going to be good. He'd tried to do a good job by getting Taylor to make up for leaving his business card at the elementary school fire. That had been such a sloppy mistake.

Lionel thought that snooty folks like Taylor were smart enough to know you shouldn't bring anything like that to the scene of a fire you were going to start. And they'd almost gotten away with it…but then Taylor got caught at that bitch's house, that bitch who was working for the police.

Lionel knew Taylor had gotten caught because he'd hidden in the field set apart from the farmhouse, too, watching and waiting for Taylor to come out of the house. He was supposed to go in when it was quiet, when he was certain the Redland woman wasn't there.

But no. He went in too early and she was home. She was too fast, too quick, and had caught Taylor.

Lionel chuckled to himself. She hadn't found him. He'd been long gone by the time the police showed up, too.

"What took you so long?" The brother in charge of Brother Wise's security team glared at him, but Lionel didn't care. They weren't going to take him away to the place of repentance again. Not when he gave Brother Wise his new idea.

He'd stayed awake all last night writing it down. They still had the major players for what Brother Wise wanted to do. And now Lionel had a new weapon, one they'd never thought of.

The next week crawled by, everyone at SVPD on tenterhooks as they waited for "the call" to take down the cult. When Saturday came around, Abi decided to make the most of the day. After yoga she headed to the store, the place where her new life would soon start.

She hadn't expected a team of enterprising women to accompany her, though.

"There's an awful lot of work here."

Abi looked around the empty office space. This part of the downstairs used to be a dentist's office, according to Ezzie. It wasn't hard to imagine, with the counters and marks through the hardwood floors that indicated where the patient chairs had been. She liked the rustic feel of the place. It was going to add a welcoming ambience to the store once she had it polished up and running.

"Where do you want us to start?" Kayla stood with all the women Abi had met in yoga class: Nika, Cassie, Zora—the wife of SVPD Detective Bryce Campbell—and Ezzie.

"Wyatt's at a friend's all day, so I'm good for whatever you need." Cassie spoke as if her warehouse hadn't been demolished by the fire, as if she hadn't had her multimillion dollar industry brought to a halt, at least temporarily.

"Are you sure you want to paint, Cassie?" Abi still couldn't believe such a successful, famous CEO was also so giving of her time. She barely knew Abi, and wasn't going to benefit from Abi's business in terms of her own corporation. Cassie was being a friend.

"Are you kidding? She helped me when I moved into my place, and then with the florist shop. Cassie's a pro!" Kayla spoke with authority. "I think I'm best left to scrubbing out any rooms you need cleaned, and then I'll measure for decorative items."

"What do you mean by 'decorative'?" Abi wanted the place to look put-together but nothing over-the-top. "I'm not much for silk plant arrangements."

Kayla grinned. "Damn, that scraps my stuffed-silk cactus idea. Just kidding. I was thinking that since you want a kind of a cabin-in-the-woods theme, I'd donate some succulent arrangements in log planters."

"That's way too generous, Kayla. You can do that but only if I can pay you for the plants."

"Don't even try, Abi. She'll never take your money." Ezzie shook her head. "Just say 'thank you.'"

Zora looked at her with the most startling emerald eyes. "You know, Abi, I had a bit of a rough time when I moved back to Silver Valley. I'd been in the Navy and all over the world, and while I met plenty of nice folks everywhere, it was still an adjustment to come home. The friendliness of the people here is for real. Accept it."

"Thanks. But I don't think we want you on any ladders, Zora." She looked purposely at Zora's bulging belly. "I don't know how to deliver a baby!"

Zora placed a protective hand on her belly. She was the picture of blissful maternity and something deep tugged at Abi's soul. Not that she wanted to be Zora. And she wasn't thinking she wanted her own family yet; that would require settling down. But wasn't opening her own shop in Silver Valley in effect "settling down"? At least for now?

"You okay, honey?" Nika touched her wrist. She remembered how Keith had done the same at the police station. She hadn't heard from him since. Abi blinked.

"I'm fine. It's a little overwhelming, is all."

"When is your contract with Silver Valley PD up?" Zora pulled her red hair into a high ponytail, preparing to dust and sweep. Zora was also a Trial Hiker; Abi had seen her at headquarters, though neither acknowledged that they knew one another from anywhere besides yoga class.

"Basically as soon as we catch all the arsonists that have been fire crazy over the last several months."

"You mean, since that cult group moved into town." Cassie placed several rolls of blue painter's tape on her forearm. "It's been on the news since that paroled felon Leonard Wise moved here almost two years ago. I for one can't wait to see SVPD arrest his bony ass and throw him back where he belongs."

"What about doing your time and all that?" Zora ran a dust cloth across a windowsill.

"Give me a break. You read the paper, right? And you're married to the dude who broke the case to start with." Kayla's exasperation with Zora was mock, as the women all were tight. Abi had seen evidence of no less since meeting them all.

"Bryce doesn't tell me everything about his work, you know. Maybe Rio tells you more?"

Abi wondered what she used to occupy her thoughts

with before she had Keith to daydream about. Not that she was doing it like a teen did when they had a crush or anything. More like she thought about how well they worked together, even when neither of them wanted to.

"No, Rio doesn't say a whole lot. He lets me know if he thinks I need to be more careful, like with the other cult members moving into town here, it's crazy. And of course you know how we met—he knows that with running a business in town, anyone can walk into my shop at any time."

Abi knew that Kayla had provided key evidence for SVPD when the former mayor had been brought down. The mayor that Wise had replaced after a lawyer from out of state had pressed charges against her was now back in office and Silver Valley couldn't be happier.

"Speaking of significant others, Abi, what's the deal with you and my brother?" Kayla's eyes sparkled and Abi couldn't get angry with the warmth that the florist gave off.

"The deal is that we're working closely together, which makes perfect sense since he's the fire chief and I'm an arson expert."

"Sounds like some heat could come from that." Zora giggled and the rest of the group joined in.

"How's it going, bro?" Rio slapped Keith on the back and helped himself to the empty seat beside him at the diner counter.

"Hey, Rio. What are you doing out so early on a Saturday? My sister throw you out?"

"Nope. Kayla left early to open her shop and make sure her employees had what they needed, then headed to yoga class. She's at Abi's new store now." The waitress came by and Rio ordered the breakfast special number one, same thing Keith was eating.

"I'm thinking you know all about Abi's shop?"

Keith focused on his hash browns. "Did you ever notice that Silver Valley Diner's hash browns are the absolute best? I think it's because they're so simple—no onions, no peppers. Just potatoes."

"Gotcha. So. You and Abi."

"There is no 'me and Abi,' Rio." Didn't Rio have a cult to bust up?

"Just like there was no me and Kayla? It's all over your faces every time we have a sit-down at the station. Don't get me wrong. You're both always very professional, and I'm sure no one else has caught your goo-goo eyes."

Keith choked on his coffee. "Goo-goo eyes?"

Rio threw back a swig from his mug. "You know what I mean."

"God, man, you are whipped. And it's my sister who's done it. Who would have guessed? Wait—you're digging for information for my sister, aren't you?"

Rio didn't answer and took a long time adding more cream to his coffee. "Kayla may have asked me what I thought was going on."

Keith groaned. "Do not tell her anything. I mean, there's nothing to tell. Aw, hell. Abi and I get along well with work. I actually like doing the detective kind of thing with her. But nothing beats firefighting in my book."

"What about after work?"

"We've only had a chance to go hiking. We might go kayaking or something, if this quiet period gets any longer."

"I'm not betting on it."

"Me neither. Any dibs on when they'll try to make

their move?" He had to ask Rio. Besides, Rio was the only one he trusted, except for Abi, to shoot straight with him.

"No idea. Claudia's getting tense, but in an anticipatory way. You can tell this is her bread and butter. The chief's not happy. He's been miserable ever since she announced she's going into the cult's crazy trailer park thing."

"She's really going to live there?" Keith used the mirror behind the counter to make sure no one was in range to overhear them.

Rio nodded. He didn't have to say anything. They both knew it was going to be a tough go for Claudia. Not the physical part—she was retired Marine Corps. A war veteran. The psychological and mental part was the bitch.

"How will we know she's okay? They'll be checking her for any wires, right?"

"You can bet on it. We've set up a way she'll leave notes for our other undercover officers to find. It's the safest way to do it for now."

"I'll bet Colt is about to crap his pants over this."

"Pretty much, yeah." Rio sipped from his mug. "He's a no-nonsense chief, the best we've seen in Silver Valley. But he has his human side like the rest of us and he deserves to be happy, deserves to not have to see the woman he cares about in danger."

Keith saw the way Rio stiffly put his mug back on the counter. "It reminds you too much of what you went through with Kayla last year at the mayor's daughter's wedding, doesn't it?"

Rio looked at him. "You know it. Yeah, that was a bad scene, the couple of times I thought she was in the worst kind of trouble." He shook his head and chuckled. "And she's not trained for any of this kind of risk, you know that as well as I do."

"I'll admit I wasn't your biggest fan as things were

going down." Keith was grateful he hadn't known the half of it while the crook mayor was being taken out, the first inroads to the cult being made. Kayla was his sister and he would die for her. She'd taken good care of him when he'd been on admin leave because of the false accusations. And now he knew she'd been a Trail Hiker, like he was.

"I wasn't my biggest fan, either. The last thing I wanted was for her to be involved. And you know she's highly capable, trained or not."

"Yes, that she is."

"Keith, stop me if I'm overstepping it, but you do know that Abi's a sure shot, right? She can handle herself just fine."

"Right."

"No offense, bro, but she's got more training than you do when it comes to bad guys. You put fires out, right? Abi can take out a criminal and analyze the toughest arson scene. She was tops in her FBI Academy class."

"How do you know that?"

"It's on her résumé. Not something I'm sure she tells a lot of folks but it was important for her to get hired by SVPD. Even without the TH connection, Colt would have hired her. She's damn good at what she does. Like you."

"I'm not feeling very good at it, Rio. Not with all the leads we have that amount to nothing when we can't catch all of them."

"We're not meant to catch all or any of them. Wise is playing with us, I'm sure of it."

Dread lined Keith's gut, making the delicious breakfast curdle in his stomach. He didn't want anyone "playing" with Abi.

Sunday morning before dawn, Abi groaned when she got out of bed, achy from the long day of cleaning the shop. Two cups of coffee, ibuprofen and several hours later, she was engrossed in her files on Wise and the arsons.

A loud knock on her front door startled her and she grabbed her weapon. She immediately placed it on the foyer table after she opened her front door and squealed in surprise.

"Dad! Mom!" She hugged each of her parents, relishing the bear hugs and loud smacks of kisses they gave her as they stood on her front steps. "Come on in." She led them to the kitchen where the morning light was streaming through the windows.

"Now hold on, Abigail. I want to take a good look around." Her father's gravelly voice was sincere as he took in her new digs.

"I see you could use some help with the final touches." Her mother fingered a bare windowsill, looking at the window frame as if she were measuring it in her mind for draperies.

"I only moved in a few weeks ago!" Abi took them on a tour of the house, pointing out details she knew they'd both enjoy. "This area is only about twenty years old, as it's an addition to the original stone farmhouse. That building may link back to the founding fathers."

"Like Ben Franklin?" Her mother was positively giddy.

"No, Mom. Franklin was more central to Philly. I'm not sure whom—they think this is the nearest house to the tavern that was discovered to be where they wrote the Bill of Rights. I haven't had time to discern the connections and all with my new business, but it's exciting, for sure."

"When will you be done with your arson work?" Her father's gravitas weighed on her, despite the lighthearted tone he tried to take.

"I don't know, Dad. There are some real bastards who

used to be in a cult in upstate New York here. They've set up shop in Silver Valley since the head honchos were paroled almost two years ago. I can't say that much more, but we're hoping we'll break it all wide open soon."

"At least you're not in the middle of dangerous operations with the police, even though you're working with them. Right, Abi?" Her mother's eyes were wide, her anxiety clear.

"Right, Mom. I'm basically an analyst, just like when I was with the Bureau." White lies with her mother never hurt. Except her father never fell for them.

"Give me a break, dear daughter. It's me, remember?"

"Sorry, Dad." She ushered them back toward the kitchen. "Why don't you let me grab you a glass of water, then tell me what motivated you to drive two hours to see me?"

Chapter 17

"Your mother wanted to see where you lived. I did, too." Dick Redland's large frame made her kitchen table look miniature as he swigged back the glass of ice water. "It's a good day for a drive, too."

"The hills are so beautiful here, Abigail. Have you hiked yet?"

"As a matter of fact, yes. And that brings me to something I need to tell you. I was going to wait until the grand opening, but I'd rather you know ahead of time so that you and everyone else can be here. I'm opening up my own business."

"PI?" Her father looked intense. Ever since she'd joined the FBI, both her parents had asked when she'd be leaving to do something more "settled." They hated the idea of her in danger.

"PI? Private investigator?" Abi laughed. "God, no. Dad, you think that all I do is go around busting down the doors of hardened criminals, don't you?"

"Arsonists need to be apprehended."

"Dad, I'm an analyst. And, no, I'm not going into law enforcement of any kind." She fought back a wince at the teeny lie. They'd never know about Trail Hikers. "You know I've always liked to hike and camp. So I thought, why not open my own nature tourist shop? I'll have kayaking, canoeing, hiking, camping—even golfing. I want to put the fun back into outdoor adventure."

"You're in some of the top fly-fishing spots on the East Coast. How far are you from the Yellow Breeches Creek?"

"Ten minutes. And, Mom, do you know what the Yellow Breeches are named for?"

Annie Redland shook her head, probably annoyed that it was the one American history fact she didn't know.

"During the Revolutionary War, the British soldiers would cross the creek in their white britches, which of course became yellow from the limestone sediment and other minerals that are unique to the tributary." Abi grinned. "I happened to read a portion of the county's history last night."

"Well done." Her mother had always been a history buff and had instilled an appreciation for it in her children.

They sat and talked for another half hour, catching up on each other's lives. Abi especially liked to hear stories of her brothers and their families. "I'd like to get home for Memorial Day. If this case is over by then, I will."

"Even if it isn't, you deserve a day off here and there." Her father stood. "How much of the land is yours?"

"None of it, yet. I'm still renting-to-own. I'm renting the office space in Silver Valley proper, too." Just in case...

"Honey, you like it here enough to start a business. Don't you think it's time you put down roots?"

"Maybe. I just don't know… I mean, how are you ever sure you want to stay somewhere? You guys have *always* lived in Philly."

"True, but we've talked about a move plenty of times."

"Like after the fire." Both her parents turned their eyes on her.

"Abi, let it go, honey." Her mother's anguish was in her eyes, the way she gripped her water glass, now empty.

"You're not still in arson, working this contracting case, because of that, are you?"

"Dad, give me a break. It's in my blood. You were a firefighter until I ruined it."

"My leaving the station had nothing to do with you, Abi. I'd served for many years and the house fire…it underscored that I'd been investing too much time in my job and not enough with my kids."

Abi didn't argue with him. It was true. Her dad was a self-admitted workaholic who'd loved the constant work being a Philadelphia firefighter had given him.

"You mean to tell me that if Donna hadn't died, if you hadn't been investigated for it, you wouldn't have stayed on at the department?"

"It might have taken me longer but I was already coming to the same conclusion, yes."

"He's telling the truth, Abi." Her mother frowned. "Please tell me you haven't pursued arson forensics because of it. Joining the FBI after college, that was one thing. But to keep doing this kind of work at the same time that you're trying to start a business, it's a bit much, isn't it?"

"I'm wrapping up my investigative work, Mom, trust me."

"It's just that… I'd hoped you'd want to settle down. Have you met anyone here?"

"She means, have you found a boyfriend, Abi?"

"Thanks, Dad, I get it." She smiled at them both. "I have, but it's nothing serious." Yet. Or it was, but she wasn't about to tell them. *Yet.*

The doorbell rang, followed by a knock. Abi was spared answering her mother, and shoved back any thought of mentally responding to the too astute observation.

"Keith."

"Don't look so thrilled. Are you okay? I saw the strange car in your driveway."

"And wanted to make sure I'm not being held hostage." She leaned against the doorjamb. "Actually, I am being held hostage—emotionally." She kept her voice low. "My parents have paid me a surprise visit."

"Your dad the firefighter?" Keith's eyes lit up. "Where is he?"

Abi groaned. "I was hoping you'd rescue me from this."

"After I meet him."

"We may have a lot of new technology that you didn't back in the day, but it's only in place to help us do our jobs better. It's the same work, all told."

"You're too easy about it, Keith." Dick Redland had the same dark brown eyes as Abi, and Keith knew the man was sizing him up. Why wouldn't he be, when his daughter had recently moved to Silver Valley and a strange man showed up at her door?

"Keith, how long have you known Abi?" Annie Redland was more about the other reasons Keith might be there. Other than what they'd already told them.

"Mom." Abi's one-word utterance sounded like the same warning his sisters gave his mother when she was digging too close to the live wires. Sex, marriage, grandchildren.

"Honey, let Keith answer." Dick patted his wife's forearm. She snarled at him. Keith laughed.

"Why don't we leave Keith alone?" Abi's mouth curled like her mother's.

"It's okay, Abi." He squeezed her hand and he wasn't sure what was more hilarious—her mother's annoyed expression or Abi's look of helplessness. A rare sight from who he saw as the goddess of Silver Valley. "Abi and I are work colleagues, in a sense, as we're both eager to get the arsonists that have been keeping my department far too busy these past several months. Of course, as you know—" he nodded at Dick "—when you work together under such dangerous conditions it's easy to either learn you despise one another or that you could become good friends."

"If Annie had worked with me when I was a firefighter, I don't think I would have gotten much work done." Dick smiled at Abi's mother, who tried to continue to look annoyed but failed miserably.

"Abi, what were you planning for your day? Before we showed up?" Annie's change of subject perked everyone up.

Keith looked at Abi. He'd been hoping to find her here on her own and to cajole her to take him on a kayaking trip. Or more.

God, he was thinking about the *more* part of his relationship with Abi often enough to make him think she had to be thinking the same thing. This kind of connection wasn't one-sided. And it was soul deep.

"Abi?" He squeezed her hand again as she remained silent.

She shrugged. "Nothing much. Other than inventory what I have for my store in terms of equipment, and figure out what I need to order."

"Don't spend your life savings on this venture, Abi." Dick spoke as someone who understood small business.

"Dad, I appreciate your concern, but I've got this. I've saved plenty all the years I've been working. As a single girl, it's not impossible to put away a small nest egg."

"But what about the cost of this house?" Her mother always chimed in to support her father, it appeared.

Keith saw the tense way Abi held her shoulders—she didn't like her parents ganging up on her.

"I told you guys, I'm renting with the option to purchase. I'm keeping all avenues available. And the arson case is my priority, anyhow. I don't plan on opening the shop until the case is closed." Keith felt a release of the tension he'd held whenever he thought about Abi leaving Silver Valley. She was going to give it a good, fair shot here. Silver Valley Adventures wasn't just an idea on paper or a whim. Abi was staying.

"You should have seen the crowd that turned out to help Abi get her shop in shape. How many folks were there to help you paint and clean?"

"A handful. They're friends I met at the local yoga class. One of them is married to a police detective and another is the girlfriend of the detective who's running the arson case at the police station. And she's also Keith's sister. Kayla. She's the local florist."

"This is certainly a small town, isn't it?" Annie smiled.

"I told you, Mom, it's a big change for me from DC. And it's nothing like Main Line Philly, either. It reminds me of Gramps's place."

"Gramps's place?" Abi had never mentioned her grandparents to him.

Abi's face lit up. "Yes, my mom's father. He and my grandmother had a huge plot of land out past Lancaster, to the north and east of here by about an hour and a half.

When I was little, I'd spend weekends with them. There was a lake for swimming and they had this huge vegetable garden my brothers and I used to play hide-and-seek in. And the berries—Mom, do you remember the raspberries?"

"I do. Your sweet little face would be covered in bright red juice, not to mention your clothes."

"And Dad used to fish there. By the way, did we mention that Dad here is going to be my consultant for fly-fishing? He'll make an angler out of anyone."

Abi's pride in her father was familiar to Keith—he felt the same way about the work his father had done in his life as a Foreign Service Officer.

"That's great. So you're retired from firefighting now?"

No one spoke and Keith could have kicked himself. "I mean, I know you were a firefighter. I'm sorry. Abi told me about the house fire when she was in high school."

"That was a sad day, for sure." Dick looked at the kitchen table, then at Abi. "But I didn't quit firefighting because of that."

"Dad, we've been through this already."

"Yes, we have, and it bears repeating. You had nothing to do with my leaving the department, honey. It was high time I did." Dick looked at Keith. "Firefighting can be hard on a family, a marriage."

Was Abi's father warning him?

Abi watched Keith charm her parents all afternoon. It was impossible not to jump to the conclusion that he wanted to impress them. Now they sat on what Abi was thinking was "their spot," her front stoop, watching the daylight fade.

"Thanks for dealing with my parents. I know they're a handful."

Keith grunted. "You haven't met mine yet. They'll be quiet, not as inquisitive up front, but they'll be testing your knowledge of geography before dinner's served."

"If they're anything like you, I'm sure they'll be wonderful." And she meant it. Because she'd come to the conclusion that Keith was a good man. Whom she was incredibly attracted to but so much more.

Could it become a lifetime of *more*?

"You look miffed. Why?" His voice was low, tugging her in. Or was it her imagination?

"It's so much easier to fall for a guy who's not so nice. Then it's easier to enjoy the moment and leave it when I need to. No strings."

He put his arm around her, lifting her chin with his other hand. "We don't have strings, Abi. I don't do strings, myself."

That was true: all she had to do was remember the piles of baked goods at the fire station from the significant others and even active-duty firewomen. "Then we make the perfect pair." She barely got the words out before his lips were on hers and they were pressed against each other, confident of their privacy in the early evening with all the farm workers in for the night. The air smelled of early summer blooms while Keith's breath fanned cinnamon and some other spice across her mouth. When his tongue tasted her lips, Abi didn't have the energy to play coy—she met it with her own, claiming him every bit as he claimed her.

"Oh, my God, Keith, you have no idea how good this feels." She wrapped her hands around his neck and licked his throat, loving the salty tang on her tongue.

"Actually, I do." He grasped her hand and hauled her up next to him as he stood. "Your bedroom, Abi."

"Yes." She led him through the front door and then paused. "All I have is an air mattress."

"The floor is fine. Hell, your kitchen counter works." He had her up against the wall as soon as the front door closed, grinding his pelvis into hers.

Abi moaned. She reached for his crotch, her fingers catching on his button fly. "Did I tell you how when I first saw you in jeans at the police station that morning, I wanted you then?" She tugged and got two of the buttons undone, enough room to get her hand inside his underwear and grasp his erection. The sheer hit of sensations from holding his hardness, knowing she'd done this to him, made her bite his shoulder.

"Stroke me, babe." Keith licked her ear, her lobe, her throat, leaving playful bites as he explored the area between her neck and shoulder.

Sensations rocked Abi as she moved her hand up and down his shaft, her center getting wetter, aching for him. Just when she thought her knees wouldn't hold her, Keith took her wrist and broke the connection. "Hell, Abi, I can't take much more of that or this will be over before we make it to the bedroom."

"Then come on." She grabbed his hand and pulled him across the living room, down the hall to her bedroom. The air mattress was big enough and firm enough for both of them, so she sat on it, reaching to remove her top.

"No, let me." Keith took her top off and stared at her breasts as they strained against the push-up bra with greedy need. He reached his hands into the cups and his fingers found her nipples. He squeezed, tweaked, and Abi cried out with sheer want.

"Babe, this mattress isn't going to handle us. Come

here." He yanked her up and in what seemed one move, stripped off her pants and panties. She stepped out of them, pulling his shirt over his head.

"Why are you wearing a T-shirt, too?" Before she grabbed it, Keith was out of his jeans and underwear, the length of his erection between them, signaling the primitive need they had for one another. Abi's hands and knees shook—she'd never shaken for a man before. Her desire for Keith wasn't a tremble or quiver—it was a full-on quaking that rumbled through her and ignited her most feminine parts.

Finally they were both naked and stood staring at one another, both breathing in gasps.

"Keith, this is craz—"

"Come here, Abi." He pulled a wrapper from his jeans that lay next to him on the floor and donned protection before he pulled her down on top of him. She splayed across him, his erection pushing into her thigh. Skin-to-skin, nose-to-nose, their eyes met and Abi stilled, save for the pounding beat in her chest. Her heart. Keith's heart. Did it matter whose? It was as if it were the same heart.

It was singularly the most erotic moment of her life. Abi opened her mouth to tell Keith but he only took it as invitation and grasped her nape, pulling her mouth to his.

His hands were on her ass, holding her as he rocked his pelvis up. Their eyes met and in one thrust he entered her. Abi cried out at the intensity. At the delicious pressure of him inside her, yes—but more at the rush of heat from her center to her scalp, back to her nipples. Keith leaned up and sucked on a puckered nipple. Hard. This was no time for sweet or tentative.

"Ride me, babe."

Abi did, and they matched one another thrust for thrust, slamming together until she thought she'd die of waiting for the building pressure to let go. When her release came she felt it through her toes, through her hair. With Keith, she felt it everywhere.

Keith groaned and then gave a loud grunt as he joined her. Abi watched him, his throat muscles tightening and then the complete bliss that swept over his expression.

It had never been like this before.

Chapter 18

"I hate you going in there, Claudia." Colt held her in his arms as they sat on her back deck, secluded by the woods and the fact that her nearest neighbors were acres away.

"I would feel the same if it were you. You know I'll be okay, right? I was in Fallujah. A crazy cult isn't going to get the best of me."

"In Fallujah you had weapons and protection. You're heading into the trailer park with nothing of the sort."

"I'm going in there with my wits about me. In war it's the same—all the weapons in the world won't help if you can't think your way out of an ambush. Trust me, Colt. I'm going to be okay, and we're going to get these crazies. It's high time Silver Valley was able to sleep well again."

"Yes, it is. Call me an old codger but I'm more worried about how you're going to sleep in that rat-trap trailer park Wise has holed up in."

"Frankly, I'm not worried about sleep. I'll be fine—I'll

be bunking with my closest female friends." She grinned. "I've already reached out to a few folks who live there. I've introduced myself as Claudia Jones, a local gal who's looking for a church home."

"And they bought it?"

She nodded against his chest. "Hmm. You know what I'll miss the most, Colt?"

"I can guess."

"Well, there's that. But this—you holding me close, hearing your heartbeat under my ears. It's a damn shame we never met before, sooner."

"Would it have mattered? You were a career officer, Claudia. And I love being a cop. I'm not sure I would have picked up and moved with you. And there's the fact that I was married for a good while myself."

She leaned up and looked into his eyes. His dear, sweet, honest eyes. "Are you sure it's what you want again, Colt? I'll understand if you want to keep things the same. It's very comfortable, what we have."

"Say no more, woman. We're going to make this thing between us permanent and legal as soon as you get the best of Leonard Wise and all of his cronies."

"And you round up the arsonists."

"Yes." He raised her hand to his lips and she watched him kiss each finger, each knuckle. "I love you, Claudia."

"I love you, Colt." They shared a smile that promised all she'd ever wanted. A place to call home and a man to share it with.

"What should I do?" Claudia looked at one of her cult "sisters," a woman she'd been offered a room with on the New Thought compound.

"Sister Claudia, you'll be peeling potatoes. We're going to need all those bushel baskets done." Mary, the leader of the woman's part of the cult, motioned at the two dozen or so baskets of potatoes they'd brought in from the farm store. They were preparing for the weekly Wednesday night "sermon" from Brother Wise.

"I'll get to it." She found that being busy with a task was the best way to overhear what the hell was going on with the cult. It was easy to judge from the outside looking in, and think that all of these women and the men were crazy in and of themselves for following a creep like Wise. But since she'd been allowed to stay in the trailer park, she'd seen that a lot of the folks seemed almost normal, if a bit too trusting of the cult's rules. Which they all called "good guidelines for good living." Claudia wanted to gag every time they repeated any of the propaganda. So far all of it was straight from the pamphlets and publications Wise had printed up for the New Thought "community." Nika Pasczenko had sneaked photos of the literature last Christmastime.

"Are you excited, Sister Claudia?" Becky smiled at her over a bowl of hardboiled eggs she was peeling.

"Excited? About what?" Claudia kept peeling the old potatoes, noting that the cult was living on a shoestring if these potatoes were any measure.

"You'll get to see Brother Wise speak tonight!"

"Ah, yes. I've been so busy learning about the New Thought that I almost forgot."

"Never forget that Brother Wise is the whole reason for our joining."

"Joining?"

"Being together in community. And there's a good chance that he'll pick a new mother tonight." By "new mother," she meant a woman or, worse, girl, to inseminate.

"Any idea who?" Claudia fought back her disgust and

rage. If the son of a bitch tried to lay a hand on an under-age girl while she was here, all bets were off. She'd take him out before the FBI had a chance to come in and officially do it. She was never an advocate of using Trail Hikers status to accomplish what overt law enforcement could, be it at the state, local or national level. But when it came to protecting children, she saw no reason to remain undercover. She'd claim she'd been undercover for SVPD if she had to, and Colt would back her up.

Colt. She missed him, missed talking to him before bed each night, missed what they did before, and sometimes again after, the talking. It'd only been three nights. Nothing compared to the months she'd spent deployed, at war. But then, she hadn't been in love with Colt Todd yet.

"Sister Claudia, stop lollygagging and get those potatoes peeled." Sister Mary was being rather bitchy. And really, "lollygagging?"

"Yes, Sister Mary." She exchanged the rusty peeler for a paring knife and went to work.

"That's better, Sister Claudia. You seem to know your way with a paring knife, don't you?"

You should see what I can do with a bayonet, bitch.

Abi woke to the predawn darkness, the moonlight illuminating the sheers on her bedroom windows. Keith's solid breathing was next to her ear as he spooned her. She took a moment to savor it all. Not just the beauty of skin-to-skin contact, or the sensuality of his breath against her nape as he slumbered. Anyone could give her physical comfort, but only Keith made her feel like the most beautiful woman on the planet. As if she mattered, her past be damned. He gave her life meaning, purpose. She'd never before had a purpose beyond her career.

Keith was the man for her.

She started to slowly flex her toes, her fingers. The air mattress had lived up to the promise on its box, holding them both better than she'd expected. Although that first round of sex had been so physical, so exertive, she was grateful they'd been on the floor.

They'd made love two more times—until nearly midnight—before falling into an exhausted sleep. She knew he'd been as tired as she had been; the last months and weeks in particular were weighing on everyone working the case. She didn't drift off, however, before she'd realized with startling clarity that she and Keith had just sealed the connection that had always existed between them. The bond that neither could deny. They hadn't had sex. They'd made love—they *were* love.

Maybe she should have told Keith about her plan for this morning. Maybe he'd be pissed off at her for not, but she'd decided to remain solo. If she found anything, she'd let Rio and Trail Hikers know immediately. With Claudia in the depths of the cult, the police and fire departments preparing for a worst-case scenario, Abi knew that this was her op. Keith was needed by his department.

Before her parents had shown up on Sunday, she'd been up at the same early hour, working on the satellite images and maps of the area. She'd thought she'd found something last week but wasn't sure enough to move on it, and besides, her brain needed some rest time to put together the bits and pieces coming in from Claudia and other sources in place in Silver Valley and the area around Three Mile Island.

As Abi eased herself out of bed, she gave Keith a kiss on his forehead, hoping that if he stirred he'd think she was getting up to use the bathroom.

Not to sneak out of her own house and escape into the darkest, deepest parts of the Appalachians.

She wrote him a quick note, leaving it on the coffee-pot she'd programmed to begin brewing in another hour. Keith was an early riser like her, but even he didn't get up before sunrise most days. How she felt about him was too much to deal with in this moment; she'd tell him once they'd wrapped up the case. Once they were safe and she was done with law-enforcement work. Because they both had to survive the next several hours or days.

Backpack, phone, hiking poles, hiking boots, high-protein snacks, water, bedroll. Night-vision goggles, hi-res digital camera equipment, portable wi-fi hot spot in addition to her phone. She had enough to survive out there for three days if she had to, and the means to get information to SVPD headquarters. And Trail Hikers.

The kitchen door gave a betraying creak as she opened it and Abi stood stock-still. The house remained quiet. She quickly slipped out, locking the door behind her.

The grass on the path to the big barn was damp but didn't soak through her sneakers as she stayed on the higher ground in the middle of the path. At the barn, she slid the door back.

Bright light spilled out into the dark.

"Keith!"

"You didn't think I'd let you do this alone, did you?" He stood in front of her, fully dressed as she was for biking, hiking and camping.

"How did you know?"

"Come on, Abi. I know when you're holding back. The piles of maps and charts on your dining room table, the lists of camping gear. You've been acting like you did when we first met—when you had to keep your under-cover status with the Trail Hikers from me. So I knew you were onto something, something you probably want to protect me from, right?"

"'Protect' is a strong word. More like keep you free to do your part of the job. Put the fires out, keep the morale of your department up. And more than anything, you have to be ready to handle the load that evacuating for an event at Three Mile Island will bring. And if there's an explosion or fire, your department needs you, Keith."

"This is where we've got a big disconnect, Abi. This case is about more than my department, more than the resurrection of my career. This is about justice and sending a message to every damned creep out there that Silver Valley isn't going to be hurt anymore."

"*Riiiight*. Which brings us back to why you think you can go with me on this?"

"What says I can't?"

They stared at each other in the harsh light coming from the old bulbs in the barn. Abi shifted on her feet. "Look, it's getting lighter by the minute out there. I have this timed so that I can disappear into the woods without being seen by anyone. If you have to come along, fine, but the minute you show any signs of not taking my lead, you're back in your station waiting for the alarms. Got it?"

"Got it." He gave in more quickly than she'd anticipated.

"I mean, no funny business out there. No heroic moves. I'm going in to take out wherever Wise is hiding out in between his propaganda sermons."

Keith held up his hands. "Look, I don't even have a weapon. I'm here to help and give you muscle where you need it."

She stared at him. Keith was a proven hiker, and he knew this area better than she did, no matter that she'd memorized maps, but those had nothing on years of experience and walking the land, knowing how too much rain could make a creek turn into a roaring river, how too little dried up any reference points related to tributaries.

He smiled. "You know you need me."

More than she was willing to admit, especially to herself. Not with a mission to accomplish.

"Yes, I do. But we have to agree to focus on the mission now. Can you trust me that we'll pick this up where we've left it then?"

His eyes sparkled. "I trust you with my heart, babe."

Abi steeled herself against throwing herself into his arms and making love to him again. Both of their lives depended upon her staying centered.

"Great. Well. I could use your historic knowledge of the area. You've been hiking and camping here for, what, almost twenty years?"

"Twenty-two. We moved here when I was twelve."

She sighed. The weight of what they were about to embark upon dowsed her earlier excitement. "I certainly can't beat that. I have two extra bikes—pick one. I'd suggest the blue one, it's the sturdiest. Do you have a bedroll?"

He lifted his pack. "Good to go. I packed for five days last week when Colt gave us our marching orders. Just in case."

She rolled her eyes. "Of course you did. I'm packed for three, so let's hope we're back in one."

"It'll take longer to smoke them out, don't you think?"

"Yes, I do. And that's okay—as long as we get to them before Wise starts his finale." She didn't have to say Three Mile Island or risk of nuclear meltdown. They both knew what they were fighting for.

They rode the bikes as far into the base of the mountains as possible, for a total of twelve miles from Abi's house. It took them almost an hour and the sun was over the horizon as they stashed the mountain bikes under a grove of Leland pines and took to their feet.

"I was hoping to be at a higher elevation by now." She shot Keith a glare.

"Now, now. You're just sore because I was onto you. Abi, we made love in a way I've never experienced before. Where's the tender lover from last night?"

She was right here, her body begging for more. But she had to keep both their bodies intact, safe.

"On hiatus." She hoisted her pack higher and kept walking, using her compass to guide her.

Keith chuckled behind her, low and sexy.

She paused and looked back at him. "We should probably keep our voices down, right? Our voices will carry in this still air."

Keith looked up at the sky through the tree canopy. "Yeah. It's going to rain, too. Pour, if the forecast is correct." He leveled his gaze on her. Would she ever tire of those blue eyes?

"Abi, getting wet will slow us down. If it starts to drop, we need to pop up a tent and wait it out."

Getting wet. Oh, God, she was really going to have to pull out all of the stops to stay on a professional track here.

"I know. Let's keep going and hope we'll get close enough to where I think they are before then."

There wasn't a track to follow like the Appalachian Trail as they were way off any established path, just as she suspected the True Believer hideout was. But the area they traversed, while overgrown, offered them a wide enough swath to hike side by side for the next hour. They quietly shared their observations and thoughts, and Abi had a sense of firm purpose when Keith revealed he thought she was on target for the cult shanty.

"You know these woods better than I do, Keith. I have a GPS coordinate I'm heading for, but you know what the area looks like. Is there going to be a place to stake out that will be close enough to get the information we need?"

"By information, you mean figure out who's coming and going, how many extra officers you're going to need up here?"

"Yes."

"Let me see where on the map you think it is. I saw your drawings in the dining room—is that where?"

"Close enough." She held out her phone.

Keith took her phone and looked at the screen, then turned it sideways and enlarged it.

"Yup, I know the perfect spot to go to."

"You agree I'm on the right path?"

He nodded. "Absolutely. I'm sure whatever intel you have led you here, but I can tell you that it's wide and flat enough for snowmobiles and ATVs. Many parts of the AT hiking paths, and other local trails, could never be traversed any other way than by foot. Especially the solid-rock walls and boulder-pocked way up the mountain. They're not going to use anything as obvious as the ski trails."

Abi did have intel, as Keith said, but couldn't share all of her information with him. It was part of the Trail Hikers code, not unlike working for the government. You only received information that you needed to, and it wasn't to be shared with anyone else, even a Trail Hiker, unless necessary.

"I know I was being standoffish about your role in the investigation. I'm sorry, Keith. You are the best person to have with me on this."

He stopped and looked at her. "You don't have to patronize me, Abi. I'll still make love to you with wild abandon."

She slapped her hands over her mouth to keep her laughter from echoing into the woods and alerting anyone unwanted to their presence. As Keith watched her giggling subside, she felt the familiar heat rise between them. Heat she'd thought they'd taken care of last night. At least for a while.

But it would never be enough with Keith. He was one of a kind, and the connection they shared was one she'd never experienced before. It was more than sex and hot kisses, more than the right line delivered at the right time to make either one of them laugh. It was deeper. A kinship.

This is what falling in love is.

Before she had time to mentally wipe away the awareness, Keith had his hands on her cheeks, cupping her face, lowering his lips to hers.

This wasn't like any of the kisses last night, the kisses that brought her emotions and sensations to a fever pitch and gave her the most incredible orgasms ever. This was tender, sweet and…loving. His lips and his tongue let her know that he wanted her, cared about her, was here for her.

But was it enough?

He lifted his face and sought her eyes with his own. "Abi, we've only just begun to get to know one another. I never thought I'd say these words to any woman, not now, and not especially in the middle of a case like this. But I've never wanted a woman the way I want you."

Want. He *wanted* her. Well, just great.

"Let's keep our focus on finding these losers, shall we?"

Chapter 19

Claudia lay on the thin mattress, the frame of the pull-out sofa poking at her ribs and back as it had last night, and the night before. Her four roommates were in various stages of falling asleep. Only after she was certain they were in deep REM could she risk going out and leaving her message.

The quickly written note lay in her front pocket. She'd gone to bed in the typical nightgown they were all expected to dress in—the kind her grandmother used to wear. Plain, flannel and left her covered from neck to toe. She felt like she was in a psychotic version of *Little House on the Prairie.*

It had been easy assimilating into the cult, proclaiming she was a believer from way back of Leonard Wise's crap. She even said she'd had a relative from upstate New York who was in the original True Believer cult and his cronies had believed her. She hadn't met him, only seen him at the compound once since she'd been here, at "sermon" night.

It was an awful mix of pathetic human beings seeking more than whatever life had given them, with power-hungry, spineless men who were also child molesters, if not in deed, then as accomplices. They all supported Leonard Wise and his insistence that the "community" give birth to new hope for tomorrow and the ever after: babies born to young girls who'd been basically sacrificed by their parents to be there.

Lucky for Wise none of the girls had been forced to have sex with the old son of a bitch yet, from what Claudia had found out. But the "night of sacrifice" was coming and there was talk about a special place the girls would be transported to.

She'd written it all out on the note, and hoped Rio and Abi would be able to do what was needed to keep the girls safe from harm. If Claudia got wind of Wise doing anything sooner, she was still prepared to end it all for the cult then. She'd take them out herself, with her bare hands.

Creeping slowly through the cramped trailer, she stepped over two of the women lying in sleeping bags on the floor.

Wise had also made a haven for mentally ill and homeless people. They were vulnerable and needy enough to accept whatever his terms were to enjoy food in their bellies, a roof over their heads. Claudia hoped that the county services would take good care of these folks once the cult was disbanded.

"Where are you going?" A vicious tone charged the whisper from a young girl who stood in front of her. She must have crept up from behind the narrow hallway that led to the back bedrooms.

"Vivian, I need you to be quiet or you'll wake the others." Claudia faked a wheeze. "I have asthma and I need some fresh air."

"I'm coming with you."

"Fine, but make it quiet and quick."

They left through the door nearest the front room, being careful to not let it slam behind them. Once outside, Claudia turned and faced Vivian.

"How old are you, Vivian?"

"Fifteen next month."

Claudia's stomach sank. "You're only fourteen? And last night you were up in front of the community as one of the women who will be sacrificing for new life?"

Vivian nodded quickly. She didn't look at Claudia in the moonlight, but the glisten of a single tear as it tracked down the girl's cheek said everything.

"Your mother brought you here, didn't she?"

Vivian nodded. "It's not her fault, Sister Claudia."

"No?"

"No. She's been trying to keep it together since my dad died in the war, and then my younger brother got sick, and she can't afford the medicine. This is the best place for us to be."

"But you're not living with her or your brother?"

Vivian sniffled and wiped her nose with the hem of her nightshirt sleeve. "No, they've made me come live here with the other girls until…until—" She stopped talking and her shoulders started shuddering.

Claudia placed her hands on the girl, trying to calm her. "Do you want to be here, Vivian, really? Do you want to be with someone like Leonard Wise?"

"No, ma'am."

"It's Claudia. And you can drop the sister part, too. How would you like to help me put an end to all of this nonsense, and we'll work together to get your family a safer place to live and medical help for your brother?"

Vivian nodded. "What do you need me to do?"

"Follow me for now, and keep to the shadows. There are security men where we're headed and we can't let them see us."

Claudia led Vivian to the outskirts of the trailer park. Vivian did exactly as she'd been told and was a natural at keeping her footfalls silent, staying away from the parking lights and beams of light that spilled out of other trailers.

It figured. The trailers that housed the men were still lit from within. Apparently the brothers of the society were allowed to stay up as late as they pleased.

"Stop." Claudia held up her hand. "The guards are right over there, by the entrance. Do you see them?"

Vivian peered into the night. "Yes. But who are they guarding us against?"

"Good question. It isn't important right now. What matters is that I get across the highway without them detecting me. Can you stay here, and if they look like they're onto me, make a distraction to bring them back here?"

"What should I do?"

"I'm hoping you won't have to do anything. But if you see them move to leave the park and go across the main road, call out to them and tell them you heard noises in the bushes over there." Claudia pointed to an area behind them. "They'll ask you why you're out. Tell them that you were only outside of your trailer in order to go to your mother, to see her, when you saw a large figure run across the compound. They'll believe you as long as you act afraid."

"I am afraid of having to face them!" Their conversation was in whispers but Claudia didn't want to keep talking—it was too risky.

"Can you do it, Vivian?"

The girl's bottom lip trembled. "Yes."

"Good girl. Now stay here, and don't fret—I'm good at this. They'll never know I was in and out of the park."

Claudia used the same route she'd taken the last two nights, skirting the guards and going around the last grouping of trailers that was either empty or full of women and pitch-dark. The darkness aided her escape.

She'd set it up with Rio to check the boulder on the main highway right before the trailer park. There was a clump of wild lilies next to it, and she'd dug a hole the first night to put the note there, up against the flat side of the boulder.

Getting out of the park was simple, and she breathed a sigh of relief once she had the note in place. Running through the tall grass, back onto the gravel that signified the park's boundary, she allowed a rush of satisfaction to put a spring in her steps. Who said more mature, retired Marines couldn't get a job done?

Turning the last corner to meet Vivian, she halted in her tracks.

One of the guards had Vivian up against a trailer, his hand covering her screams.

Claudia gave him a hard hit to his kidney, then the other as he fell. Once he was on the ground, she crushed his balls with her foot.

She looked up at Vivian. "You okay, honey?"

Vivian's huge eyes stared at her. She nodded.

"Then let's get back to the trailer."

"The next time we camp together, let's opt for a more scenic route." Keith slapped his forearm against the early infestation of mayflies that had decided to swarm exactly where they sat, under a large pine tree and behind a grouping of bushes that hid them from anyone on the wide swath of land laden with ATV tracks.

"It's worth the bites to be able to catch these idiots." Abi wasn't ready to call it a night yet, but so far they hadn't witnessed anything untoward and the sun was rapidly sinking on the horizon.

"We need to get some rest. I think tomorrow will be a long day." Keith looked steadfastly forward, using his binoculars to scan the trail and the side of the mountain as it fell away below them.

"I brought my smallest tent."

"Which is why we'll use mine. I packed a double."

"I'm sure you did."

"Hey, we don't have to sleep together if you'd rather not." He lowered the binoculars and looked at her. "Seriously, Abi, as much as I can't wait to be inside you again, I'm at your beck and call for this stakeout. Or whatever it is we're doing."

"We're staking out, for sure. And if we're lucky, we'll do some apprehending."

"I thought you said the police would take care of that?"

"They will, as will the FBI, when we're going for the jugular on the cult. Until then, we have to be ready to do whatever. Well, *I* do. You're not officially certified to participate in anything legal-wise."

"Yeah. Trail Hikers–wise, I'm pretty much an observer, too."

She sighed. "I know that it sucks for you, and I feel your pain. Trust me, it'll feel just as good when all the arsonists are behind bars and we have Silver Valley back to its usual sleepy-town self."

"Do you believe that, Abi?"

"That we'll catch them? Hell, yes. That Silver Valley will ever be sleepy again? Probably not. But we can hope."

He kept looking at her and she elbowed him. "Quit it."

"I can look at you as long as I'd like to, Abi. It's not harming anything."

Maybe not, but it was making her wish they were out here camping for other reasons than a stakeout.

Keith laughed, low and throaty. "I can't help teasing you. You are so damned beautiful. Do you know that?"

She looked at him and for the first time in her life, she *did* know it. "I can't believe otherwise when you're next to me."

"Then we're going to have to do whatever it takes to keep it this way. To move forward, next to one another."

Abi couldn't agree more. But she was still afraid, deep down, that Keith could change his mind. He was a firefighter and had always been able to put his job first. Was he really ready to commit to something more with her?

"This is all we need."

"Yes, sir."

Colt stood next to Rio as they stared at the note from Claudia.

Wise looks very frail. Stated that the time to impregnate the girls is very soon. They must have some kind of hideaway in the Appalachians. Abi may already be on it; did you send Keith with her? Will need other help to bring it all down. Also much talk about a final explosion, the holocaust of the unbelievers. I think it's about TMI.

Rio had picked up the note last night, basically forbidding his boss to do it. He knew if Colt got anywhere near the compound, he'd want to go in and get Claudia out.

Rio was correct. It had all but killed Colt not to get the note himself.

"Is there someone else you need to notify at Trail Hikers?" Rio was looking at him, and Colt knew that Rio saw into his soul. Colt was experiencing what Rio had— seeing the woman he loved at risk of losing her life over some crazy cult's doings.

"I have the contacts to call, and I'll get on that. The FBI needs to know about this, too."

"We can tell the agent who's due to report here within the hour." Rio stared at Claudia's note.

"No, that's too late. They need to know we're in need of more bodies on the ground. As soon as Abi finds their hideout, we're going to take it down." Colt's phone buzzed. "Hang on."

"Colt Todd."

"Chief Todd, this is FBI agent Andrea Locklear. I'm still about twenty minutes out, but I have to share some recent information with you. If you haven't heard already, we've made a connection between the True Believers, aka New Thought, cult and the Army War College."

"We know about the DOD employee Taylor, Agent." Really, the Feds were implying this was news?

"No, sir, it's not about that. It's deeper—Mr. Taylor unwittingly gave out information to two international students who are, in actuality, terrorists. They've been absent from class for the past week and we think they're working to bring down Three Mile Island with a cyber attack, along with the other international terrorists who went missing when they came into the country. We've finally connected all the dots."

Colt held up his hand to Rio as he listened. "I'm going to put you on speaker, Agent Locklear. Can you please repeat what you just said?"

Colt watched Rio's face reflect everything he was feeling. Anger, shock, resolve.

"The governor would normally call in the National Guard for a physical threat against TMI, but with the sensitivity of the systems being breached, we'd prefer to have this handled at the lowest level possible, with no media involvement. We're counting on Silver Valley PD and all the surrounding police departments to provide perimeter security while we at my agency bring in the bad guys."

"I understand, Agent Locklear, but you understand *this*. I've got God knows how many underage girls only hours from being raped by a cult leader and his fanatic followers. My people are on the ground looking for where the crime is expected to occur. I can't do anything until they move the girls and try to harm them. But when they do, this entire cult will come down."

"Roger that, Chief, but we've got bigger problems with the terrorists and cyber, *and* possible physical, attack on TMI."

"Roger this, Agent Locklear, that's your problem. TMI is a federal facility. I will not, repeat *not*, have my officers taken off the cult case for this. If it's a cyber attack, there's nothing we can do about it anyway, except clear local civilians of the area."

God, he'd already lived through this once, as a young boy back in the seventies when Three Mile Island had come close to a disaster. Not that it mattered.

For Claudia he'd go to hell and back.

Snuggled in the small tent with Keith, it felt more like a lovers' getaway than a stakeout. Abi ignored the guilt that preyed on her overachieving workaholic self with this realization.

"Relax. We're out of here in two seconds if we hear anything."

"Hmm." She nestled her bottom against his pelvis and felt his erection through their cargo pants. They'd remained dressed for expediency. "I feel like a couple of teenagers who sneaked away from their parents."

"Except we're allowed to do whatever we want." He nuzzled her neck.

"Keith." She wriggled onto her stomach and faced him. It was pitch-dark save for a sliver of moonlight at the far corner of the tent, across their feet.

"What?" His voice and his touch were all she had to go on. But she imagined his eyes, liquid heat for her.

"I've never wanted to blow off an op as badly as I do this one." She kissed him. Her aim was off in the dark and she hit the side of his mouth first, but then his tongue sought hers and the kiss deepened. Their pelvises were up against one another and his erection made her mad. She needed to please him, but not now, not here. When Keith stroked her breast she groaned as much from desire as regret. "We can't do this now."

"I'm in love with you, Abi."

His declaration bolted through her.

"I know. I mean, I'm falling in love with you, too." It didn't hurt to admit it or make her feel trapped. It was freeing to tell Keith how she felt. She laughed at the relief of it.

"What's so funny?" His hands were stroking her back, his nose bumping hers.

"I've never felt so alive before. So happy." He kissed the tears that tracked down her cheeks. Tears of joy.

"It's mutual, babe." He took in a deep breath, then quickly expelled it. "Let's get this wrapped up so that I can wrap you up in my arms without anything in our way."

"Roger that." She pulled back. "No more distractions. I'm going to take a quick look." She reached for her night-vision goggles.

"Do you want to do shifts as I suggested earlier? So that we can each get some rest?"

"I do, but not yet." She unzipped the tent and hoped the insects had calmed down for the night. It helped that they hadn't lit a fire and weren't using any lights. A distant droning sound caught her attention, especially as it grew louder. "This might be what we've been waiting for."

Keith was next to her and they were crouching behind the bushes, searching for the source of the engine noise.

Abi's gut tightened as she spotted two vehicles, about a half mile away on the wide trail. "I've got two contacts, and they look a hell of a lot like ATVs."

"Yup, that's what I think, too."

She stood and began to move. "You stay here. I'm going closer to see what we've got."

"I thought this was solely an info-gathering mission." Keith's voice had an edge of tension she understood. She felt it, too. If these were the cult members, they were past the point of trying to fake their way out of an arrest. Wise's men were playing for keeps.

"We need to confirm their identity if we can, and see where they go." She prayed that whatever kind of bunker the cult had built up here in the mountains was very close. It would be impossible to follow the ATV vehicles for very long. A quarter mile, tops.

As they sat under the bushes, the drones grew closer.

Abi made out two people on each of the two ATVs. As they drew closer she saw what looked like weapons, automatic rifles, slung over their backs.

"Right now, I really hate that Pennsylvania is open carry," she whispered more to herself than to Keith.

"I've seen guys carry their hunting rifles or a handgun in a holster every now and then. But not automatics." He was looking through his NVGs and obviously knew his firearms.

"We can't go after them now." She only had her handgun and a knife with her. Even with the element of surprise, taking out four men armed with AR-15s wasn't her idea of good odds.

"Were you really planning to?"

"Yes. No. I don't know—I was waiting to see what the situation was."

And now they knew. The cult was armed and dangerous. As Abi and Keith watched, the vehicles turned almost ninety degrees in front of them and stopped. From their perch, Abi and Keith were approximately thirty feet above the armed men.

Incredulity hit Abi as the ground appeared to open up under the ATVs. The vehicles and their passengers sunk down as harsh light spilled out from what she could now see was an underground dugout of some sort. Two other men waited inside what looked like a garage and one was on some kind of control box.

"I'll be damned. Hydraulics." She willed the faces to turn toward her, toward the lens of the video camera she was operating, to reveal their identity.

"Yes, ma'am. The cult must take in a lot of money." Keith's voice sounded as stunned as she felt.

"It makes sense with the connections Wise might have."

Keith looked at her in the predawn light. "What kinds of connections? Or can't you tell me?"

"Frankly, I don't know, not for sure. We know that several of the cult members are affluent, or were, before they turned funds over to this new evolution of his cult, New Thought. And none of the crimes that have been committed over the past two years can be directly attributed to him in a court of law. Until now."

"Until now is right." She heard Keith change position. "What do we do now, Abi?"

"I keep taking photos, and shooting this video. We call it all in to Rio and the contact at Trail Hikers. Then we wait to see what Rio wants us to do."

Rio and Colt watched the computer screen as Abi's digital stream of video ran. Agent Locklear was with them.

"Gentlemen, I'm going to have this sent to my headquarters. In the meantime, I need you to keep your people there as long as possible."

"Done." Colt watched Rio make short work of texting Abi to stay put with Keith. He asked her how much time she had with their supplies and her reply was "as long as we need."

"Abi says they're set to stay out there for the duration."

"I'm glad the reception is good on the AT, with the way it covers the higher elevations of our area. She cannot get caught." Colt's insides hadn't untwisted from the knots they'd been in all night. "Claudia's message is proof that they're getting ready to move the girls, and it's going to be soon." He looked at Agent Locklear. "Can you get us backup ASAP?"

She frowned. "Normally, yes, but we've got Three Mile Island to worry about."

"Right." Colt looked at the computer screen, his mind suddenly alert and clear. He knew what had to be done, and if he had to be the one to do it, he would.

Chapter 20

After they sent the video to Rio, Keith and Abi watched the sun come up together. "What do you think Rio's going to order next?" He spoke quietly, next to her ear.

"I thought he was going to keep us out here, on lookout, but now I'm not so sure. If all hell is about to break loose with TMI, they'll need us back there."

"I hope it's not until you get what you want out here, Abi."

"Yeah, well, me too. But I go where the mission needs me."

That was what worried him most.

Keith's uneasiness amplified with each moment they waited near the site of the underground bunker. It was as if he had some kind of telepathic connection with Abi. He literally felt her concentration, her gears turning. *Churning* might be more like it.

"What are we going to do, Abi?"

She turned her liquid-brown eyes on him. One blink. She'd decided.

"Wait—before you say anything—I support whatever you need to do. But I don't want to see you put yourself at risk. Remember, 'no heroics'?"

She smiled. "Right." She straightened. "We can't go down there and hunt around—that's too obvious, and I'm sure there are cameras, wire trips, motion detectors. We're lucky they're not up here. Our spot here is high enough to be out of their range of concern."

"With a contraption like that hydraulic lift, they're thinking they have a pretty protected spot. If you weren't the expert you are, no one would have found this." Keith stared at the ground below, marveling at how, if he hadn't seen the lift lower the ATVs into the man-made bunker, he wouldn't have believed it.

"They're going to come back up—they have to. For whatever reason. Not to mention the cult members they'll be bringing out here. This is the perfect spot to hide your flock if you're a crazy cult leader and you believe it's the end of the world."

"But what about their post-apocalyptic plans?"

Abi smiled. "You know, you'd make a good intel analyst, Paruso. Yes, the post–Big Bang plans. They think they're raising this new breed of believers, right? So of course there have to be underground bunkers. Do you know what this entrance we've found most likely leads to?"

"Leads to? As in an underground hidden bunker isn't enough?" He scanned the horizon. "There's no mining in this county, no caves nearby. The only other structure near here is the quarry." Realization squeezed his lungs like a tight, painful band. "The quarry, damn it."

Abi nodded.

"They're not coming back up here because they've

found a way out through the quartz and limestone bedrock. I saw that there was an abandoned quarry not far from the trailer park compound, and it's on the land Wise bought." Abi spoke as if she was figuring it out aloud. "This is their secret-getaway-escape hatch, so to speak. The quarry has to be what—three hundred feet lower than this? At its rim? So they've used the natural limestone and quartz openings to make an underground road to the quarry, where they can bring in whatever size vehicle they want." She paused. "If they can come and go either through here or there, we're going to need backup at both places." She looked at him. "How fast can I get to the quarry?"

"We can get there in twenty-five minutes, thirty tops. If we run."

"Not 'we,' Keith. You have to go back in now. Your department needs you. I'm trained to do this, and Claudia will be coming in for backup."

"It'll take too long for you to go on your own. Let me take you there." He heard the pleading in his voice, felt how far his love for her had taken him. But it wasn't to a low, groveling place. It was where he belonged. Where he wanted to be.

"Only if you promise that you'll leave right away and help with the TMI threat. It's your one chance to prove that any accusations against you were false. Trust me on this, Keith."

She was right. And he wanted her to be in place in time, to do her job with the least chance of danger to her. Because he'd never be able to control Abi's decisions. But he'd never be able to live without her, either. He knew that now.

He looked at her, standing with the mountain rising behind her, the sun flashing off her eyes. Abi was a warrior, a woman, his love.

"Follow me."

* * *

Claudia stood in the group of women closer to her age, wanting to do anything else but this. The evening meal came and none too soon, as Claudia's knuckles were raw from peeling potatoes.

They were all taking turns serving dinner to the men of the flock as they filed by the large buffet set out at the back of the community room.

"As soon as the brothers are served, we can eat." Sister Mary spoke quietly, her eyes downcast. She placed her hand on her stomach.

"Are those growls I'm hearing?"

She nodded. Claudia said nothing as another group of men arrived, all dusty and dirty from God knew what, for their plates of food. It was clear that this was a highly unusual event, to have the community get together on an occasion other than a regular sermon night.

"You're lucky those walls didn't collapse on you, Brother Gregory." One of the young men guffawed as the other's face turned red.

"If you would have told me that we weren't going back the way we'd got in, I wouldn't have gone so quick."

Claudia mentally reviewed everything Abi, as well as other analysts, had found out about the secret True Believer/New Thought hideaway. The last set of maps she'd looked at showed possibilities that were near a quarry. She'd consulted the top geologists in the country and discovered that it wouldn't be inconceivable for a series of narrow underground caves to exist adjacent to the quarry. Several of the dig sites had been shut down for safety concerns, but that wouldn't keep criminals from using them. And since Wise had one on his property, she had to believe it was for a purpose.

"What are you looking at, Sister?" Another man had

walked up to the table, and she recognized him as Brother Lionel. He had more bruises on his face and arms than she thought possible and still moved around with a sense of purpose. Ugly purpose.

"Nothing."

"Nothing what?"

"Nothing, Brother Lionel."

"That's right." He looked around at the other women at the table. The remaining men scattered, taking their plates to eat in peace. Brother Lionel sneered. "Do you realize the glory we're about to see realized? Brother Wise is leading us all to our salvation, and there's no time, no room, for anyone to be concerning their selves with anything but the preparation. That means keeping the men fed and strong. And keep the younger women, the ones fit for birthing, healthy. Ya got it, Sister Claudia?"

"Yes, Brother Lionel." Claudia knew then that there was no viable plan for her, Sister Mary or the other "older" women. The men were going to protect themselves and the women who could bear the future children of the cult. She might not have time to get another note out for Rio and Colt to use, so she was needed to act quickly.

She looked forward to watching these bastards go down.

Lionel left the trailer and headed out to accomplish what Brother Wise had told him to. He wasn't going to stay for the sermon; he couldn't. Because, at the end of the sermon, the New Thought mothers would be safely tucked away and soon be impregnated. The other women—no one needed them. He'd have to circle back and get rid of the older bitches. The young mothers would take up where they left off.

Lionel had his job to do. It was the final fire, the

flames that would let the world know that what Brother Wise preached wasn't made up or crazy. It was the truth.

And it was too late for those who hadn't already heeded the call.

"What kind of timeline are we looking at?" Rio addressed FBI agent Andrea Locklear as they sat around the SVPD conference table with Colt.

Keith listened in on a phone as he hid near the quarry, but Abi was already in place to go into the underground bunker as soon as the opportunity presented itself. Keith could see her from his vantage point and relayed her action to the group. Colt knew Keith was full of fear; he was in the same place. They both had to trust that their women would survive.

Andrea worked a laptop and her phone as if she'd been born with them attached. "FBI and NSA are working together on the cyber part of this. I'm not even privy to that, but my director for this op is saying we have twelve hours, tops."

Colt slammed his fists on the table. "That's not enough time to evacuate all the civilians in Silver Valley!"

"No evacuation is happening. A cyber attack doesn't mean they'll blow up Three Mile Island. It does signify that they want to show the world that they can take over the systems of the nuclear plant. But to actually blow it up?" Andrea shook her head. "Don't see it happening."

"But it could, Andrea." Rio spoke.

"Doubtful. I think the most that has happened here is that the fake students at the Army War College were sent in by their terrorist organizations. They were sent here to feel things out on the ground, without having to worry about being placed under any kind of surveillance by our government. They're simply students, right? They were able to find out from Taylor and his family about the cult, which only helped them. They've used the cult's activities as a screen, to predict how we'd react."

"And now that they know how we handle fires and emergencies? You mean they didn't know that already?" Keith whispered into his mic.

"I can't explain everything—you all just have to trust me on this. Higher levels are taking care of the cyber attack and any resulting threat to the nuclear plants. But this has tied up our resources to the point that we can't be as much help with the final apprehension of Wise and his cult leaders, as I said before.

"What you need to do at the local level is the heavy lifting with bringing down the cult and keeping those civilians involved safe. We all know how ugly it gets when a crazed sociopathic cult leader is cornered." Andrea's words hit Keith in the gut.

"You still there, Keith?" Rio's voice.

"Yeah."

"You need to report back here ASAP. Your department needs you. They're already on their way to where Wise has sent men to set off flares and fireworks in a perimeter around TMI."

"I'm needed here, Rio." His department knew what they were doing.

"You have to come back and lead your department. Rio's right. Let Abi do her job." Colt's voice was barely audible. Keith's phone signal was weak. Damn it.

"Roger." It went against his gut instincts to leave Abi, but his other instincts told him his team needed him, too.

No, not gut instinct. *Heart* instinct. Abi was his heart, and her life was at stake.

Lionel ordered six teams of five men each to the places where they'd planned for months to establish a ring around the Susquehanna and Cumberland valleys. The center of the "ring of fire," as Brother Wise called it, was the famous Three Mile Island nuclear power plant. Brother Wise said that man's evil need for power was underscored by the existence of Three Mile Island, even after it had suffered a near catastrophic nuclear accident in the seventies.

"Do not speak to anyone as you go to your firing point. Do not launch. Repeat, do not launch your rockets until the signal is given. Does everyone have a fully charged phone?"

The men nodded and murmured their compliance. "We've practiced this enough. Once you launch your rockets, you may be approached by law enforcement. Do not resist. Let them see that you're not afraid to go to jail for the best reason ever. You are representing the New Thought, the True Believers of years ago come back. You are the servants of Brother Wise and are bringing salvation to the world by letting them know the truth."

"Amen!" The men clapped and stomped their feet together, in the practiced move that was unique to their community. Lionel had never been more proud or excited. He was in charge, for now.

And if anything happened to Brother Wise and his immediate circle of trusted men, Lionel was ready to take over their entire flock.

"Brother David, do you have your kayak ready?"

"Yes, Brother Lionel."

"Then go now—you need extra time. Be quick and silent."

Brother David was going to be the one closest to the nuclear reactors. The only way to reach them was via the river. Brother David had rowed crew when he'd been at a university, still under the influence of the world's evil ways. He was strong and good with the oars. And he'd shown no fear during their practice run on the small private lake in the Poconos a month ago. Brother Wise had a friend up in those mountains who owned a cabin on the shores of a remote lake. They'd practiced an entire weekend until everyone was sure the fireworks would go off without a hitch.

Leonard let the rush of exaltation surge through him. Soon the world would know who was really in charge.

Chapter 21

Abi felt Keith's supportive gaze on her the entire time she was crouched near the quarry's entrance to the cult's bunker. The opening hadn't been difficult to spot; the fake Japanese maple trees placed in front of steel doors set into the hollowed-out entrance were a giveaway. From a distance it appeared as if weeds or wild trees had started to overtake the base of the abandoned quarry. Up close, the camouflage was ridiculous.

Her phone had died and it didn't matter; she'd be here when the busloads of women and girls came in. Claudia's note and the FBI agent's further intel had helped her figure out Wise's next steps.

And more importantly, hers and Claudia's.

The bastard had already sent his minions out to surround TMI, and the international cyber terrorists were at work to freeze the facility's systems. Abi couldn't worry about any of that. She had to do what she could—save the young girls being bussed in here at any moment.

Tires crunched on gravel and the lumbering sound of a school bus shifting gears echoed against the quarry walls. She looked up for Keith's gaze, his reassurance.

Keith was gone.

As he'd promised her, he'd left to do his work—with his department. She sent up a prayer that he'd be safe, that the work around TMI would be straightforward, no life-threatening fires, no nuclear meltdown. From her FBI work, she had every confidence in the national law-enforcement agencies and their ability to lock out the cyber terrorists. The arsons set by the cult around TMI could be handled, too. That was Keith's job. It was Leonard Wise and his unpredictable behavior with innocent girls that she was concerned about.

She forced her thoughts from Keith and mentally rehearsed her plan before the goons arrived with the girls, and hopefully the other women, too. As the school bus drew closer, she strained to see the profiles in the windows. All young girls. Pure evil. Whatever happened over the next few minutes, she had to keep the girls from going into this bunker. Once they were behind digitally programmed steel doors and under hydraulic lifts, she'd have little ability to free them.

Keith was hot, sweaty and nearly to where they'd stashed the mountain bikes yesterday. He was switchbacking around the side of the quarry, getting farther and farther from Abi.

Colt's words echoed in his mind, but not as loudly as Abi's. She'd implored him to do his job so that she could do hers.

But Keith *had* done his job. He'd prepared his department for all eventualities, ensured each and every firefighter had the best training money could buy and that he could give them, too. He slowed down, stopped. No one would ever think twice about him leaving Abi on the side of a mountain to go do his work as a firefighter. No one would blame him. In fact, he'd face recrimination for not being there with his department, not leading them into the fight against the cult and its attempts to light fires around Three Mile Island. The very thing he was hell-bent to achieve—complete redemption from the citizens of Silver Valley—wasn't important to him any longer. He'd been crazy, trying to show that the accusations against him were false, even after they'd been dropped.

He took a long last swig of water from his plastic pouch. A funny, tingling feeling began in the center of his chest and ran up the back of his neck and down his spine. It wasn't cardiac arrest, but it had to do with his heart. Abi.

He turned around and ran back toward the quarry.

Claudia lay between two back benches on the floor of the dilapidated school bus, covered with the tote bags each of the girls had been instructed to take with them to the "refuge." She'd looked into the bags—sanitary napkins, cheap perfume, toothbrushes and toothpaste. That's what the sick Leonard Wise was sending his virginal sacrifices into a goddamned bunker with. The good point was that the bags were light and she could stand with little effort. The bad side was that she was on the floor of an old school bus, being banged and jolted as it ground up the mountain.

"Are you okay?" Vivian's eyes peered through the bags as the girl pretended to tie her shoes. She'd agreed to help sneak Claudia on board and had enlisted three of the others to help. None of the underage girls were under Wise's spell, unlike their mothers, who'd been left at the trailer park. Presumably to rot, but Claudia feared for their safety, too. She hoped Colt was on it.

"I'm fine. Be ready as soon as the bus stops. How many men are with us?"

"Two. The bus driver and the guard."

"Does the guard have a weapon? A gun?"

"Yes, a long, rifle-looking one." Vivian's quick response made Claudia smile. This girl might be a future Trail Hiker.

"Good girl. Now sit up and be prepared."

Claudia acknowledged the adrenaline that surged through her system in anticipation of what she had to accomplish. It made her hands shake, her heart pound in her rib cage. She'd felt it before, in Fallujah. As soon as the bus stopped, Wise's cronies were done. She had to disarm the man with the rifle, no doubt an AR-15, as had been reported in Wise's stash of assorted arms.

She'd never been more proud or grateful for what she'd learned during her first basic training, Plebe Summer at the Naval Academy. The Marine Corps Officer Basic Training didn't hurt, either. They both prepared her for this moment.

"That's it, Colt. We've taken out six of the eight suspected fire starters, with Detective Campbell and Officer Pasczenko apprehending the seventh now." Rio sat between Colt and Agent Locklear in the command vehicle.

"All on the ground?" Colt had to confirm they were secure before he could go where he really wanted to be. Not Silver Valley Police Department, not in this communications van outside of Three Mile Island.

"All but one or two. Trail Hikers got two of the men to talk and there's one man, possibly two, on a boat, probably a kayak, headed for TMI." Rio looked at his notes as he spoke, checking off each item, accounting for all of SVPD's officers.

"Chief Todd, I just got a report that the cyber terrorists have been arrested, all six of them." Agent Locklear looked as pleased as punch as she delivered the news.

"Six? I thought there were four at most."

Agent Locklear shrugged. "We catch them as we need to." She stood from her laptop and stretched, bent over, as she was taller than the comms van was high.

"So it was all a ruse, so that Wise can do God knows what at that quarry. He never counted on the cyber terrorists, but wouldn't have cared, either. Goddamn it!" Colt wanted to tear the electronic panels off the inside of the van.

Rio's eyes filled with concern and understanding. He knew what it was like to have the woman you loved in danger. "Yes, sir."

"That's it, then. FBI's on the cyber part and Special Ops will get the remaining rats in the water." Scuba teams were positioned throughout the Susquehanna to take out Wise's attempt to draw national attention to his cult.

"Yes, sir. I'll bring in the rest of the department, Chief. We can all meet back at headquarters." Rio all but pushed Colt out of the van.

"Good job, everyone." Colt nodded first at Rio then at Agent Locklear. She lifted the corner of her mouth.

"Claudia's got this, Chief Todd. And Abi's well prepared for it, too." Agent Locklear's expression revealed nothing, but by the nature of the case and the level of Trail Hikers involvement, Colt knew the FBI agent knew who Claudia and Abi were. What they were capable of.

And what they were up against at this very moment.

"I know." Colt grabbed his coat. "Rio, call in to the station and tell them I want the ATV waiting for me at the bottom of the AT entrance on Silver Pike Highway."

"On it."
Colt fled.

Abi waited for the bus to stop, then ran up behind it at the one moment she could approach it from the rear with the least risk of the driver seeing her with his side mirrors. Giving a light tap on the back door, she waited. Meanwhile, the side door of the bus squeaked open. She dropped to her stomach and saw the booted feet of the guard or driver make their way to the bunker's steel doors. Peering around the side of the bus, she saw it was the guard. He had an AR-15 slung over his back. When a second pair of large, booted feet hit the ground, the driver's, Abi knew she had less than a minute to save a busload of girls.

She pounded on the back door again, this time harder. It didn't matter if the men heard her—she had to get them free. Shuffling, a shout of "Quiet!" and the door flew open. Claudia stood at the back door, tote bags falling from her shoulders and onto the girls grouped around her. Several had started to whimper.

Claudia turned to an older girl. "Vivian, now!"

Vivian motioned for the girls to follow her. "This way!" The girls jumped off the back of the bus, Abi helping them down, urging them to run as fast as they could. "Head for the ridge, up there. Stay to the side of the quarry. Get as far away from the bus as you can." She counted twenty-two in all.

Shots rang out and Abi didn't waste time to look; she knew what an AR-15 sounded like. She met Claudia's commanding gaze. Claudia nodded, shoving the last five girls off the bus.

Worst case, at least the girls would survive. They had to. Abi knew Claudia agreed. Best case, the girls would survive and Claudia and Abi wouldn't, but they'd take out the driver and guard in the process.

The very best scenario would allow Abi and Claudia to take out the men, then wait for the one who'd caused all of this. The one man who had wreaked havoc on Silver Valley and threatened these girls.

Leonard Wise.

Abi knew Wise was her target, but since Keith had told her he loved her she'd had the hardest time keeping him out of her immediate thoughts. And remarkably it wasn't affecting how she did her job. In fact, she felt she had more clarity than ever before. Finding true love did that to a girl. Unfortunately for Wise, he'd targeted her man when he'd coached that couple to bring false charges against Keith. She didn't take kindly to anyone who threatened or hurt her loved ones. This one was for Keith, too.

Abi gripped her weapon and headed for the bunker.

Colt sped along in the department's ATV, willing the new engine to go faster, damning the city for not funding a helicopter for SVPD.

"Hang on, Claudia. Hang on," Colt shouted over the noise, feeling like a madman and not caring. He had five more minutes. Five minutes to get to the quarry, five minutes to back up Claudia and Abi. Or not—an AR-15 bullet killed instantly.

As he fought to maintain control of his sanity, he spied a male figure running along the same route. What the hell was Keith doing out here? He was supposed to be with his department.

Colt slowed the vehicle down. "Hop on."

Before he said the words, Keith was seated behind

him. "Go! There's a school bus of girls and Abi's alone to deal with it."

Yup. He and Keith were heading for the same destination.

Shouting over the engine, Colt filled Keith in on the operation so far. All that he knew, anyhow.

"No one told me Claudia would be going into this, too." Keith's voice was hoarse, his trepidation palpable.

"It's her job. She's had the same great training as Abi. They've got it, don't worry." Why the hell was he trying to console the fire chief? He was as worried as him, for the same reasons.

"Shouldn't we slow down, go on foot as we get closer?" Keith's shout saved them from giving away their presence. Colt wouldn't have stopped until he'd driven into the quarry and taken out every one of the males in the damned cult.

It would have cost Claudia and Abi their lives.

Colt slowed the ATV and pulled off the beaten track, then killed the engine. Keith was off the seat and running before Colt had a chance to pull his weapon. Son of a bitch, getting old sucked. Thank God for gym time and adrenaline. Colt ran behind Keith, skidding to a halt and diving onto his front behind the wild shrubbery that rimmed the perimeter of the quarry.

What Keith pointed to made his heart stop.

"You bitch. I should kill you right here in front of all the future mothers." The gunman held the AR-15 up, pointing at Abi's forehead. She wasn't worried about him, though. It was the driver standing near the now open steel doors that concerned her. And what if there were more men inside the bunker?

Keep him talking.

"You can't upset them. They'll never conceive at all if they're stressed. A woman's cycle is very sensitive, you know."

Sweat poured down the man's face and his eyes narrowed. "Brother Wise will decide who becomes a mother!" Behind the armed loser, Abi made out Claudia as she crept toward the bus driver who hadn't detected her presence yet. The driver appeared riveted to the scene playing out in front of the bus between Abi and the guard.

"Look. Neither of us wants the girls to get hurt. Why don't you get them off the bus safely, then you can take care of me? You know Brother Wise will not be happy if the girls see anything bad happen."

He paused, actually appeared to listen to her. He cocked his head at an extreme angle. "You know, you might be right. But no bitch decides what I do!" He was foaming at the mouth, his missing teeth allowing for spittle to fly.

Please, Claudia, do it, do it!

As if she'd heard her, Claudia's creeping turned into a flurry of motion. The bus driver screamed as Claudia took him out. Abi saw the retired Marine Corps General's feet hit kidneys, groin, stomach. The gunman kept his rifle on Abi as he turned his head to see what was causing the commotion. His last mistake.

Abi grabbed the end of the rifle and in one smooth move the gunman was flying over her, landing against the bus and sliding into a heap with a satisfying "Oof!"

He held on to the weapon and Abi kept the barrel away from her, away from where she knew the girls were hiding. Using every skill she knew, she wrestled the AR-15 from the creep. It cost him his consciousness as she hit him in the head when he tried to grasp her ankles. She sank to the ground next to the bus's tire.

"Where are the girls?" Claudia was next to her, appearing out of sorts in her torn, cultic dress but none the worse for wear.

"I sent them where we'd planned." Abi wiped her brow, thinking. The girls were hopefully halfway up the quarry by now, if not out entirely, huddled together at the meeting point.

"We saved them, and SVPD will get the rest of the women from the trailer park. Now we wait for Wise to show up." Claudia rested her arms on her bent knees, her hands dangling.

"Whoa—did you break your hand?" Abi pointed to the huge swelling of two of Claudia's fingers.

Claudia laughed. "Yeah, probably. And I'll break the other one if I have to."

A loud, whopping noise caught their attention and they looked up to see a helicopter descending into the canyon. It wasn't SVPD or an emergency life flight.

"We didn't know about the helicopter." Abi looked at Claudia, who stared at the aircraft.

"No, but it doesn't matter. It has to be Wise."

They started to crawl under the bus in unison, no words needed. The bus driver lay unconscious at the bunker entrance, not visible to anyone more than ten feet away. The armed guard that Abi had knocked out was on this side of the bus, and she and Claudia quickly dragged him under the bus with them. The scene Wise was landing in looked calm, deliberate. As far as anyone knew, the girls were in the bunker already, just as Wise had planned.

The helicopter landed not one hundred feet from them and before the blades stopped turning, two burly armed men got out and helped a frail, thin man to the ground.

Leonard Wise had come to reap his reward.

* * *

Keith watched Colt stare through his binoculars. He had left his behind when he'd originally run from the quarry, thinking he was going to help his department.

When he'd left Abi to die.

"Is it Wise?"

Colt didn't answer for several beats. They watched the three men egress the helicopter and walk slowly toward the entrance to the bunker. "Yeah, it's him. The bus driver is still out, lying by the door—I can make out his feet. No idea where the other man is, but he's nowhere in sight."

"Any sign of Abi or Claudia?"

"Not yet. Wait—damn it!" Colt threw the binoculars at Keith, who caught them and immediately started focusing on the bus.

"They're under the bus. They're going to have to take down Wise and the two men. I'm heading in."

Colt stared at Keith. "You have to stay here. You don't have a weapon, and you can be the lookout for the police department. Talk to Rio." Colt pressed the speed dial for Rio before he handed Keith his phone. "You're our comms link." Colt disappeared into the brush that surrounded the quarry's edge, headed for one of three paths that led to the bottom. He'd be behind the helicopter within five minutes.

"Rio here—Colt?"

"No, it's Keith. Colt's going into the quarry. A helicopter with Wise and two bodyguards landed. Abi and Claudia are under the school bus. No sign of the young girls, and it appears Claudia and Abi disabled the bus driver and a second man, probably another guard."

"I've got units headed in, Keith. They're going to have to park a good half mile away and run in on foot, to stay out of earshot. Unless Wise and his guards are neutralized by then."

"Roger." Keith kept the phone to his ear, watching Colt's progress with the binoculars. Once he ascertained that Colt was doing all right, he swung the glasses toward the bus. Wise and the two men were drawing perpendicular to the front of the bus. He told Rio as much.

"Keep the information coming, Keith, and whatever you do, don't even think about going in there after Abi. Do you hear me? Colt, Claudia and Abi have this, Keith."

"Roger." He'd stay there as long as he could—as long as Abi and Claudia appeared to be in command of the scenario. If things went south, all bets were off.

Abi took the safety off the AR-15 and aimed at Wise. Claudia was running out from behind the bus, her feet nearing the men's. Abi considered herself a good shot but it was never easy, targeting a bad guy so close to a colleague. She wanted to close her eyes, just for a second, and imagine Keith next to her, telling her he loved her. She'd have to settle for the warm feeling that knowing how he felt gave her. Abi was close enough to hear Claudia's voice, and as Claudia distracted the men, she crawled on her stomach until she was out from under the bus and up against the front right tire. Still hidden from Wise but able to stand and take him out when needed.

"Brother Wise, it's been awful. We were ambushed and a group of strange men led the girls into the bunker, after the doors were opened. Two of our brothers were sacrificed." Claudia sounded just like the religious zealot she wasn't.

"Calm down, Sister Claudia. Tell us what happened. For real this time." Abi saw Wise shrug off his escorts and he looked from one to the other, nodding at each.

They hoisted their weapons, also AR-15s, from their backs and held them aimed at Claudia.

"Why are you pointing those at me?" Claudia wrung her hands, still playing the distressed cult believer.

"We're just keeping you safe, Sister Claudia." Wise's tone was a conciliatory monotone.

Abi took deep breaths, keeping her hands and arms still against her adrenaline rush. It would be so easy to take all three of the losers out right now. But Claudia wanted them alive, if at all possible. No martyrs for any True Believers who were left after the takedown.

"Oh, Brother Wise, please, tell me what to do."

"Come with us, sister." Once again Wise nodded at his goons and they started to turn in semicircles on either side of him, sweeping the area to protect their prophet.

Claudia fell behind Wise and the thugs. Abi waited until they were closer to the bunker. She wasn't going to let Claudia go inside alone; she'd never come out. Not alive.

When Claudia coughed sharply three times, Abi made her move. She ran toward the group from behind, keeping her steps as quiet as possible on the graveled base of the quarry. Before the guards reacted, she knelt and aimed.

"Drop your weapons now or Wise is dead."

As the guards spun to look at Abi, Claudia moved. She wrapped her arm around Wise's throat, throwing him off balance. His eyes bulged as he clawed at Claudia's arm. His efforts were futile. The guards aimed at Abi, at the AR-15 she had in her hands.

"Drop your weapons. Kill her and I'll break his neck." Claudia had taken several steps away from the goons, Wise's weak kicks laughable as she firmly held him.

"Do what she says. Drop the rifles, brothers." Wise coughed out the command.

The "brothers" dropped their rifles and held their hands up.

"On the ground." Abi took over their apprehension, using zip-tie handcuffs. She looked up at Claudia.

Claudia had let go of Wise and was patting him down. She bent to feel along his legs and Wise used the one tiny window Claudia gave him. With a garbled shout, he brought his elbows down on Claudia's head. Claudia fell over and Abi, certain the thugs were neutralized, ran to her. Blood oozed from a head wound. Abi started first aid and looked to see where Wise was headed. She'd thrown the rifles carried by his guards under the school bus. If Wise made a move toward the bus, she'd take him out.

Instead he headed for the bunker doors. Abi saw how slowly he was going and took a moment to check on Claudia. She ripped off the sleeve of her blouse and used it to staunch the blood flowing from Claudia's wound. SVPD had to be very close if not here already.

"Claudia, can you hear me?"

She moaned. Tears of relief ran down Abi's cheeks. They'd done it. They'd taken out the cult and Wise was moments from being arrested. "Hang tight while I finish off Wise."

She crept forward, her eyes on Wise, knowing she had to take him out before he got into the bunker. He'd made it to the entrance and didn't even pause to look at his fallen cult members, the men she and Claudia had knocked out. Instead she saw his gnarled hand move around the keypad. Abi raised her weapon to fire.

And then the ground shook, a large boom knocked her onto her back and a dark cloud blocked the sun.

Keith was halfway down the path into the quarry when the explosion hit. He'd decided to go in and help Abi and Claudia, since Colt had disappeared from his view. He rolled onto the ground, holding his ears. Once the percussion of the blast stopped echoing in the quarry, he opened his eyes. A huge dust cloud poured from the bunker entrance but, thanks to the summer wind, blew up and out of the quarry. Keith's heart felt bigger than possible for his rib cage to hold. He only needed, wanted, one thing.

To find Abi.

He got up and started to run down the remaining twenty yards of path onto the quarry floor. He felt like a rabid animal, acting only on instinct. Keith had never faced losing all that mattered to him like this before. He'd thought his job had been everything, but he'd been wrong.

Abi lay next to Claudia, their forms still and covered in white dust. As he reached them, Abi sat up, coughing. Claudia followed.

"Abi!" Keith reached them and crouched down, grasping her shoulders. "Are you okay?"

Abi nodded. "I'm fine. Claudia—"

"I'm good." Claudia's voice rasped with dust as she struggled to sit up.

"Don't move, Claudia. You were unconscious." Abi tried to move toward her but Keith held her in place.

"You just survived a major blast. Stay tight." Sirens wailed behind them and he heard the familiar beat of the life flight's blades. The helicopter wouldn't be able to land in the quarry as Wise's craft had, not with the amount of loosened gravel and dirt.

"Where's Colt?" Claudia ignored Abi's and Keith's admonitions to stay put as she got unsteadily to her feet.

"I'm right here." Colt jogged up to them and didn't hesitate to take Claudia into his arms, holding her for what seemed like an hour. Keith watched them and had to give them both credit. They'd decided to make a go of it as a couple, even with the high stakes of both their careers. Something inside Keith snapped—or was that his heart breaking? He loved Abi. But love meant you didn't put the one you loved through hell. Hell was what he'd just experienced as he'd wondered if Abi was dead or alive. As a firefighter, he'd be asking her to go through this every day, with every fire alarm.

Abi deserved better. He couldn't knowingly hurt her. Ever.

"What happened, Colt?" He had to ask Colt something before he lost his resolve and pulled Abi into his arms. She'd already shaken off his hands and was on her feet. He stood next to her.

"Colt?" Abi wanted to know, too.

Colt looked up from his embrace of Claudia, his hand holding the top of her head to keep her bleeding under control. His grin was as white as the quarry dust. "I didn't have to do anything. Wise had the opening booby-trapped with explosives. The bus driver was supposed to disarm the trap before they put the girls in there. When Wise tried to get in, he blew himself and the bunker entrance to smithereens."

Abi stood still and Keith watched her take it all in. She finally turned to him.

"You didn't go to your department, Keith. Why?" Her eyes sparkled through the dust particles, her smile a whisper.

Keith knew what Abi wanted. She wanted the happy

ending that Colt and Claudia were having. But he couldn't give it to her.

"I needed to know you were good." His voice was hoarse and he couldn't blame it on the dust. If there were tears on his cheeks, she'd surely see them—the powder that caked all of them would only highlight the sign of his tumult.

"I'm good." She looked at her feet and then back at him. She grabbed his hands and shrugged. "All in a day's work for a firefighter, right?"

"Right." He let go of her hands, saw the confusion on her face. Keith pushed her hair back from the side of her face. Wiped away the tears that streamed down her cheeks, too. She knew. "Abi, I'm sorry—"

"Don't do this, Keith. I know what you're thinking. You're going on emotion. It's scary to see an op play out. But I'm not going to be doing this kind of work anymore. Not all the time." Her hand pulled on his forearm and he dropped his hand. Abi's chin lifted and she stared at him, her eyes pleading as tears fell. She was filthy, her front covered in dirt and quarry dust, her hands torn up from her adventure, her hair matted and snarly. His chest tightened. He'd never seen such a beautiful woman in his life. There'd be none after Abi, no one ever like her.

"I'd never ask you to quit your job, Abi. You're the best. You need to be able to work for Trail Hikers whenever they need you. And it's not you. It's me."

"I don't understand." Her lips trembled and the sight of Abi in pain over him hurt.

"I'm a firefighter. I don't pick and choose missions, or work in dangerous situations part-time. I do it every day, all day. I'm always on call, always an alarm away from the last fire I'll ever battle. I can't ask a family, a wife, to go through that constant anxiety."

Abi's eyes brightened. "You said 'wife.'"

He shook his head.

"I can't, Abi."

"You'll change your mind." She held his gaze and he saw sorrow, compassion, soulful comprehension. "We belong together. We're not done, Keith."

Shouts and the pounding of feet running into the quarry surrounded them as police, EMTs and firefighters arrived. Abi broke eye contact and turned away.

"Chief, anything you want us to know?" Tiger stood next to him, holding out an SCBA.

Keith shook his head. "We won't be needing those. There's nothing to put out—the blast closed up the entrance." Tiger relayed Keith's message to the other firefighters. All Keith could do was stare at the pile of rubble, tons of rock that had been a bunker entrance only moments earlier.

And the woman standing near it.

Abigail.

Keith did the hardest thing he'd ever done and turned away. Put one foot in front of the other. No matter what Abi thought she wanted, no matter that she believed he'd change his mind. He wouldn't. He loved her too much.

Chapter 22

The first week after Wisc's death and the demise of the True Believer Cult blurred into two, then three, as Abi waited for Keith to come back. To text, call or show up at her house. She wanted to go to him but sensed he needed space. As she worked side by side with Silver Valley PD to wrap up all loose ends of the case, the weeks turned into a month and she had to accept that Keith had been speaking his truth. He wouldn't be with her no matter how much he loved her—in fact, his love was keeping him away. She spent twelve-hour days at the station to distract herself from the emotional pain of their breakup, eager to close out what she hoped would be her last law-enforcement venture.

She had a business to open and get off its feet. Her heart ached at staying in the same town where she could run into Keith again, knowing he'd chosen to let go of what they had. But she'd fallen in love with Silver Valley, too. She wasn't going to let a second love pass her by. If she couldn't have Keith, she could have her new life in her new hometown.

"Abi, you're done. Let the police officers finish this." Rio stood in front of her in the conference room as she filed paperwork into a dozen storage boxes that covered the huge table.

"I will, Rio." Abi kept filing.

"Abi." She looked up. Rio's expression was grave, his eyes seeing everything. "You need to go now. The case is closed."

Abi looked away. She couldn't handle what she saw in Rio's glance. Understanding, yes, but also compassion, sprinkled with pity. Abi didn't need anyone's pity, not even Rio's.

"I'm sorry we didn't get him alive, Rio." Her voice was low as she fought tears through her words. "He deserved to be locked up for the rest of his life, not die a martyr."

"Yes and no. And it doesn't matter. You saved the lives of dozens of girls, and the women all have a chance at reentry into a normal life. The men who weren't arrested will start over, too." Rio put his hand on her shoulder. "It's okay."

Abi sighed. Rio was right. It would have to be okay. Because she was done and she had to start over. Even if it meant she was going to be without Keith. She'd all but got down on her knees and begged him not to leave her when he'd broken up with her at the quarry. Broken up? They'd barely had a chance to enjoy their newfound love. The hope of a future had withered three times as quickly as it had blossomed.

"We'll see you tomorrow, right?" Rio referred to Silver Valley Police Department's social event of the decade. The wedding of Colt Todd to Claudia Michele.

"Of course." It would be her last officially related function she'd attend. After that, no more law enforcement unless Trail Hikers needed her on an extraordinary case.

"He'll come around, you know." At Rio's words she straightened her spine.

"No, he won't." She didn't bother to ask Rio how he knew so much about her and Keith. Keith's sister Kayla was engaged to Rio, after all. "And it's okay, Rio. I'm on to the next chapter in my life. It would have been great if Keith wanted to join me, but, well…" Her throat constricted and she swiped at the tears on her lashes.

Rio put his hand on her shoulder. "Hang in there, Abi."

She'd hang in there, all right. She was going to throw herself into her reliable new love, Silver Valley Adventures. And do her best to accomplish the impossible: let go of the one man she'd ever loved so completely.

Keith stared at the fire department's work schedule on his phone as he waited for Rio in the diner. He still couldn't make heads or tails of it and it had nothing to do with the small screen.

Go to her.

Abi's face as he'd walked away from her in the quarry had haunted him for the past month. But no matter how many times he went over it, he came to the same conclusion.

If he loved Abi, he had to let her go.

It made sense on paper but the hole in his heart was still screaming, still raw. He didn't want Abi to ever feel like this. Out of control, unable to protect the one she loved.

"Hey, bro." Rio settled into the bench across from his in the red leather booth.

"What's so important that I had to meet you here with only hours before Chief Todd's wedding?" Keith didn't feel a need to hide his annoyance from Rio, the man who'd seen him at his worst and in fact had saved his firefighting career last year. Without Rio acting like a bulldog with the couple who had brought the negligence charges against him, Keith might still be out of a job.

"You've been pouting for the last month, Keith. Time to man up and go after the woman who's got your heart."

Keith felt like steam was coming out of his ears. "Leave it, Rio. None of your damned business."

"Oh, but it is. You see, *my* beloved, *your* sister, is distraught that you're keeping yourself from the love of your life. She's got it in her head that your stubbornness is going to cost you everything."

"Answer me this, Rio. How do you promise my sister to love her forever when you can be taken out at any time? When you go to work each day not knowing if you'll come home?"

Rio sat back and looked at him. "You're kidding. You really don't get it, do you?"

"Get what?" Keith wondered if the diner's AC was broken. He felt hot and cold and clammy at the same time.

"It's because I know how precious life is that I'm giving it all to Kayla. And besides, man, it's her choice. I'm just damned grateful she said yes."

The diner door's bells jingled as more customers poured in; the sound of clanging pots and clinking plates roared in Keith's ears as he stared at Rio and absorbed his words. But all Keith heard was his heart pounding in his throat.

Rio didn't appear to notice that Keith was in the middle of the most important realization of his life as he waved a waitress over and asked for coffee.

Keith reached for his wallet and pulled out a bill. He slapped it on the table as he got out of the booth. "It's on me. I've got to go."

Rio's expression turned from stunned to delighted. As Keith pulled open the diner door he heard his friend's shout. "Finally!"

"Dang it." Abi used her eye makeup remover to take off the sloppy job she'd done with the black liner. Her hands were shaking the way they did when she had to do something she absolutely did not want to. Today she had to go to a wedding of all things and face the one man she wished she'd be spending the rest of her life with. Instead they'd be like strangers, as if they had no connection.

Pounding on her front door stilled her. She forced herself to calm down and not overreact, but it was difficult. Her instincts were always trained to assume danger lurked around every corner. Her bare feet relished the cool hardwood floor as she padded down the hallway and looked through the windows that framed the front door.

Keith. She'd know his frame, his shape, his bearing anywhere.

Opening the door with more calm than she thought possible, Trail Hikers training be damned, she pasted a smile on her half-made-up face. "Keith."

"Hi, Abi." He was in a T-shirt and old jeans, his hands in his pockets. "Do you have a minute?"

"That's about all I have. The wedding is in less than two hours, and I'm supposed to help with greeting the guests. Come on in." She didn't wait to see if he followed her but instead went to the kitchen. "Want a glass of water?"

"I didn't come here for water, Abi."

"It's been a month, Keith. No phone call, no texts, not

even an email. And now you want to talk?" She pointedly swept her gaze over his disheveled appearance. "When we both need to get ready for the wedding?"

He actually looked chagrined, regretful. "That's on me. I'm sorry. You're right—I should have come sooner."

She eased her back against the counter and crossed her arms. "Well, you're here. Go ahead and say whatever you need to." Abi didn't think her heart could hear his crappy excuses for why he couldn't be with her again, but, whatever. "Wait—is this so that you'll feel comfortable at the wedding? Did you come here to do some kind of firefighter damage control, so that I don't make a scene in front of our friends?"

His fingers on her lips silenced her. He leaned in and she smelled *him*. Soap and firehouse. The promise of sex, and more. The warmth from his fingers radiated down to the place between her legs, where she pulsed for Keith.

"I'm here to ask you one thing, Abi."

She shook her head and pushed his hand away from her mouth. "I can't do this again, Keith." She'd barely started to breathe again without her heart hurting.

"Abi. I didn't give you the one thing I thought I would never take from you. Your own choice. By trying to protect you, what I was really doing was controlling you. I was trying to control what's between us, to save both of us from potential hurt in the future. That's not possible. And I can't live without you."

"You're just realizing that now?"

"I'm a slow learner." The ghost of a grin etched hard lines in his face. "Tell me, Abi. If you had a choice to accept the risk of losing me each day, and allowing me to accept the fact that I could lose you during one of your Trail Hikers missions, would you do it?"

She shook her head. "I'm not doing Trail Hikers ops anymore."

"You will, Abi. You have to. You know it. And I want you to do it. And I want to be the one there for you when you come home."

She wanted to believe him. So badly.

"You'll let me make my choice about being with you? You won't take it back again? Because I can't handle it again, Keith. If you're asking me if we can start again, you'd better mean it this time."

He stepped closer, only inches from her, and cupped her face with his hands. "Abi, please forgive me for being so blindingly stupid. For putting you and putting us through this past month of hell. Can you forgive me?"

She fought to keep her eyes open and on him, instead of closing them and pressing her lips against his like she wanted to. "I forgive you, Keith. If you ever pull a stunt like this again—"

His lips silenced her and Abi couldn't pretend to hold back or deny what she'd missed for the past month. What her whole life had led up to. Being with Keith.

He kissed her with his lips, his tongue, but more, with his heart. When he lifted his head she had no doubt he'd come back to her. For good.

"Aren't you going to the wedding, too?" Her breath was a whisper. All she wanted was to be with him.

"Yes. But there's something I have to take care of first." He kissed her again and pulled her pelvis up against his. Her breath stopped at the feel of his hard length.

"Keith, we have no more than thirty minutes before I have to be out the door. And you need a suit, don't you?"

"It's in my car."

She wrapped her arms around his neck and pulled him to her. "I've had a real bed delivered since the last time."

* * *

Abi sat with Keith on the right side of the wedding seating in the refurbished barn, near the back. She'd been shooed from her role as guest-greeter by Kayla as soon as Rio had spotted Abi and Keith together, holding hands.

His firm thigh was pressed against hers, his body heat a potent reminder of what they'd shared only an hour ago. Abi smoothed down the skirt of her fit-and-flare pink dress as she wiggled her painted toes in the silver, glittery sandals that matched her clutch. She hadn't had an occasion to dress up in too long, and wanted to make a break from her usual professional clothing. Make it clear to everyone, but especially herself, that she was beginning a new chapter in her life. A new business, a new home—she'd transferred her rental lease to a mortgage. And now she had the one man she wanted to share it all with. To start anew with.

"Hey, sexy." Keith's voice thrummed in her ear.

"Aren't you on the wrong side of the aisle? You're a friend of the groom."

"*And* the bride. Remember, Claudia read me into TH, too." He whispered this into her ear, too, bared by her updo. The single tendril the hairdresser had artfully twirled near her ear vibrated with Keith's breath.

"Not the place for it, Paruso."

His hand grasped hers and she nearly jumped out of her seat. She hissed. "Not the time for it, Paruso."

Keith stood, refusing to let go of her hand. "Walk with me, Abigail. We've got twenty minutes before Colt and Claudia get hitched."

Abigail. He'd called her Abigail. It sounded like the sweetest music on his lips.

Abi allowed Keith to lead her out the barn's side door into the bright morning sunshine that reflected in the budding trees and fields that lay before them. The barn was historic and from the ridge on which it lay all of Silver Valley was visible.

She turned to him, relishing the love in his eyes. For her. She'd be happy to drown in their ocean-blue depths. "How lucky are we, Keith?"

He lifted her chin. "I'm the lucky one, Abi. Blessed."

"Keith." A whisper.

As she met his gaze she found that she wasn't drowning in their depths, she was awash in…light. Laughter. Love. The promise of more. Tomorrow's hope.

"I love you, Abigail Redland. I was a fool to walk away from you. When I saw you down in that damned quarry and didn't know if you'd made it, I came unglued. And I know that's what I'm asking you to go through every damned time I walk into a burning building. But I can't live without you, Abi, and I don't want to."

She stared at this man who came off so tough, because he *was* tough. Sexy, because he *was* sexy. Loving…because he was lovable. Her man.

"Paruso, you are a fool. You think because you showed up here in this killer suit—" she fingered the lapels of his lapis-blue jacket "—and put some gel in your hair—" she mussed his short locks with her fingers "—that I'm going to go all to jelly and agree to your…what is it that you're proposing, exactly?"

"You know damned well, Abigail." His eyes burned with need. "I want you in my bed, in my life, next to me for the rest of eternity. You and me. Together."

He got to one knee and took her hand. With his other hand he held up a small velvet box. "How did you do this so quickly?"

"The Silver Valley jeweler's a high school classmate.

I wanted to do this at your place, but we got distracted. Now may I continue?"

"Yes."

"Abigail Redland, will you be my wife? Will you agree to be true to yourself, do whatever job you want to do and know I will always do my best to come home safe and sound each day to you?"

"Yes, yes, yes. A thousand times, yes. I love you, Keith. You're *my* firefighter."

She wrapped her arms around him as he pulled her to him and his lips met hers with complete command, desire and love.

* * * * *

If you loved this novel,
don't miss other suspenseful titles in the
SILVER VALLEY P.D. *miniseries:*

HER SECRET CHRISTMAS AGENT
HER CHRISTMAS PROTECTOR
WEDDING TAKEDOWN

Available now from Harlequin Romantic Suspense!

COMING NEXT MONTH FROM

H HARLEQUIN®

ROMANTIC suspense

Available May 9, 2017

#1943 CAVANAUGH ON CALL

Cavanaugh Justice • by Marie Ferrarella
When detective Alexandra Scott is transferred from Homicide to
Robbery, her new partner is *quite* the surprise: Bryce Cavanaugh
is just as headstrong and determined to get his way as she
is. When they go head-to-head while solving a string of home
invasions, fireworks are sure to ignite!

#1944 PREGNANT BY THE COLTON COWBOY

The Coltons of Shadow Creek • by Lara Lacombe
Thorne Colton knows his life is way too crazy for a relationship,
which is why he pulls away after an amazing night in
Maggie Lowell's arms. But when a pregnant Maggie is
endangered by a bomb planted in her car, Thorne is drawn back
into her life, determined to protect her and their unborn child.

#1945 A STRANGER SHE CAN TRUST

Escape Club Heroes • by Regan Black
Just before closing time at The Escape Club, a woman stumbles
out of a taxi and into the arms of off-duty paramedic Carson Lane.
Melissa Baxter doesn't know who she is, but she knows she
can trust Carson to keep her safe. Now the two of them must
bring a killer to justice before he can silence them forever!

#1946 REUNITED WITH THE P.I.

Honor Bound • by Anna J. Stewart
Her star witness is missing and assistant district attorney
Simone Armstrong has only one person to turn to:
Vince Sutton, P.I. Only problem is, he's her ex-husband—and
she put his younger brother in prison. Once they team up, it
becomes harder and harder not to remember how good they
had it, but a killer from Simone's past is determined to put a
stop to their second chance at happily-ever-after—for good!

HRSCNM0417

"Is that..." Thorne's voice was husky and Maggie realized he was now standing next to the bed. She'd been so focused on the screen she hadn't even noticed his approach. "Is that the nose?"

Maggie's gaze traveled back to the head, which was shown in profile. She ran her eyes along the line of the baby's face, from forehead to chin. How could something so small already look so perfect?

"Yes. And here are the lips." Dr. Walsh moved an arrow along the image, pointing out features in a running commentary. "Here is the heart, and this is the stomach and kidneys." She moved the wand lower on Maggie's belly. "Here you can see the long bones of the legs forming. And this is the placenta."

Maggie hung on her every word, hardly daring to breathe for fear of missing anything she might say. She glanced over and found Thorne leaning forward, his expression rapt as he took everything in. He must have felt her gaze because he turned to look at her, and in that moment, all Maggie's hurt feelings and disappointment were buried in an avalanche of joy over the shared experience of seeing their baby for the first time. No matter what might happen between them, they had created this miracle together. They were no longer just Maggie and Thorne; they had new roles to play now. Mother and father.

"Congratulations," he whispered, his brown eyes shining with emotion.

"Congratulations," she whispered back. Her heart was so full she could barely speak, but words weren't needed right now.

Thorne took her hand in his own, his warm, calloused fingers wrapping around hers. In silent agreement, they turned back to the monitor to watch their baby squirm and kick, safe inside her body and blissfully unaware of today's dangerous encounter.

I will keep you safe, Maggie vowed silently.
Always.

Don't miss
PREGNANT BY THE COLTON COWBOY
by Lara Lacombe, available May 2017 wherever
Harlequin® Romantic Suspense books
and ebooks are sold.

www.Harlequin.com

HARLEQUIN®

A *Romance* FOR EVERY MOOD™

JUST CAN'T GET ENOUGH?

Join our social communities
and talk to us online.

You will have access to the latest
news on upcoming titles and special
promotions, but most importantly,
you can talk to other fans about your
favorite Harlequin reads.

Harlequin.com/Community

 Facebook.com/HarlequinBooks

Twitter.com/HarlequinBooks

 Pinterest.com/HarlequinBooks